TERROR BENEATH THE BAYOU

By

Steven Amory Twitty

TERROR BENEATH THE BAYOU

Print Edition

CHAPTER 1

CLEE RODEN AWOKE AS THE first traces of dawn tinted the tops of tall pines. Musty odors of decaying vegetation permeated the air as a sporadic breeze played high in the trees. Another hot August day in South Louisiana, not something Clee looked forward to. In the deep shadows of The Swamp, where he lived, temperatures would be sweltering by noon.

Clee yawned and belched, bringing up the rancid taste of bile. He hadn't slept well the previous night, needing something more than the strawberry wine Pete Baxter had reluctantly shared, for only strong liquor could numb the flaring pain of Clee's stomach cancer but with money low and whiskey too expensive, he had to make do with whatever came his way.

Clee rarely ventured into town anymore to ply his chosen trade of panhandling. Not being as quick on his feet as he had been in years past, he no longer wanted to cope with the occupational hazards of his profession. Chased from one too many trash dumpsters and picked up once too often by police for begging had him restrained from straying too far from his moldy sanctuary. Even so, he would do anything at the moment for a drink with his stomach gnawing a hole clean through him.

Withered arm muscles strained as Clee raised himself from his timeworn bed of collapsed corrugated boxes. The one-acre wooded plot on which he lived rose ten feet above the surrounding marsh, a stationary raft of underlying clay capped with tall, spindly pines, stunted oaks draped in moss and layered in trampled leaves. The Swamp, as the locals referred to the one hundred-fifty acre lowland, was wedged between Union Town and abandoned factories of the town's failed industrial park.

Clee squinted and caught sight of Pete near his own shelter on the opposing side of their wooded knoll. Struggling to his feet, Clee tried to draw comfort from the last of the night's cool air and the hope of the taste of liquor.

"Man, I've gotta get something to eat," Pete remarked when he saw Clee stirring. Looking at the old man he asked, "You hurtin'?"

"Hurtin' bad," Clee groaned, clenching his teeth at another jab of pain. Breathing in shallow pants, he lowered himself back down on his makeshift mattress, hopeful his partner would take pity.

"Go to the hospital," Pete chided.

"You know they ain't goin' to do nothin'," Clee mumbled. Having visited Union Town General on previous occasions, Clee could expect nothing more than a handful of wimpy painkillers, questions from the police and harassment from do-gooders out to save his soul from damnation. Clee figured Hell couldn't be any worse than the life to which he had been driven.

"Them pills they give you are better than nothing," Pete remarked, tired of listening to the old man's incessant bitching and moaning.

"If I can just get a little whiskey. I'll be all right," Clee pleaded. He recalled a time when Pete had been a pretty fair friend, back a couple years ago when they had first met, and the old man remained hopeful he could stroke some compassion from a hardened soul.

Pete ignored his neighbor. A bellyache wasn't his problem. Walking down the gentle slope of the knoll, he took up position and unzipping his pants, urinated into a tangle of honeysuckle vines ringing their tiny bastion in uneven clumps. Usually able to flush out a host of flies when he pissed here, this morning showed no activity. Shifting his stream in another direction he received no better results.

"I can't keep bringing back enough drink for both of us," Pete protested as he finished up. He had paid the old man back ten times over for the times he had been the one in need and he wasn't about to add to the tally. Clee had shot his wad and anyone who couldn't bring something to the party was of no use to Pete.

"I'll go tomorrow," Clee promised as a knot of pain subsided. Swallowing with dread anticipation of the next bout, he added with flagging hope, "If I can just get a drink."

Pete shook his head while zipping up his pants. Time to find a new partner, he thought. Having to put up with the old man's mooching was bad enough but the constant complaints about his belly were getting unbearable. And what if the old codger died? The authorities would get involved and that was the last thing Pete wanted. He figured he had it made living out here, away from prying eyes, relatively comfortable, and the less attention he drew, the better.

Pete realized he didn't even like being around Clee anymore. The guy was a sight to behold, a walking corpse with slumped shoulders, dry leathery skin and sunken eyes. And his black-rimmed teeth, two missing top front and a bottom one chipped off at the gum, reminded Pete too much of his own failing pearly-whites.

"Get off your dead ass and start producing," Pete said. "I'll be lucky to get anything to drink myself. I've gotta eat first and handouts ain't been too good lately."

Clee remained silent, too ill to speak.

"Hey, look at this!" Pete exclaimed, amazed. He moved further down the knoll toward a sinkhole which served as their garbage pit. But the sinkhole was gone; garbage, pit, everything, replaced by an eight foot diameter shaft piecing straight down into the ground. Cautiously Pete edged closer and looked in. He couldn't see bottom.

"Clee, come see this. There's a friggin' hole over here. Must go all the way to China."

Pete picked up a discarded sardine can and tossed it in. He listened. One thousand one, one thousand two, one thousand three. When he reached ten and still hadn't heard the tin hit bottom, he stopped counting. "Damn, that's deep," he muttered, shuddering at the thought of falling in.

Something struck Pete as peculiar about the opening, other than the fact it had not been there the day before: Its shape, perfectly round, as if some machine had bored straight down into the earth. But Pete was certain no machine could reach that deep.

Pete bent down for closer inspection. A uniform fringe cleared around the hole's perimeter exposed roughed chert, as if someone had purposely swept away the ground cover and poked the cleared earth repeatedly with the sharpened point of a pencil. The shaft's grainy sides had the same indentations along with vertical grooves, some a mere inch in length and others long enough to disappear into the blackness below.

"You gonna take a look at this?" Pete called to Clee.

"Man, I'm dyin'. You gotta get me something to drink." Clee could only think about his belly.

"Yeah, yeah," Pete said tiredly, too hungry to fool with the hole or Clee any longer. With enough money for a pint of chocolate milk and a candy bar or two, he would run the bus fare trick in town and see if he scored enough for a bottle of hard stuff. He didn't plan on sharing any with Clee. Not this time. Well, perhaps he'd save him a swig or two.

"You stay away from this hole, old man," Pete called. Marching around the knoll, he disappeared into the bushes on a well-worn trail.

THE STRIP OF PINES BEHIND Red Dot Market was no longer the tallest in Union Town. Hurricane Bonnie, in 1986, the year before, had taken care of that distinction, spawning a tornado that made quick work of the market's metal roof and shearing off the treetops, strewing them across the parish. Since the clipped trees still acted as a windbreak from winter storms that came barreling out of the northwest, Carl Shuck, Red Dot Market's sole proprietor, had not bothered to have what remained cut down.

Pete emerged from the tangled brush of The Swamp and scurried up a rocky slope behind Red Dot Market to a weedy patch of untrimmed grass. With a quick glance to the grocery's still empty parking lot and the occasional car passing by on Front Street, he ducked into the sheltering trees. Having just downed a slab of chocolate he had bought at Cecil Natera's convenience shop next to the bus station, he worked his tongue over what remained of his upper molars.

Billy Nagel, locally known as Wreckerman, was already holed up in the stand of decapitated pines. "You alone?" Wreckerman asked Pete from a mat of palmetto fronds, legs crossed Indian fashion. A forty-seven year old bear of a man with long black hair, streaked with gray and tied in a shoulder-length ponytail, Wreckerman was a local boy who had burned his brains out on drugs and couldn't hold down a job, even if he had wanted to. He lived with his grandmother and most of his time was spent stretched out on her sofa watching daytime talk shows, drinking beer and waiting for his unemployment checks.

But for the last six weeks, Wreckerman had been obliged to show up each morning at Red Dot Market for a full day's work. He owed Carl Shuck money and that was the way Mr. Shuck and the circuit court judge had agreed he would pay it back. Tips Wreckerman made hauling groceries for customers were his to keep but half of his hourly wages remained in Mr. Shuck's pocket. Making enough to afford a few more six packs and not having to break a sweat doing it suited Wreckerman just fine.

Wreckerman claimed to be a Viet Nam vet, a decorated one at that. Claimed also to have taken up drinking to forget the women and children he had been ordered to kill in some unknown village in Cambodia. To the unseasoned ear his stories were fascinating, stories from which legends were born, but the residents of Union Town took no notice to these tall tales. The closest Wreckerman had ever come to Southeast Asia was through rented video movies featuring his hero and Hollywood creation, John Rambo, blasting through unlikely scenes in the Mekong Delta. Wreckerman had a problem dealing with reality but you didn't say that to his face. The man had a temper.

"YEAH, THE OL' MAN'S SICK again," Pete said of Clee. "What've you been up to?"

Wreckerman smirked when he said, "Running recon." Reaching behind his back he produced a black plastic garbage bag from which he unwrapped an unopened fifth of Evan Williams Bourbon. "My Green Beret training comes in handy. In and out like the wind."

Pete's eyes nearly popped from his head when he beheld the whiskey. He didn't know where Wreckerman had acquired the bottle and quite frankly, didn't care, just so long as the big man was in a sharing mood. Pete glanced through the trees as if expecting someone else to join them. "You drinking all that yourself?"

"You can have a bit," Wreckerman said, twisting off

the cap. Sniffing at the sharp fragrance wafting forth, he pressed the plastic pour spout to his lips and upended the bottle. "Damn that's good stuff," he moaned. He wiped off his mouth with the back of his hand and relinquished the bottle to Pete, watchful the promised swig didn't turn into a gulp.

"Why don't we cross over to the industrial park?" Pete suggested after sampling the golden liquid. Obligingly, he surrendered the bottle to its not-so rightful owner. "I saw the law over at the bus station. Ain't no reason for them to go snooping around the factories."

"I got a better place," Wreckerman said, not having intended to stick around with his booty anyway. Mr. Shuck would be arriving in a half hour to open his business and Wreckerman wasn't doing any work this day. He had a bottle to kill and someone's undivided attention for his war stories. Getting shit-faced wasn't fun unless he could bend an ear and giving up a portion of his bottle was well worth the sacrifice.

Pete smiled at Wreckerman's agreement to move on. Indian and Juke Box, two other street-bums, hadn't been over from Opelousas for several weeks but Pete was loath to take any chances. This bottle of bourbon was just too tempting to split with anyone else.

The two vagrants slipped out from the pines, half sliding, half walking down the washed out, gravel strewn embankment. A trail led into The Swamp's denser interior where thick underbrush, faded from summer heat and ebbing ground water, snagged anything coming close.

Deftly Wreckerman threaded his way through the dry brambles, the bottle held across his chest like a loaded weapon. He stepped lightly as if the slightest sound would bring down on them the entire North Vietnamese Army.

Brittle reeds, tightly clumped and set out from stubby hardwoods, announced changing environs. Denser foliage yielded to exposed clay tattooed with a ground cover of tufted grasses. A sweep of Wreckerman's long arm brushed aside tall reeds to a half-acre clearing.

Wreckerman knew The Swamp better than anyone in and around Union Town. Hunting rabbits and turkey there as a boy, he had covered every inch of ground between there and Palmetto. When wanting to make himself scarce, Wreckerman knew just where to go.

"Don't you go blabbing to nobody about this here bottle," Wreckerman warned Pete. Wreckerman had liberated the bottle from Clara May Runyun's back porch after she left for her weekly hair session at Jean Mackey's home-based salon and he couldn't afford being fingered as the pilferer. He was on probation for busting up a dryer at Carl Shuck's Laundromat and adding theft to his transgression would land him in jail again.

"Ain't no worry about me telling no one," Pete promised. "You take care of me and I'll take care of you."

Within the grassy clearing a ten-foot square of paint speckled canvas covered the ground, emptied beer bottles and cans scattered about. The tattered pages of a Playboy Magazine protruded from under one edge of the ground cloth and opposite, a sun-bleached rabbit skeleton. Completely decomposed, the animal's remains lay in a dark, oily blotch with no lingering trace of skin or fur.

"I used to hunt down here," Wreckerman reminisced upon seeing the remains. "That was back before Nam."

"Oh yeah?" said Pete. His host was about to launch into another long line of war stories and Pete knew what he was in for, but he would gladly suffer through whatever Wreckerman had to say so long as he continued to get a taste from the bottle.

Wreckerman swept the rabbit bones off the canvas with the side of his foot as he went on. "Me and Cal Wissnant shot the hell out of rabbits and birds down here. Gave me good target practice for shooting slant-eyes." He paused, took another draught from the bottle and said, "Did I ever tell you about the time we liberated Lai Mai?" Wreckerman had no idea if such a place existed in Viet Nam or anywhere else on the planet but it sure sounded like a good slant-eye name and Pete would certainly not know the duplicity.

"Maybe," Pete commented, and then asked, hoping Wreckerman might postpone his tale. "You ever shoot deer around here?"

"Used to see all sorts of wildlife in The Swamp," Wreckerman said, accommodating Pete this one request before getting on with his story. "But since that damn industrial park was built I haven't seen nary a rabbit or bird, much less a deer." Motioning to the bones he said, "He must've died of loneliness." Chuckling at his own witticism, Wreckerman shook his head in disgust. "Leave it to the friggin' politicians to ruin a good hunting spot by building a bunch of damn factories." He passed the bottle to Pete and leaning back on an elbow, prepared to tell his tale.

"Why do you reckon The Swamp is drying up?" Pete asked, truly interested in Wreckerman's opinion about the changing environment. After all, this was Pete's home and it bothered him The Swamp appeared to be dying.

"I'll guar'ran'damn'tee it was them factories what done it," Wreckerman said. "Just like chasing off all the game." Taking back the bottle he said, "I watched them drive the foundations for the buildings. Sure went mighty deep. Betcha did something down there what let the water drain off, like breaking through into an underground cave or something."

"Yeah, a cave. That's what it's gotta be," Pete said and he told Wreckerman about the deep hole he had discovered that very morning.

"That's a cave all right," Wreckerman said with authority. "No telling how big it is. Could go all the way to the Mississippi."

"Ya reckon there's any gold down there?"

"Could be," Wreckerman said. Drawing himself up and leaning closer to Pete, a serious look on his face, he added, "Keep what you found to yourself. We'll have every cave explorer in Louisiana prowling around here if you don't. Won't be no privacy no more and they'll end up making this a friggin' park."

"Who am I going tell?" Pete asked.

"Well, ya best be careful."

Wreckerman didn't wait for Pete to pursue his line of questioning. "Lai Mai," the big man said, nodding his head in mock recollection. "There were six of us on Special Forces patrol. We'd covered a lot of ground inside North Viet Nam and were on our way back to headquarters when Charlie opened up on us, just outside a village. It was just before daybreak—"

Pete settled in for what would be another long discourse, satisfied Wreckerman's explanations of the dry marshlands around Union Town and the deep shaft he had discovered alongside his flop were correct. The only thing Pete had to worry about was some outsider finding the cave entrance. Concealing the hole with branches and brush would take care of that problem.

THE LATE AFTERNOON SUN HUNG low in the sky when Pete stumbled up the knoll to his home, his mind hazy with alcohol and his eyes begging for sleep. Spending the entire day with Wreckerman, he hadn't bothered to go back to town and the little he had eaten that morning plus the whiskey in his belly would have to hold him until tomorrow. With only three cents left in his pocket he would have to really hustle in the morning.

Clee was nowhere to be seen and Pete figured he had finally gotten off his dead-ass to rummage through someone's garbage can or mooch money from anyone who looked him in the eye. Either way was fine with Pete. Drunk, he was going to get some sleep before the old man returned moaning and complaining about his belly.

Realizing his bladder was about to burst, Pete made for the far edge of the knoll and took up position in his usual spot, focusing as best he could on the dark outline of the strange hole. At least, Pete thought, his garbage wouldn't pile up anymore with a cave the size of Nebraska in which to throw it all. He took a few unsteady steps past the honeysuckle and watched his urine arch into the bowels of the earth.

"The world's deepest piss-hole." Pete chuckled to himself.

Something caught Pete's attention. Within bushes, twenty feet from where he stood, lay a pair of pants and a shirt. And more. Pete finished, zipped up and with uncertain curiosity moved around the hole for closer inspection.

"Damn!" Pete gasped. A skeleton! A human skeleton still garbed in clothing and lying in a pool of a black oily substance. The skull's empty eye sockets stared straight at Pete, its jaws open as if caught screaming.

Pete recognized the clothing and the shoes. They were Clee's!

"What the..." Pete stammered. He looked more closely at the skull. Two teeth, top front, were missing and a bottom tooth was chipped off at what would have been a receding gum line.

Pete backed away, horrified, unable to take his eyes from the gruesome sight. It was Clee! There was no doubt about that. But Pete knew this was impossible. Clee had been alive that very morning and now his bones were as sun-bleached as the rabbit skeleton back at Wreckerman's hideout.

Pete's thoughts raced as fast as his heart. Did cancer do that to Clee? When people said that someone was 'eat up with cancer', is that what they meant, they were literally eaten up? Maybe, Pete thought, someone killed the old codger. But why, and how had his body decomposed so quickly?

Pete took another step backwards, unable to find answers to his questions while those hollow eye sockets followed his every move, cursing him for not having been there to save him.

Pete's whiskey-laced mind fumbled with what to do. He couldn't tell the police. If law officials put two and two together they would get murder. How else would they explain Clee's remains and the fact that he, Pete, had not said anything about them until now? No one would believe the old man had died that same day. No matter what Pete said, the evidence would all look like he was the killer.

Wreckerman! Yeah, Wreckerman would know what to do.

Spinning about, his heels digging into exposed chert, Pete teetered on the edge of that gaping hole, momentum forcing him on. With arms flailing in a desperate attempt to catch himself, Pete's world swirled and blurred as the abyss swallowed him.

Pete threw out his arms and found a handful of leaf-covered ground. He dug his white-knuckled fingers into the cold clay. His chest slammed against the lip of the hole, dashing the wind from his lungs. Three ribs cracked like dry twigs.

Pete clung on, his body quivering with exertion to hold on, every gasp for air a spear through his chest. Slowly, with excruciating pain, he reached up his other arm and found another handful of earth.

The searing pain in his chest spread through Pete's body. Numbness crept down his outstretched arms. He toed the straight-sided shaft for a purchase but continued to slip further into the chasm.

Something tugged on Pete's pants leg. He tried to gain a purchase but whatever had been there was gone. He could hold on no longer and then –

One thousand one, one thousand two, one thousand three. Pete Baxter never made it to ten.

CHAPTER 2

"MAN, THERE AIN'T NO SECURITY system, I done told ya." Jeff Mackie was talking, a scruffy-haired, eighteen-year old from Union Town. A face pock-marked with acne and close-set, bloodshot eyes were his most notable features and the faint moonlight in which he now stood gave his skin the pallid hue of a recently exhumed body. His nickname, 'Weasel', was fitting for the small-time junkie he was.

Two o'clock in the morning found Jeff standing before a previously cut hole in a once formidable security fence topped with strands of now sagging barbed wire. A pair of wire cutters protruded from Jeff's back pants pocket and his flashlight spot lit a metal-sided building within the once protected compound.

Jeff's partner, fifteen-year old Rod Franklin, cowered at the bottom of the embankment, keeping to moon-shadows. Having just made it through The Swamp without stumbling across those tramps who supposedly lived there was a great relief but now he was adding to the experience by breaking into an abandoned factory. Not a typical day's workout for Rod.

Making quick inspection of the rusted ends of previously cut fencing, Jeff said, "Come on, let's go." He slipped through the cut fencing.

Rod didn't budge. "I don't know," he called up, ready to give up their plans and go home. "What if we get caught?" He didn't care anymore if Jeff knew he had lost his nerve.

"Damn you," Jeff said, shining the light on Rod. "What's the friggin matter? You want in on the deal or not?"

"Well, yeah," Rod answered, "but…"

"But nothing, you chicken shit. Either you're in this or you're not." Jeff said. "Why don't you go back to your mommy," he sneered. "I can do this myself."

Rod wished he had never agreed to come on this outing. If his stepfather found out what he was up to the old man would strip the hide off him. The son-of-a-bitch got physical when he was angry.

"Are you coming?" Jeff snapped.

What the heck, Rod thought. His stepfather would never know. The old sot was drunk last night and would sleep until time to open his diner later in the morning. All Rod had to do was get back before his mother woke up. Not that he worried she would tell her husband. Rod knew better than that. They kept a lot of secrets from the old man. Rod's main concern was his mother's disappointment knowing he was still hanging around with

Weasel.

Rod peered around in the twilight sensing he and Jeff were well hidden. No one would see them. No one would know.

"Yeah, I'm coming," Rod said, convinced this was his big chance to get out of a nowhere town, in nowhere Louisiana, and far, far away from his stepfather. Rod was a bastard child and Dick Driskoll, his mom's third husband, never let him forget it. Rod hated the man for that but what he despised more was the abuse his stepfather dealt his mother. Each time Rod crossed his stepfather his mother would intervene and she always suffered as a result. When Rod tried to stop the beatings, he scored his own bruises for his intrusions and his mother fared even worse.

Rod could see only one way to rid himself and his mother of their problems, not to give his stepfather any more excuses for violence against his mom. Steal anything of value from this old factory, sell it and buy some marijuana from Weasel's friends over in Morganza. After reselling the dope in Baton Rouge for a good profit, he would head for California. What he would do when he got to the West Coast Rod didn't know and at this point, he didn't care. The main thing was to get out of Union Town.

Rod scampered up the embankment and ducked through the opening in the fence. In the eerie moonlight the single-story building looked like a straight-walled canyon, broken only by a metal door before them and an access ladder to the roof at the building's west end. The door was decorated with; *Cajun Snax Foods; No Admittance – Emergency Exit Only.*

Rusty gouges from previous forced entries scarred the door's face and gave Rod hope that for all of his trouble, there was still something left inside for Jeff and him to pilfer.

With a nervous glance either side, Jeff grabbed the door's handle and pulled. It didn't budge.

"Gimme a hand," Jeff said.

Rod slipped in beside Jeff and on their third heave the door popped free, creaking hinges echoing throughout the tomb-quiet building. Darkness from within oozed through the open doorway.

Rod's breath caught in his throat at the sight of the eerie blackness within. This was his limit. He was going no further. No matter what Jeff called him, Rod was not taking another step forward.

The silver shaft of Jeff's flashlight pierced the gloom, casting a circle of luminescence over a dusty, concrete floor.

"Damn, this place is big," Jeff mumbled. He took a half-hearted step inside. Before him a bulky, black iron machine squatted among scattered shipping boxes draped in pallet strapping. The machine's stainless steel side panels had been tossed aside, exposing rusted drive shafts and gears. A dial-studded control panel hung askew.

Jeff swung his light from side to side, revealing similar equipment and piles of refuse. His junkie friends had indicated a lot of stuff was still left for the taking; copper wiring, electric motors and pieces of stainless steel, even some computerized controls and Jeff hoped they were right. This place was a lot spookier than it looked from the outside and though he wouldn't admit it to his partner, he was scared too.

From his left a yellow forklift rail cut a line parallel to the rear wall to a cinder block partition separating the production area from the factory's offices. Jeff wondered if anything of value remained in that portion of the building. Running the light up the wall to the ceiling he could just make out steel trusses strung with cables.

"Come on," Jeff urged Rod.

"I'll wait here," Rod replied in a faltering voice, quickly adding, "just in case someone comes."

That was fine with Jeff. Compared to the blackness within, the moonlight appeared as bright as sunshine. With the door held open he didn't feel entombed.

"Okay," Jeff managed with feigned determination, not wanting his partner in crime to see his own fears.

Jeff moved cautiously toward the monster machine before him, trying to ignore the silent darkness encasing him. He glanced behind him and croaked in a fear-shackled voice to Rod, "Keep that door open." He pressed on.

The machine's control panel was missing all of its switches. Jeff nudged open its front cover. The copper wiring had already been stripped out and further inspection revealed nothing of value.

"Have you found anything?" Rod called anxiously.

"Not yet," Jeff answered. Waiting for his echo to die away, he gathered courage once again and moved to the next machine.

A sound like a windblown twig rustling against a window pane halted Jeff. Uncertain of its origin, he shone his light around a wider perimeter but saw nothing. He swallowed nervously, his skin crawling when he realized it could be rats. Jeff hated rats.

Under a low-set conveyor Jeff located an electric motor. It had to be worth something. Dragging it out into the open, he discovered a nearby wooden crate filled with scrap iron and more electric motors.

"I got some stuff," Jeff called.

"Good," Rod said. "Hurry up."

Relieved at Jeff's success, Rod edged out of the doorway and took a precautionary look around. The door was midway along the building, the back wall running two hundred feet in either direction with the ladder at one end and beyond, a weedy, wrap around yard.

A car crossed Krotz Bridge, a quarter mile away on Old Simmesport Highway. The auto's headlights flickered among bridge supports then disappeared beyond the factory's corner. Rod couldn't tell if the vehicle had turned onto Industrial Boulevard, the single access road into the park, or had continued north. Only a police car would be out this time of morning.

Rod switched on his flashlight and looked at his watch. Jeff was still going deeper into the building. Rod had not figured on this foray taking so long.

Inside the building, Jeff once again heard the rustling sound. Gooseflesh crawled up his back like an icy hand. Grabbing a two-foot length of iron round-stock from the crate, he pressed on. Any rat venturing too near would get its head smashed in.

"You little bastards. I've got a surprise for you," Jeff threatened, reaching deep inside himself for another spoonful of courage.

With weapon at the ready, Jeff crept deeper into the factory inspecting each piece of machinery he came to, his mouth so dry he could no longer swallow. He snipped off a coil of electrical wire from another control panel and stuffed it into a pants pocket. The pickings were slim and if he didn't find something of greater value soon he would get the hell out of Ratsville.

A stale, rancid smell of rotten eggs caught Jeff's attention. The sulfurous stench, borne on a wisp of air, turned his stomach.

Jeff's heartbeat raced to full gallop when he once again heard movement, closer now. He panned his light over nearby machines and then onto a portion of concrete floor in front of him. The entire floor in this section sagged on an increasingly steep grade, ending at a gaping hole. Jagged cracks intersected the abyss like blackened veins in a dead eye. Thick, fetid air wafted from the bowels of the crater, settling over the floor like marsh vapor. Inching forward for a closer look, Jeff could hear the earth breathing.

The hole had been chiseled from the concrete in a perfect eight foot diameter circle, exposing the floor's internal grid-work of reinforcing bars.

A shadow moved along the edge of hewn concrete but dropped out of sight before Jeff could get a good look. With rats all around him, Jeff didn't have to be persuaded he had had enough. Nothing could keep him in this creepy place any longer.

Stepping back onto more level ground, Jeff didn't dare take his eyes from the hole. His light was the reason those rats remained out of sight and he was going to keep it that way, at least until he got closer to the open doorway. The very thought of those filthy creatures scurrying around nearby made him ill.

Click! Jeff swung his light up into the rafters, from where the sound had emanated. His heart pounded in his chest. This place was crawling with rats!

Jeff dashed through the maze of debris and machines for the open doorway, his flashlight's beam leading the way. To hell with what his friends had said and to hell with everything in here.

High among peaked rafters came a low pitched buzzing from the rapid beating of wings. A chorus of grating sounds rose up from all sides. The very building seemed to come to life.

Adrenaline surged through Jeff's veins. He ran without conscious thought, wanting nothing more than to be outside, to be free of this black Hell and all it contained.

Contorted shapes of monstrous machines leaped from the darkness. Jeff bounced off the wooden crate of scrap iron and motors, tripped and went sprawling to the floor. The flashlight was loosed from his grip and sailed through the air. It struck the concrete floor with a sharp, metallic thud and went dead. The length of steel roundstock skittered into the darkness.

"Hey, what's going on?" Rod called. Whatever Jeff was doing, he sure was making a lot of noise. When Rod got no answer he called again. "Jeff, what the hell's going on?"

Jeff groped frantically about for his flashlight. Realizing the futility of the situation, he found the corner of the crate and pulled himself up. His right thigh throbbed pain. Touching his wound, he gasped at the feeling of blood but there was no time to check his injury. The sounds around him were getting louder, getting closer.

Finding the dimly lit doorway then never taking his eyes from his only avenue of escape, Jeff hobbled on. Within the moonlit portal, Rod's silhouetted figure was urging on his partner, or was he? Rod's frantic movements were as if he was warding off a swarm of attacking bees.

Something darted through the air past Jeff, passing within inches of his right ear and making Jeff's head spin from fear. Jeff ducked and sidestepped. He ricocheted off some gloom-shrouded machine, gasping from more than pain and exertion.

The flying phantom circled in a tight pattern high over Jeff's head. It swooped down again, slamming into his right shoulder. Instant, searing pain drove deep into the Jeff's flesh like a hot dagger. His face twisted in agony and he fell to his knees, clawing at his shoulder as if attempting to dig out a hot ember embedded within. Watery blood streamed down his back, staining his sweat-streaked shirt.

Jeff struggled to his feet and stumbled on, crazed with a pain that boiled through his body. He had lost all sense of direction and all feeling in his body. Fire-white flashes exploded before his eyes and then, Jeff Mackie was no more.

CHAPTER 3

When Dip-stick didn't show up for breakfast Maurice knew something was radically wrong. Dip-stick never missed his morning meal. The old hound's daily routine revolved around it; chase rabbits for an hour or so at dawn and be on the back porch waiting for Maurice let him indoors. After that, wherever Maurice went, Dip-stick followed.

Maurice cooked his usual breakfast; two fried eyes, sunny-side up, three strips of bacon and burned toast.

After eating, he called his dog from the back porch. No response. Oddly, no answering bark or lumbering crash through underbrush that had overtaken once plowed fields.

"Dip-stick, here boy," Maurice called again, wondering if the bitch on the Planchard farm was in heat. Dip-stick might have been old, nearly ninety in human years, but he could still get it up. Even so, Maurice thought, the old mutt hadn't missed his share of eggs for a piece of ass since he turned seventy.

Breakfast scraps were dumped into Dip-stick's food bowl and a day's ration of dog food poured over this.

Dip-stick preferred to eat the dried chunks first and then lap up the greasy eggs at the bottom.

Not long after seven o'clock when Dip-stick still had not returned, Maurice became anxious. It just wasn't like his dog to disappear, especially on a Wednesday, the day he rode to town in the back of the flatbed truck. That weekly trek and hunting were the two things Dip-stick lived for.

Maurice stepped through the screen door onto the back porch. Wooden floor planks creaked protest at his two hundred eighty pounds. At sixty-eight years of age, he still enjoyed his own cooking and gave himself a lot of practice.

Across a weedy field that made up his side yard and had once been planted in tobacco, Maurice could just make out the shingled roof of the Planchard place. Hurricane Bonnie had spared a stand of younger, hedge-rowed trees between their houses which suited Maurice just fine. The Planchards and their two young sons were likable enough neighbors but Maurice appreciated his privacy.

"Where is that dog?" Maurice mumbled. He stepped off the porch into the backyard and called yet again, worry gnawing at his gut. Dip-stick could have tripped in a gopher hole and broken a leg or had a heart attack. After all, he was old.

Dip-stick had been a throwaway, one of many unwanted puppies left at the parish landfill by irresponsible owners. Those puppies not killed by coyotes or run over on the road were mercifully shot by Spencer Neumann, the parish's long-standing sanitation engineer. Spencer justified his actions as being more humane than leaving the poor creatures to an even ghastlier fate. To Maurice it made some sense since few people in Union Town took in strays.

It was after one of Spencer's multiple executions that Maurice happened to drop by the dump with his weekly load of kitchen garbage. Within an overturned bucket of old crankcase oil he had found a sole surviving puppy overlooked by Spencer. The poor creature was cold and hungry and whimpering with fear, its white fur stained gritty-black with used oil. After Rounder, his previous dog, had died a few years earlier, Maurice had never considered a replacement but he couldn't resist this little grease ball and hauled him home for a good washing and a bowl of warm milk.

That had been nearly thirteen years ago and now Maurice wondered if old age had finally caught up with the mutt. Dip-stick had been acting strange lately, taking to worrying a patch of ground in the side yard as if something were buried there and just three days ago he had dug a hole big enough to bury a twenty-pound bag of dog food. The crazy hound then sat on the edge of his excavation howling like there was no tomorrow.

"I bet you're at it again," Maurice said under his breath, relieved he finally knew his dog's whereabouts. He marched to the corner of the house. If Dip-stick had opened up that hole again he would get the strap.

"Dip-stick!" Maurice was angry. "Dip-stick, come!"

But the side yard was empty except for a pile of freshly dug dirt and a gaping hole. Dip-stick had indeed been busy this morning. The hole was twice as big as before and deeper.

A muffled bark caused Maurice to look across the half mile of open field to the Planchard place. "Dip-stick, here boy," Maurice called. Immediately came another muffled bark, now sounding as if Dip-stick were inside the house. Maurice went through the backdoor into the kitchen. No Dip-stick.

Confused, Maurice returned to the side yard, calling again. The barking was clear but still faint. Moving closer to the hole, Maurice realized Dip-stick had dug down another foot in his previous diggings and had fallen through into some type of cavern. Maurice looked in. Dip-stick barked.

"Lord have mercy," Maurice stammered. He knelt down for a closer look and his senses were assailed by a putrid smell of sulfur and rot rising up from the bowels of the earth. He coughed from the foul vapors. "What have you gotten yourself into now?" he muttered to his dog.

A single shaft of morning sunlight tattooed the cavern floor illuminating Dip-stick's broad head. The hound whined as if Spencer Neumann were down there with him. The dog's left front leg was broken.

"You hold on," Maurice called down. He hustled to the house and returned with a flashlight, a ten-foot aluminum ladder and a long-handled shovel. "Move out of the way," Maurice called to his dog as he hacked at the ground with the shovel. Dip-stick didn't obey his owner's command until a dirt clod bounced off his hindquarters. With a yelp of more surprise than injury, he hobbled into the shadows.

Maurice worked as fast as he could, slowly enlarging the hole. The sulfurous odors rising up from the excavation were almost overpowering. Sweat poured from Maurice's body and his arms quickly grew tired from wielding a tool he hadn't used in years but he wasn't letting aching arms and back stop him. When Dip-stick died it would be from old age, hopefully while he was humping the Planchard bitch.

Finally, the opening was large enough for Maurice to get through. He tossed aside the shovel and dragging the ladder into position, lowered it into the cavern. It reached bottom with barely an inch to spare above ground.

Maurice shoved the flashlight into a pants pocket and swung a leg onto a top rung. Hefting his bulk into position, he started down realizing he and Dip-stick would be forgoing their usual trip into town for a longer trip to Opelousas. Union Town had no veterinarian.

The enlarged opening was just large enough to accommodate the ladder and Maurice's own bulk. One last breath of fresh morning air and Maurice disappeared below the surface, his white-knuckled hands gripping tight the ladder. Here he was, well past his prime, already tired from a younger man's labor, descending into some great hole to save his dog. Maurice knew he would be lucky to get himself back out much less with a load in tow but no one else was available to help and he feared if Dip-stick wasn't rescued soon, he might succumb to the foul subterranean vapors. Maurice pressed on.

After the first anxious gasps Maurice found the subsurface air breathable. By the time he reached bottom he had forgotten all about the foul fumes, his sights now set on getting Dip-stick and himself out.

Dip-stick limped over to his master, tail wagging at the arrival of his savior. Maurice checked his dog's injured leg. Not broken after all, just badly bruised but still warranting professional attention. He gave Dip-stick a reassuring pat on his head before switching on his flashlight, intrigued that a cave had been under his property all these years and he had never known of it until now.

To Maurice's surprise, the cave was actually a tunnel, a perfectly symmetrical, eight-foot diameter excavation running straight as a die, north and south. Dappled markings on the moist chert walls reminded Maurice of the tidal flats along the Gulf Coast where, during low tide, marsh crabs emerged from their burrows to forage for food, their claws leaving identical signatures in the soft mud.

"This thing ain't natural," Maurice commented to Dip-stick. "It's been dug." The tunnel was too perfect to have been a freak of nature.

With further contemplation of his find, Maurice added, "Ya know what, Dip-stick? What they're saying about a New World Order is true. This here is one of them secret tunnels NATO is using to infiltrate America with foreign troops. It might even lead to where they hide their black helicopters."

Dip-stick whimpered as if he too had drawn the same conclusion.

"Let's get the hell outta here," Maurice said. "If we get back soon enough from the vet, we'll call the Emcee on that radio talk-show." He smiled at having real proof of the US government's covert operations with foreign countries and it had been right under his feet all the time. He wondered how much he should charge for an entrance fee.

Dip-stick turned from the ladder, his attention no longer on his master or his own rescue. A growl rumbled deep in his throat, his hackles raised.

"What is it, boy?" Maurice shined his light into the

dark emptiness.

Dip-stick snarled and growled louder.

"Dip-stick, be quiet." Maurice ordered and listened for sounds of someone approaching. He heard nothing. No voices. No footsteps. No movement. But Dip-stick sensed something.

There! What was that? Maurice quieted Dip-stick again. A sound from deep within the tunnel played on the edge of his hearing.

Urgency raced Maurice's heart. Returning his flash-light into his pants pocket, he grabbed up his dog and mounted the ladder. The last thing he wanted was to be caught down here. This was most certainly a top-secret operation and him being a civilian, the enemy, he would be in a heap of trouble if caught.

The sounds were closer now, muffled scraping and dull thuds as if every crab from the coastal marshes had found entrance into the tunnel and were scurrying toward him.

Sunlight from above beckoned Maurice. With Dip-stick securely cradled under an arm, he ascended the ladder. The necessity to get free of this foul place twisted his stomach and the expectancy of a restraining hand at any moment rose as bile in his throat.

Halfway up the ladder Dip-stick went ballistic. He snapped at the blackness and barked furiously, his mouth frothing, his eyes wild, hell-bent to tear apart whoever was approaching.

"Hold still!" Maurice yelled at his dog but Dip-stick thrashed about so hard, Maurice lost his grip and his dog tumbled head over tail, striking bottom with a sickening thud. Up in an instant, injuries forgotten, Dip-stick lunged into the darkness with viciousness Maurice had never before seen in his dog. There came a great yelp of pain and then, silence.

"Dip-stick?" Maurice called. He waited for anything that would let him know his dog was all right. "Dip-stick. Come boy." Maurice fumbled the flashlight from his pocket and switched it on. "You hurt my dog and I'll kick your ass," he bellowed at anyone down below. But Maurice saw no one. No military personnel dressed in black Ninja suits. No weapon toting paramilitary guards. No one. Just cold damp earth.

There! Dip-stick lay on his side fifteen feet away, not moving.

"You sons-of-bitches," Maurice hollered. He lowered himself back down the ladder. He wasn't leaving his dog behind, dead or not.

The creature moved into the patch of sunlight where the ladder sprouted upward.

"What the…?" Maurice exclaimed, never before having seen a bug of such huge proportions. The damn thing was twelve inches long and half as wide. Another monstrous insect, a clone of the first, joined its twin. The odd arthropods sported two short antenna, four legs and human-like eyes. What was more, those eyes were fixed on Maurice.

Maurice lowered himself down the ladder with unrelenting resolve and never taking his eyes off those two unlikely bugs. He shook the ladder and shouted in an attempt to scare them away but to his horror they were coming closer. And what if there are more?

There were more. Hundreds more, clinging to the ceiling above him and covering the walls.

Maurice was painfully aware now no other humans were below ground. These creatures had surely killed Dip-stick and there was no mistaking their intentions to kill him too.

His heart pounding in his ear, Maurice glanced at the hole above him. Safety waited at arm's length. Just get through that hole was all he needed to do and once on the other side, in his own world, he would call for assistance to wipe out all those bugs and retrieve Dip-stick's body.

Maurice inched his way back up the ladder. Fear rose with each step as he drew within inches of a creature clinging to the ceiling above him. Slipping his fingers around the smooth metal of the ladder's top rung, Maurice took a deep breath and reaching deep within himself, he mustered all the strength he could. Almost there. Almost... With a whoop, he catapulted himself upward and burst forth from the foul vapors. He spread-eagle his arms on the hard ground, his wide girth filling the hole like a giant bung.

Sharp claws pierced Maurice's back. Pain exploded through his body. His legs went numb and failed him. His fingers ripped furrows into the topsoil as he fought to keep from slipping back into the darkness below, his guts twisted in searing pain. A blinding white light exploded in his eyes. He gasped one final breath of sweet morning air and screamed so loud his vocal chords burst. His eyes rolled back in his head and he dropped into the underworld.

CHAPTER 4

THE EASTERN HORIZON BETRAYED A sliver of dawn as Sheriff's Chief Deputy Justin Hebert parked his cruiser in a slot fronting Saint Landry Parish sheriff's headquarters. The one-story brick building was set on a grassy lot in mid-town Opelousas with two Bradford pear trees flanking a narrow walkway from the parking lot to a front porch. Adjacent poles flew the American and Louisiana state flags.

Inside, Justin greeted Tanya Garcia, the daytime dispatcher, as she returned the common desk shared with the night-shift dispatcher to her own layout.

"I like your hair," Justin commented to Tanya with an approving nod.

"I don't know if I do," Tanya remarked. A chubby woman, more hip than waist, her once long ponytail was now a mere bob.

Justin flipped through a log journal for the previous night. "Looks like a quiet night."

"Maybe around here it was," Tanya said. "What about your date?"

"Nothing special," Justin remarked.

"Amy, that girl I told you about the other day still wants to go out with you," Tanya reminded her colleague.

"I'll think about it," Justin said. He was in no hurry to become involved in another relationship just yet. He sauntered down a short hallway to a break room crowded with tables, chairs and a coffee machine. A backdoor opened onto a flagstone walkway that swept in a long arch, past a forty-foot radio antenna, to the building's front.

Justin poured a cup of coffee and took a seat at a table, mulling over his date from the night before. Since the loss of his wife, Pam, to a drunk driver just over two years ago, he had agreed to dates over the last nine months with a half dozen friends of friends but all had been unfulfilling. He now wondered if he was pushing things too fast. Until he reconciled his wife's untimely death, it would not be easy to get involved with someone else.

Sheriff Arthur Maxwell joined Justin in the break room. A solidly built man with a crew cut he had maintained since the Marine Corps, his African heritage had given him sharp facial features and rich ebony skin. "Morning, Justin," Maxwell said to his chief deputy, "Gerald starts this morning, doesn't he?"

"Yes sir," Justin answered.

"Let's try to make his first day interesting," the sheriff said. "Also, I'd like to see you in my office after this morning's briefing." Having spoken his piece, he returned to his office.

Gill Stuart, Dwight Claremont and Ricky Fuentes strolled in moments later, jabbering. Gerald Wilson, the sheriff department's newest rookie, brought up the rear.

With coffee poured and seats taken around a common table, the conversation drifted from home projects to baseball scores. Gerald, being the newcomer, had little to say. A half hour later they moved across the hall into a conference room.

"I know you have all met Gerald," the sheriff said. "Let's make him feel at home." He regarded the rookie and added with a smile, "Watch your wallet around here. These guys are dangerous."

Holding aloft a postcard, the sheriff continued. "Doug sends his love from Arizona," he announced. "It seems retirement agrees with him. I'll post this on the bulletin board in case one of you feels like writing him."

"Here's to endless days of golf and beer," Dwight said, raising his cup in mock salute.

"Gill," the sheriff said, "you and Ricky will need to be in Eunice and on LSU's campus by nine thirty. Report to Frank Doogle's office. He's coordinating all security for the governor's secretary. I'll be there by ten."

"And leave all those tender young college girls alone," Dwight chided Gill.

"Now on to less pleasant things," the sheriff said.

"We've been given another arrest warrant for Gus Reyes. Contempt of court, again."

There were moans within the ranks. Dwight spoke up. "Gill and I went last time."

"Justin and Gerald will handle this one," Sheriff Maxwell said.

"Good luck, kid," Dwight said to Gerald. "Just remember to duck."

Gerald shrugged, missing the point.

"You'll find out," Dwight said with a smile.

"Justin," the sheriff said, "contact Chief Gallo when you get to Union Town. He'll have a back-up unit for you."

"Any questions?" Sheriff Maxwell asked. "No? Then that's all."

"Gerald," Justin said as everyone stood to leave, "have a seat in the break room. I'll be right back."

Justin followed Sheriff Maxwell to his office at the end of a short hall. The sheriff closed the door and took a seat at his well-organized desk. Justin remained standing.

From a bottom desk drawer, the sheriff pulled out an unmarked manila folder. "Don't touch the page inside," he said as he handed the file to his chief deputy. "The Feds will be getting involved and it hasn't been fingerprinted yet."

Justin opened the paper cover, raising a questioning brow as he perused the single page document. A Nazi swastika formed a letterhead. Below this, printed in red, were the words, 'Watch your back, Boy.'

"I received this yesterday," Sheriff Maxwell said, grim-faced. "It was mailed from Eunice. No return address."

"A neo-Nazi group?"

"Probably not," the sheriff said. "I dealt with neo-Nazis when I was on the force in Baton Rouge. They are, I guess you could say, a little more professional than this." He took back the folder and filed it away. "Whoever sent this is an amateur just trying to scare me."

"One of the Brandons?" Justin asked.

"A definite possibility," the sheriff said. "Certainly their style. If you hear anything that might be related to this, let me know."

"Positively," Justin said.

Gerald stood when Justin returned to the break room. His supervisor's tall stature and broad shoulders were reassuring to the rookie for whatever they would be facing.

"Let's go," Justin said.

Gerald downed the last of his coffee and tossed the paper cup into a waste bin as he followed his supervisor to their cruiser.

Justin pulled his vehicle into morning traffic and drove east out of town.

"I hear you're living in Union Town now," Justin

said.

"Yes sir," Gerald replied. "I moved there last weekend."

"Do you have family there?" Justin asked, wondering why a twenty-two year old man would move to a small and isolated community like Union Town.

"No sir," Gerald said. "Mom and dad live in Eunice. My father owns a chicken farm." A school bus halted traffic and a group of children piled on board. "I moved to Union Town to be close to my fiancé."

"Oh, who's that?" Justin asked as traffic began moving again.

"Cindy Neumann," Gerald said.

"Spencer's daughter?"

"Yes, sir."

"When's the wedding?"

"In November."

Strip malls and wood-frame houses fell away as the cruiser broke free of city traffic. Justin would take State Highway 190 to Port Barre and on to Krotz Springs. State Highway 105 would then take them north to Union Town.

"Whatever got you interested in law enforcement?" Justin asked. Gerald struck him more as an accountant than a law officer.

"It's a lot more interesting to me than raising chickens or working behind a desk," Gerald commented.

"It has its moments," Justin said. "I think you'll find that out this morning."

"Exactly what's going on?" Gerald asked. Dwight's warning had worried him since the briefing.

"Gus Reyes isn't too fond of law enforcement," Justin explained. "At least not since Maxwell was elected."

"Why is that?" Gerald asked.

"It has to do with George and Bill Brandon," Justin said.

"Bill Brandon, the mayor of Union Town?" Gerald asked.

"The one and only," Justin said.

"So the feud between the mayor and Sheriff Maxwell is real?" Gerald asked.

"Brandon would like it to be feud," Justin remarked. "As for the sheriff, he couldn't care less what either of the Brandons thinks of him."

"Why the bad blood?" Gerald asked.

"You may recall when Mayor Brandon's brother, George, was sheriff of Saint Landry Parish," Justin said.

Gerald did not.

"Well," Justin explained, "George and Bill used to control Saint Landry Parish's bootlegging and George used his position as sheriff to increase their control."

"I have heard talk of the bootlegging," Gerald said.

"It is still a problem but not as much as when George Brandon was sheriff. The Feds came in and shook things up a time or two but never had sufficient evidence to make arrests. Then when Maxwell was elected, he uncovered incriminating evidence on George and handed it over to the district attorney. It was enough to put George in a federal pen. Bill came out of it all without a scratch but Gus Reyes ended up serving two years as an accessory."

"Hence, the bad blood," Gerald said.

"Correct," Justin said, "but Sheriff Maxwell's not one to be intimidated. He spent eighteen years on the Baton Rouge police force, four of those years on the vice squad, so he knows how to deal with people like the Brandons."

"Ricky told me the sheriff was shot in the line of duty," Gerald said.

"He took a bullet to his right thigh during a drug bust," Justin said. "After that, he left the police force and moved to Opelousas, where his daughter lives. A few years later he was elected sheriff."

"Gus Reyes doesn't have a gun, does he?" Gerald asked with trepidation.

"No, nothing that extreme," Justin said. "He'll cuss up a storm and throw things. That's about all. Dwight was carrying on this morning because Gus beaned him with an ashtray during his last arrest."

Scruffy lowlands yielded to stands of broad oaks and spindly pines as the two sheriff's deputies entered the Town of Port Barre. Justin pulled his cruiser onto the gravel parking lot of Vincent's Cafe. "Have you had breakfast?" he asked his partner.

"No sir," Gerald said.

"We'll get a bite here," Justin said. "No need to get to Union Town too early. Gus works third shift at a truck stop outside Lafayette and he's usually on his way to getting drunk about now. We'll let him get some sleep first. He's not as violent when he's groggy."

They took seats in a booth along a plate-glass window over-looking the nearly vacant parking lot. Larry Parker, a Union Town police officer, sat in a corner stall. He nodded greeting to his two compatriots, drained the last of his coffee and strolled over to Justin's table. "What brings you guys over to these parts?" he asked Justin.

"Giving our new deputy a lay of the land," Justin said. Introductions were made.

"Cindy's fiancé, right?" Parker asked.

Gerald blushed at having more of his private life known than he liked. "Yes sir," he said.

"And you, what brings you to Port Barre?" Justin asked Parker.

"Doing a bit of personal work for Mayor Brandon," Parker said. "He needs a delivery boy this morning and I drew short straw."

"How are things at the department?" Justin said to the policeman.

"The usual mess," Parker commented, rolling his

eyes. "Chief Gallo is off with the mayor nearly every day and we're down to four officers; me, Doff, Todd and Jack. Word is, we are going to swing shifts."

"Hang in there," Justin said.

Parker nodded and sauntered off.

A tall blonde waitress with too much lipstick and eye shadow took the two deputies' breakfast orders.

"Believe it or not," Gerald said to Justin, "I actually applied for a job on Union Town's police force."

"So, you've met Chief Gallo," Justin said.

"No," Gerald said. "The police dispatcher gave me an application and said she would call once Chief Gallo had reviewed it. A few days later I got the job with the sheriff's department. I called the police department to let them know I had accepted another job and was told Gallo hadn't even looked at my application."

"That doesn't surprise me," Justin commented. "Chief Gallo is Mayor Brandon's gopher and doesn't have time for much else. His department runs itself." Their breakfasts came and after a leisurely meal they got back on the road.

The landscape between Port Barre and Krotz Springs consisted of open fields and bayous with occasional home sites. Once through Krotz Springs and on Parish Highway 105, the terrain became marshes and pine thickets with a grassy levee separating the two lane from the muddy waters of the Atchafalaya River.

The two deputies passed Krotz Springs-Union Town fire station where Fire Chief Stan Wilton, a bald, heavyset man, and his on-duty crew were taking inventory of gear laid out in the front yard. Stan waved greeting to the passing cruiser.

A mile on, the marshes and pines ended at Calvin Wissnant's junk-cluttered yard. Calvin sat on his battered Suzuki 500 parked under a rickety carport, gunning the two-wheeler's smoking engine.

"Where's your apartment?" Justin asked his partner.

"On Burton Street," Gerald said, "in front of the old community center."

"So you have a panorama of The Swamp and industrial park," Justin commented.

"Fortunately, I only see one edge of the industrial park," Gerald said. "There's a bunch of trees that block the view."

"Why don't we swing by the bank?" Justin suggested. "I'm sure Cindy would like to see you in uniform."

"That would be great," Gerald said.

CHAPTER 5

CINDY NEUMANN WATCHED HER FATHER devour his usual breakfast of scrambled eggs, bacon, biscuits and black coffee. He was a stocky, big-boned man of fifty-nine years and thanks to his daughter, well-fed, but in need of time off from his beer drinking.

"Daddy, don't forget, I won't be home for dinner tonight," Cindy said. She was a full-figured girl with brown hair and blue eyes.

Spencer made no comment.

"There is leftover stew in the 'fridge."

"Who's going to cook for me when you're living in Opelousas?" Spencer grumbled between bites.

"Daddy," Cindy admonished, "we're going to live here, in town. You know that."

"You'll forget all about your old father when you're a married woman."

Cindy grinned at her father's feigned trepidation. Since her mother's disappearance to someplace other than Union Town, Cindy had taken over the household chores. For two years now, she'd juggled her domestic work with her job as a bank teller at Union Town City

Bank and doing a good job with both.

"Well, gotta go," Spencer said, rising from the table. He scooped up two multi-vitamins and downed them with the last of his coffee. Cindy handed him his bagged lunch.

"I'll order a chocolate pie for you from Therma's," Cindy promised as her father headed for the front door.

Spencer waved appreciation for the dessert and stepped through the front doorway of their dated modular home. The squeaky screen door slammed shut behind him. He tromped down the front porch steps and crossed a patchy, untended lawn, hefting his bulk into a tattered, early-model pick-up truck. Lighting his first cigarette of the day, he started his vehicle's engine.

Following his daily route that he could drive with his eyes closed, Spencer motored a mile across town to a dusty lot cut from sedge and encircled by aging metal fence posts holding up four strands of barbed wire. He extricated himself from between steering wheel and seat back, unlocked a metal gate and swung it open.

As Spencer returned to his pick-up, Calvin Wissnant rode up on his motorcycle. He followed his boss across the rutted lot to a white rear-loading, garbage truck and both men parked their vehicles next to an open-sided, tin shed.

Spencer grabbed his lunch from his truck's seat and a Remington, semi-automatic 0.22 caliber rifle from a gun rack hung over the back window. Sliding out, he and Calvin ambled over to the eight-wheeler. They hoisted themselves in, the gear thrown on the seat between them.

"I brought another box of shells," Calvin said, scratching his potbelly. He shoved the bullets into the vehicle's glove compartment.

With a growl and a belch of black smoke, the garbage truck's diesel rumbled to life. Spencer found first gear and drove between their personal vehicles and the open-sided shed housing an aluminum crusher straddling a mound of flattened cans.

Exiting the compound, Spencer bounced the truck over a single line of railroad tracks to Colliers Road, a narrow macadam strip running due south from town.

Calvin loaded a pinch of snuff between cheek and gum. "Ya reckon there'll be any puppies around today?" he asked in a hopeful tone. His own two mutts, both which he had saved from execution six months earlier, had disappeared a week ago. They were damn good dogs, had some beagle in them, and would have made fine trackers. Calvin figured someone passing through from Krotz Springs or Palmetto had seen that same potential. He had plans to visit both towns to claim what was rightfully his and kick the dog-napper's ass but in the meantime, he would see about replacements.

"I guess we're due for a litter," Spencer replied. "Been a few months since we've seen any."

A mile out of town, Colliers Road made a sharp curve to the right and disappeared into haze-shrouded scrub. Spencer slowed his vehicle at the dogleg but continued straight onto a well-used, dirt track. Dropping the truck's transmission into a lower gear and kicking up a billow of dust, he passed within a hundred yards of Maurice Dubois' place.

Spencer checked his rear-view mirror. Maurice's dog, Dip-stick, usually caught up to the truck at this point to challenge the vehicle to a good-spirited race, at least until the mutt spotted a rabbit and took off in another direction. Today, Dip-stick was a no-show.

A half-mile from the main road Spencer swung his truck wide and parked next to a lone pine overlooking one of three landfills scattered about the parish. The gaping hole was fifty feet deep and the length and width of Union Town High School's football field.

Spencer slid from his vehicle's cab and for a long moment scanned the surrounding acreage for stray dogs. Seeing none, he strolled over to a D-4 bulldozer parked alongside a tin shed.

"Do we need to top-up the fuel?" Calvin asked.

"Naw," Spencer said as he climbed aboard the machine and switched on the ignition. "Still have nearly a full tank." He cranked the dozer's engine and after letting it warm up several minutes, shoved it into gear and drove the creaking monster to the pit's edge. Satisfied with his new position, he switched off the engine.

Calvin trotted up and handed his boss the rifle and extra box of shells before climbing aboard himself. He took up position on the hood, legs dangling off one side.

Spencer chambered the first round, a Triple-X long-range cartridge. Short-range bullets would certainly do and were cheaper to buy, but Spencer liked the power of the longs. When he shot something, Spencer wanted a clean kill, especially when it came to puppies.

Placing the semi-automatic weapon across his lap, Spencer scanned the trash heap from end to end, finally focusing on the side directly opposite where the few rats he and his assistant had seen lately were showing up. The only movement this morning were plastic bags and paper dancing to and fro in a southerly breeze that brought with it the rank odor of rotting trash and the sharp smell of sulfur.

"I sure hope there's something to shoot at today," Calvin said. For the last month or so they hadn't seen much of anything, no birds and only a handful of rats. Three buzzards had drifted lazily overhead a week before but had been too high for a good shot.

"We'll see," Spencer snorted, not much of a talker when on the hunt. He continued his search for prey.

Movement caught Spencer's eye. Straightening up, he shouldered the rifle, his heart picking up pace with the expectation of a kill. Calvin estimated the point in the trash heap his boss had sighted on. By the time he spotted the target, Spencer got off a shot. The report was followed instantly by a dull 'thunk'.

"Got him," Spencer said proudly. He waited to see if the rodent would reappear. When it didn't, he handed the weapon to Calvin.

"That was the biggest damn rat I've ever seen," Calvin said excitedly. He spit a wad of snuff-tainted saliva, his eyes glued to the spot where Spencer had just bagged his first kill of the day.

From behind a stand of twisted aluminum tubing emerged another dark shape, the same size as the animal Spencer had just shot, at least a foot long. The beast crawled along the mounded refuse and halted, still in plain view. Calvin took aim, inhaled, held his breath for a brief moment, blew out and squeezed the trigger. Crack. Thunk.

The target didn't move.

Spencer grabbed the gun for his next turn. The monster rat was a sitting duck. Taking more seasoned aim, he squeezed off another clean shot.

"Jesus!" Calvin exclaimed even before the sound of the discharge had echoed away. "You knocked that bastard for a loop." The bullet's impact had thrown the rat into the air where it hung for an impossibly long moment before dropping slowly out of sight.

"I hit under him," Spencer growled.

"That was a crow," Calvin declared. "Wasn't it?"

"Didn't look like no crow I ever saw," Spencer said.

Both men waited for further movement. A full fifteen minutes passed before a word was spoken.

"We must have put the fear of God in 'em," Spencer commented. "Time to get to work." The rats had another reprieve until next week.

Calvin stepped down onto the dozer's sloped tread and jumped to the ground. Spencer got the diesel rewound and descended the pit's gently sloping side. He lowered the machine's blade and spread out a pile of recently added garbage as if landscaping someone's front yard.

While his boss worked below, Calvin entered the storage shed. The building was crammed with an array of hand-tools hung from nails, hoops of electrical wire stuffed in old buckets and stacks of boxes filled with treasures Calvin had salvaged from the pit.

He took a moment to peruse a wooden shelf cluttered with items bound for a weekend flea market in Opelousas. One particular piece, an oval stone exposed along the pit's edge by a heavy rain the previous week, caught Calvin's eye. He picked up the fist-size rock, still amazed at its lighter than expected weight. The stone was chipped on one end revealing a multi-colored, crystalline core not found in the more common rocks of the area. He returned the stone to the shelf. With luck, it would fetch him enough for a case of beer.

Calvin pulled a utility-size plastic bag from a storage bin. He exited the shed and set about gathering paper, plastic and other debris scattered topside by the wind. The sulfur stench was much more potent today than usual.

As Calvin zigzagged across the barren ground filling his bag, Jim Linderson, Union Town High School's biology teacher, drove up in his blue hatchback. The auto's rear was overfilled with junk.

"Morning, Calvin," Linderson called to the parish employee. Linderson was a short, plump man with wire-rim glasses perched atop a pointed nose. He squinted in the bright morning sunlight.

"Howdy, Mister Linderson," Calvin said. "It's gonna be a hot one, ain't it?" He walked over to see what valuables the teacher might be disposing of.

"Sure is," Linderson said. "Where should I leave this stuff?"

"Any wet trash?" Calvin asked. Any household garbage would be tossed directly into the pit.

"Nope, just junk from around the house."

"Toss it on the ground. I'll take care of it."

Linderson untied the hatchback's trunk lid and pulled out what he and his wife had culled from their garage. Some items, like an old minnow bucket and badminton set, were still usable and he laid these off to one side certain Calvin would find them of interest.

With his car emptied, Linderson dropped the tie-down cord in the open trunk and strolled to the pit's rim. Shading his eyes Indian fashion, he looked across the mounded debris, wondering what kinds of trash people were disposing of these days. It sure did stink.

"Where are all your birds?" Linderson asked. Flocks of sea gulls and a handful of crows were usually picking over kitchen scraps but today there were none.

"I guess they flew north for the summer," Calvin joked. Shaking his head, he said in a more serious vein, "Haven't seen nary a gull or crow around here for a couple of weeks." He spit. "Don't bother me none. I hate the damn things."

"I hope they come back," the biology teacher said. "I'm planning to bring my senior class out here to study bird behavior."

"Bird behavior?" Calvin replied, baffled that anyone would be interested in some old dirty gulls. "I can tell you all about that. They eat garbage, shit, and squawk."

"Oh, there's a bit more to it than that," Linderson said. Calvin had graduated high school the last in his class and had certainly never shown an interest in the sciences. The only time the lad ever wanted to understand animal behavior was during deer hunting season.

"If you ask me," Calvin said, "all them damn birds are good for is target practice."

Linderson gave Calvin a disapproving frown.

Calvin dug the wad of snuff from his mouth with an index finger and flipped away the spent tobacco. He spit out the remaining fines and wiped his finger on his pants. "If you want to study something," he said, "you oughta study them rats we shot at this morning. Biggest damn things I ever saw." Adding in earnest, "And they can fly."

Linderson raised a brow. "Flying squirrels I've heard of," he commented with a chuckle, "but flying rats? Now that's a new one."

"We shot one this morning," Calvin said. "I'll show you if you want to see."

Linderson looked at his watch. The only thing for him back home was more cleaning and he was not particularly interested in getting too involved in that. When his wife went on a cleaning spree she didn't let up until the house was spotless, inside and out, and it was him who usually caught the bulk of the grunt work during her binges. Besides, he told himself, if the birds didn't return to the dump in the first few weeks of school, he would need an alternate project for his students. This might be identifying the reason for the birds abandoning the dump site. Smiling to himself, he considered it might even include flying rats.

"Is it easy to get to?" Linderson asked. He didn't intend to walk out in the middle of all that garbage. The stench was nearly overpowering where he now stood.

"It's over there," Calvin said, pointing to the opposite side of the pit. "You can stay up top. I'll go down and see if I can find the thing."

Linderson followed Calvin, glad to be moving upwind of the trash heap.

"It's right over there," Calvin said when they reached their new position. "Over by that aluminum… Christ! Would you look at that?" Down in the pit, a hundred feet away, a perfectly round, eight foot diameter hole angled into the trash.

Amazed at the unusual shaft, Calvin descended the pit's sloped wall and made his way across the heap toward the opening.

"I wouldn't go too far out there," Linderson cautioned. "It looks unstable."

Calvin halted, thirty feet from the hole. He bounced his weight on the pile and prudently changed his mind about going any further. Linderson was probably right. Spencer hadn't worked the dozer on this side of the dump for quite some time and there was no telling how solid the trash was in this area.

Calvin focused on the spot where he figured the dead rat had fallen, a good ten feet from the cave opening. "I don't see nothing", Calvin called up. "It might have made it back into the hole." With nothing in clear sight, he carefully picked his way back across the refuse like crossing an enemy mine field. Scurrying up the pit's chert wall, he joined Linderson.

"You know," Linderson said, "I believe there is something moving down there." He pointed. "See that black plastic garbage bag? The one with the milk carton hanging out of it?"

"Yeah."

"Just below that. There's something in the shadows and it certainly looks bigger than a rat. Could be a raccoon."

"I'll get the gun."

"No, don't shoot it. If it falls deeper into the hole we'll never know what it is."

"It's a flying rat, that's what it is."

"If it is," Linderson said, smiling broadly, "I'll make sure it's named after you." He was pleased at just having found a fieldwork project for his seniors; ecosystem of the Union Town landfill.

Linderson and Calvin returned to the front side of the dump. "You be sure to warn Mister Neumann about that hole," Linderson said to Calvin. "That dozer is a lot heavier than you are." With a hopeful nod he added, "And I'd appreciate it if you didn't shoot any more wildlife."

"Yeah, sure," Calvin said, not bothering to mention that Spencer wasn't about to give up zapping a few rats for some stupid high school science project.

Linderson sauntered to his car and closed its hatchback.

"Mister Linderson," Calvin said, "can you take a look at something? It's some type of rock I found last week, after that big rain we had."

"Sure, where is it?" Linderson was far from an authority on geology but he did know the basics.

Calvin ran to the storage shed and returned with his prize rock with the chipped end. He handed it to Linderson. "What do you think?" he asked.

Linderson rolled the rock over in his hand. "It's not very heavy," he noted. "I'd say it's a geode."

"A what?" Calvin asked.

"A geode," Linderson repeated. "It's a rock with a hollow center and over time, crystals form inside."

"What do you think it's worth?"

"I really have no idea," Linderson confessed, "but it's certainly worth keeping."

"And what about that?" Calvin asked, pointing to the rock's chipped end. "That dark part."

Linderson perused the rock's exposed core. Just under the chipped surface lay a brownish structure, a half inch long, half as wide at one end and tapering to a point.

"That's interesting," Linderson said. "It almost looks like something embedded inside but it's probably some type of crystal."

"Awesome, thanks," Calvin said.

Linderson handed Calvin his rock and slipped in

behind his car's steering wheel. He rolled down his window, his curiosity piqued yet again. "By the way," he said to Calvin, "where are all the flies?" Linderson had not seen any of the insects among the trash and now saw none inside his car. On previous visits, when he had left a car door or window open, the interior was full of the pests.

"I guess they left with the birds," Calvin said.

Linderson took one last look over the dump, disturbed by what he was seeing. Something was keeping the birds and flies away and that same something could be the source of that god-awful stench. He decided then and there to call the EPA. Whatever someone in the parish was dumping nowadays could very well be toxic.

CHAPTER 6

"PARTY DOWN. POSSIBLE DOA. UNKNOWN cause. Number Two Industrial Boulevard," Doris Greely, Union Town's police dispatcher radioed. "Larry, what's your ten-twenty?"

"Just now entering town," Officer Parker radioed. "Responding."

"Responding," radioed Bill Moley, a Union Town paramedic and ambulance driver. Bill had just come on duty with his partner, Malcolm Friar. The two men had been on their way to Union Town Hospital for a cup of coffee when the call came through.

Justin thumbed his own radio's mike. "Doris, this is Justin. I'm on Front Street, near the bank, responding also."

Justin switched on the cruiser's blue trip-lights and caught up with Larry Parker's police cruiser as the officer turned onto Old Simmesport Highway. They sped north toward Krotz Bridge.

"Nothing like starting your day with a bang," Justin commented to Gerald.

"Or your career," Gerald said. He tightened his seat

belt.

"Justin," Police Officer Parker radioed his back up. "This is Cajun Snax's factory. You might as well take over at the scene. You know the layout as well as I do and it'll be good training for the rookie."

"Ten-four," Justin responded. If this call was anything other than natural causes, the sheriff's department would assume responsibility for the crime scene anyway and it would certainly be an enlightening experience for Gerald.

"What do you reckon it is?" Gerald asked. A break-in or vandalism was one thing but a possible DOA, now that was something else.

"Won't know until we get there," Justin commented. "It might be Clee."

"Who's that?"

"One of the town characters," Justin said. "He drifted in a couple years ago from somewhere up north. Not much of a troublemaker. Works an occasional odd job and does a little pan-handling on the side."

"Why do you think it might be him?" Gerald asked.

"Just a hunch," Justin said. "Clee has cancer and refuses treatment. I figured a call like this would come through one day."

Passing over the mud flats at Krotz Bridge, the view took in withered marsh grass and reeds along a dry creek bed cutting a path through thick scrub and pines. A hundred yards ahead a cluster of nine aluminum-sided buildings lined a single access road, Industrial Boulevard, all set on a weedy plateau of fill-dirt.

Gerald's trepidation for seeing his first corpse was tempered by Justin's remark about this Clee guy. Killed by disease, not a knife or gun. Still, it was more unnerving than arresting someone for contempt of court.

The cruisers slowed at a dead caution light marking the entrance to the industrial park. A wooden marquee overgrown with briars and honeysuckle displayed the names of the nine resident factories, all closed. Tall grass and weeds had taken over the once manicured right-of-way.

Cajun Snax was the first building on the right. The single-story structure had a production/warehouse area and adjoining managerial offices. A concrete sidewalk cut a line through a weed-strewn lawn to a glass-paneled front door.

A youth, maybe eighteen years old, dressed in jeans, work boots and a T-shirt, stood beside a red twin-cab pick-up truck curbed near the offices. The lad waved frantically at the approaching patrol cars.

Justin pulled his cruiser wide around the truck's rear, parking diagonally to the office entrance. Quickly scanning the area, he saw no one besides the excited youth. Satisfied of his and Gerald's own safety, Justin stepped out into the sultry air and slipped his nightstick into its ringed holder. He donned his hat. A relentless August sun made South Louisiana an unpleasant place, even at this early hour.

Police Officer Parker took up a similar position at the opposite end of the building, four hundred feet away. He too saw nothing suspicious.

"It's Mr. Tullis!" the boy called fearfully, pointing toward the offices.

"What happened to him?" Justin asked. The poor kid was scared, real scared.

"I don't know," the boy stammered. He was on the verge of tears. "I saw him through the front door. He came running out of the back of the office, screaming. I think he had a heart attack."

"Calm down," Justin said. "Where did you last see him?"

The youth motioned toward the front door again.

"Inside. I tried to help him but the door is locked."

Justin was well aware if this was a coronary he had to act fast. A life could be dangling from a thin thread and precious seconds were ticking by. But he also knew not to rush into an unknown situation such as this, especially since something wasn't right with the boy's description of Tullis' actions. Why had Tullis been in such a hurry to vacate the building and why had he been screaming? A heart attack victim can barely catch his breath, much less yell.

"When did this happen?" Justin asked.

"Fifteen, maybe twenty minutes ago," the boy replied. "You have to help him!"

"We will," Justin consoled. "Is there anyone else in the building?"

"Ed and Joe. They went in with Mr. Tullis."

"Where are Ed and Joe now?"

"Still inside, I guess."

Justin looked the boy in the eyes and asked, "How did they get into the building if the front door is locked?"

"Around back. There is a rear door that is open. Mister Tullis sent me back to the truck to get his big flashlight. I was changing the batteries when I heard him scream. I looked up and saw him running toward the front door. It was horrible." He started to sob. "I didn't know what to do."

"What's your name?" Justin asked.

"John Harriman," came his feeble reply. "Aren't you going to help him?"

"Go with me up to the front door, John."

"No!" John's blanched color faded even more. His jaw knotted with tension. "Please, I can't. What if he… Please, don't make me go."

"I see someone on the floor just inside the doorway," Gerald called. Curiosity had drawn the young deputy like an ambulance chaser to an auto accident. He could make out a pair of brown work boots jutting above the door's metal base. Two legs came into view. The person stretched out on the floor was enormous.

Gerald slowed his pace sensing something was wrong. One more step and the rookie deputy nearly fainted. "Jesus!" he stammered. He staggered backwards and spewed up his egg and biscuit breakfast.

"Wait here," Justin ordered John. He hurried to his partner's aid.

"Doris," Justin radioed the police dispatcher when he beheld what lay beyond the door, "I need a coroner out here. Send whatever back-up units you have available." Civilians with police scanners would soon start showing up for a look-see and Justin would need crowd control. "Chief Gallo, do you copy?"

No reply.

"Doris, see if you can locate Chief Gallo," Justin requested.

"What's going on?" Police Chief Gallo replied over the radio.

"We're at the industrial park, Cajun Snax," Justin began. He didn't know if the chief had caught Doris' original transmission.

"I didn't ask you where you are," the chief said. "I asked you what's going on."

Justin drew an impatient breath, held it and continued in a professional tone. "Appears to be a male, age and race impossible to tell," he reported. "Unknown cause of death."

"Well, hell," the chief said tiredly. A woman's bedroom voice spoke softly in the background, audible over the air. Chief Gallo said, "Let me get hold of the mayor. I'll be out there directly."

Justin radioed Doris again for someone to bring keys for the building's door and asked her to get in touch with Sheriff Maxwell to appraise him of the current situation. "Tell the sheriff," Justin said to the police dispatcher, "I'd like him over here as soon as possible."

"I'll let him know," Doris replied.

An ambulance swept onto Industrial Boulevard and joined the other vehicles in the parking lot. Bill and Malcolm climbed out. Bill retrieved an over-sized medical case from the rear of the modified van.

"Looks like one of those days," Malcolm said to Justin. He looked at Gerald and said, "Are you all right?" The rookie deputy was still hunkered over, breathing rapidly from his ordeal. A feeble moan was all he could muster to attest to his improving condition.

"I say it's a gunshot," Bill's gravely voice interjected. Bill Moley was a hefty man, with a double chin and thinning black hair. He was a volunteer fireman who headed up Union Town's paramedic service and grew monster tomatoes in an organic garden behind the fire station.

"Ten to one says it's a coronary," Malcolm countered.

He and Bill had a running duel as to who could correctly identify causes of death. Most cases were cut and dry; a drowning in the Atchafalaya River last year and an occasional auto accident or heart attack, but this one would definitely be a challenge.

Malcolm, an oval-faced twenty-two year old with ebony hair, olive skin and a lean build, held a part-time job as Bill's assistant. The remainder of his time was spent working for Olan Barnes, the town's mortician and owner of its only funeral home.

"Can a heart attack do that to someone?" Gerald asked. Having recovered enough to speak, he was still unwilling to look at the body again.

"Sure can," Malcolm replied, chuckling. "You should have seen Wayne Roberts, back a couple years ago. He had a massive heart attack while screwing his ol' lady. By the time we got there he was bloated like a toad in heat." Laughing again he added, "She must be some piece."

"A coronary, maybe," Bill pondered out loud for Gerald's benefit, "but look how discolored the skin is. A bullet's impact can create enough systemic pressure to rupture every blood vessel in your body. Turn a white man as black as Rufus Jackson." With a shake of his head he added, "I've certainly never seen a corpse in this condition. Hard to tell how long he's been here. A week, I'd say."

"That I agree with," Malcolm said.

"That doesn't make any sense," Gerald commented to Justin concerning Bill's last comment. "The claimant told you he saw his boss alive this morning."

Justin nodded. "That's why I requested Doff Green. This is now considered a crime scene."

As seen through the paneled-glass front door, what was supposed to be the late Bob Tullis lay belly-up on a beige carpet, black slacks and bright green shirt stretched to near tearing over his severely bloated, six-foot frame. His eyes had popped from their sockets and lay like deflated balloons on bulbous cheeks. Syrupy ocher oozed from nose and ears and a swollen tongue forced open his mouth. The body's exposed skin was translucent purple-green underlined with an irregular pattern of blackened lines that had once been blood vessels.

"You guys might as well take five," Justin said to the paramedics. No one was doing anything until Doff had taken photographs, the area had been gleaned for evidence, and the coroner on-call had officially pronounced the poor stiff dead.

"Ain't gonna be any fight from me," Malcolm said. "It's too early in the morning to deal with the stink in there anyway. Right, deputy?" He winked at Gerald.

Gerald was not amused.

Justin ordered Gerald and Parker to cordon off the crime scene. Retrieving his note pad and clipboard from his cruiser, he returned to Mr. Tullis' truck. Young John

Harriman had a few more questions to answer.

"Mister Harriman, I'd like you to tell me what Mister Tullis was wearing this morning," Justin said. He would not put the boy through the trauma of looking at a body he felt was not Tullis.

"Is he dead?" John honestly didn't know.

"Just answer my question."

"I don't remember," John said in a shaky voice. He was having a difficult time remembering anything at that point.

"Take your time."

John thought, trembling with uncertainty, and then said, "He had on dark colored pants and a gray shirt."

"And you're sure of that? Dark pants, gray shirt."

"Yes sir."

Justin jotted down the information, convinced now the dead man was definitely not Tullis. The victim had on dark-colored pants all right but his shirt was unmistakably green. Justin would have reconsidered his assumption had young John Harriman remembered to point out he was red/green color-blind.

From what Justin knew now, it seemed quite possible Tullis had entered the building from the rear and stumbled upon the body when he had come into the front offices. His reaction to his gruesome find might have made it appear to John as though something had been physically wrong with his boss. Mr. Tullis could very well have retreated into the factory area. But in any event, Justin needed more information before he and his team made entry. He wouldn't jeopardize himself or his subordinates in such an unknown situation.

"What's Mister Tullis' full name?"

"I think it's Arlin," Harriman says. "I don't know his full name."

"Are any of you from around this area?" Justin asked John.

"No sir," the young man said. "We're all from Natchez, Mississippi. We came down yesterday afternoon and stayed at a motel in Simmesport."

Justin scribbled the information on his note pad. "I want you to tell me again exactly what happened," he instructed.

John took a shaky breath. "We got here about six thirty this morning to haul some equipment up to Natchez. Mister Tullis rebuilds and sells used food processing machinery." He halted, adding, "This was my first day on the job."

"How did you alert the police?" Justin asked. There were no public phones in the industrial park.

"Mister Tullis has one of those new Dyna TAC mobile phones," John said. "In his truck."

The fact neither Tullis nor the other two men, Ed and Joe, had exited the building nor attempted to contact the authorities bothered Justin. Something definitely was not right.

"Justin, this is dispatch," Doris radioed.

"Go ahead, Doris," the deputy responded.

"I just spoke with Sheriff Maxwell. He's on his way to your ten-twenty."

"Ten-four," Justin said.

Justin's requested back-up arrived. The first vehicle carried Joel Dubonnet and Andre Loux, members of Union Town's rescue squad, and the second, Police Officer Jack Moore. Behind them in separate cars were Police Officer Doff Green and Olan Barnes, the coroner on-call.

Orders were given for Joel and Jack to block the industrial park's main entrance with their cars. Word would have already spread about a supposed murder and soon everyone in town would come by for a firsthand look.

Justin showed Doff and Olan the body and filled them in on what he already knew about the case.

"Christ," Doff said when he viewed the remains. "This guy's been here awhile."

"The claimant's name is John Harriman," Justin informed the two men. "He's a little confused right now. Says the deceased was his boss who had a possible heart attack a half hour ago."

"Confused is right," Olan remarked. "A half hour plus a few days."

"Let's air this place out so I can get some photos," Doff said. He produced a ring of keys kept on file at the police station and unlocked the glass-paneled door, swinging it full open.

"The offices haven't been secured yet," Justin informed the others. To Gerald he asked, "Are you up to going inside?"

Gerald nodded with some effort, determined not to let his weak stomach get the better of him.

Justin drew his pistol and moved across the threshold. He called out to anyone inside. No response. "Are you ready?" he asked Gerald.

"Let's do it," the rookie said with as much resolve as he could muster. He took a deep breath of fresh outside air and followed his superior, stepping wide around the cadaver and averting his eyes from the gruesome scene. When he could no longer hold his breathe, he exhaled and reluctantly drew in another.

To both Gerald's and Justin's surprise and relief, the air in the office was stagnant and hot but held only a heavy sulfur smell laced with a musty odor, far from the sharp, pungent stench of rotting flesh they had expected. Even standing next to the corpse there was no hint of an offensive smell. It appeared as if John Harriman was indeed correct and the victim had died a mere half-hour before.

An L-shaped hallway connected the reception foyer

and offices with the factory's production area. Justin again announced loudly the presence of law enforcement. Failing again to illicit a response, he led the way down the hall, past two opposing offices littered with scattered papers. Beyond these rooms the corridor took a ninety-degree turn to the left, past another office and two adjoining bathrooms and ended at a service door to the production area. All of the offices were clear.

The service door was locked from the opposite side and none of the keys Justin had been given fit its keyhole. When Justin's attempt to raise someone within the factory failed, he and Gerald returned to the front. Doff was busy with his Nikon 35 millimeter.

"We'll secure the rest of the building," Justin told Doff. "Parker," Justin said, "take the east end of the building. Gerald and I will secure this end. Meet us around back."

Gerald drew his weapon, his anxieties growing as he followed his supervisor to the building's rear corner. The rookie deputy had trained with the revolver at the police academy in Lafayette to supplement what training the sheriff's department offered but this was the first time he had taken the pistol from its holster in the line of duty. The gun's cool steel felt good in his sweaty palm.

The Swamp's dense foliage pushed up hard against a fifteen-foot embankment at the building's rear. Vines snaked up the steep grade to gain a hold on the useless security fence. Longer tentacles had reached the buildings back wall and service ladder to the roof.

Officer Parker appeared at the building's far end. The three lawmen advanced, closing the gap between them.

Justin pointed out to Gerald a hole cut in the fence opposite an emergency exit. "We used to get a lot of break-ins just after the park was closed down," Justin said.

"Why did the factories close?" Gerald asked.

"Ground subsidence," Justin said. "The industrial park was built on fill dirt over a trash dump and it's been plagued with sink holes from day one."

Justin held up a halting hand. A patch of color beyond the fence at the bottom of the embankment caught his attention. He slipped through the opening in the fence for a closer look.

"Dispatch," Justin radioed, "all communications go to channel five." He switched his own unit to the emergency channel which would isolate transmissions to official walkie-talkies only.

"I have human skeletal remains outside the building," Justin radioed. "Request back up at my position. We'll be making entry."

From where he stood, Justin could tell the skeleton was that of a youth, a boy by the clothes and the victim had been there for some time, his bones bleached white. No hair was visible, only a black, oily substance beneath the remains.

"What do we do now?" Gerald asked nervously.

Nineteen years of law enforcement had taught Chief Deputy Justin Hebert one important rule, one that he constantly drilled into his men. A simple rule but one that saved lives: 'Expect the unexpected.' This rule was rolling around in Justin's mind at that very moment. Anyone inside the factory could be armed and as frightened as young John Harriman, a dangerous combination in any scenario.

Officer Parker reached their position. "The Rumpsin twins," Parker remarked, when he viewed the remains.

Justin frowned and nodded affirmation.

"Who are the Rumpsin twins?" Gerald asked.

"A couple of kids abducted from the Lake Charles area about five years ago," Parker said.

"I remember that," Gerald said. "Their bodies were found here in Union Town."

"Yes, they were," Justin answered. He had never forgotten the horrible condition of the bodies; mounds of maggot feces and scabs of dried skin riddled with bore holes. And bones, dirty brown and stinking of death. But Justin saw none of that here. No signs of maggots, no apparent smell, and bones white enough to have come from Mr. Bones, the resident teaching aid in Jim Linderson's biology classroom.

"We haven't had any missing persons reports filed at

our department," Officer Parker said. "Anything in Opelousas?"

"Nothing," Justin said. He regarded the building knowing whatever fate had befallen this youth had to take second seat to the job at hand. Mr. Tullis and crew had to be located and the building secured before any further work could be done.

"Oh shit," Parker said, grim-faced. "Look who's coming."

Frank Dyer, one of Union Town's six parish councilmen approached, followed by Officer Moore. Frank was short and thin with protruding ears, a near bald head and a prominent Adam's apple. He didn't look happy.

"Parker," Frank said as he stepped up to the fence. "The mayor wants to know what's going on here."

"We have two bodies," Parker reported, directing the councilman's attention to the skeletal remains, "and possibly three persons inside the factory."

"Jesus Christ," Frank exclaimed when he beheld the bones.

"Mister Dyer," Justin said, "this is a crime scene and you are not authorized to be here. Please return to the front of the building." To Officer Moore he said, "Jack, I'll need you to secure this rear door while we make entry."

"These police officers take orders from Chief Gallo," Frank protested. "Not a sheriff's deputy."

"Mister Dyer," Justin said in growing consternation, "Chief Gallo was made aware of the body in the office area and he has not provided any input."

Frank huffed. "The mayor will hear about this," he snapped and stormed away.

"Okay, we're making entry," Justin said to his team. "Remember there are three individuals still unaccounted for."

To Gerald, Justin said, "You stay with me. Any questions?"

"No sir," came Gerald's uneasy reply.

Justin took up a position against the factory's wall. As he swung open the door, a putrid odor of sulfur wafted out. "This is the sheriff's department," he said loudly. "Arlin Tullis, can you hear me? Joe, Ed, can you hear me?"

No response.

Justin radioed those at the factory's front that he and his men were entering the building.

"Justin," Officer Green radioed, "Olan says we may be dealing with chemical contamination. Are you aware of any chemicals stored in this building?"

"No, I'm not," Justin said, "but I do detect a strong sulfur smell."

"Be alert to any chemical spills," Doff advised.

"You heard Doff," Justin said to his subordinates.

Both Justin and Parker were well acquainted with the

interiors of all these factories from past call-outs. The abandoned buildings had become havens for vagrants and vandals and Cajun Snax's facility was no exception. Since the factory ceased operation two years before, Justin and Parker had worked break-ins here numerous times and they knew the building had never contained chemicals of any kind.

Justin quickly reviewed the building's layout for Gerald's benefit. "Make sure you stay with me," he stressed to the rookie. Undisciplined curiosity could be a killer.

Gerald took a calming breath and shook tension from his hands.

"Parker, you take the east end," Justin said. "Gerald and I will take the west."

Justin led the way into the factory. A wedge of sunlight flowed through the doorway illuminating dead machinery shrouded in eerie silence. If Joe, Ed or Mr. Tullis were indeed inside, they were being awful quiet. Too quiet.

CHAPTER 7

DOFF COMPLETED PHOTOGRAPHING THE CORPSE. "It's all yours," he said to Olan.

Olan stepped forward. "I'm wondering if this man's death is chemical related," he said to Doff. "Give Justin a heads-up and find out from the claimant where his boss was before they arrived here."

"This could be Tullis after all," Doff commented.

"Maybe. I need you to get a hold of the hospital," Olan said. "Have them track down Doctor Martin. The remains around back need to be examined and I have my hands full here."

Doff radioed Justin and then hurried off to track down the other Union Town coroner and speak with young John Harriman.

Olan donned latex gloves and squatted alongside the corpse. "I've never seen anything like this," he commented to Bill and Malcolm. "I can see clear through the skin to the vertebra in the neck and sutures of the skull." He wiped his brow, adding, "The boys in New Iberia are going to love this one."

"Is it my eyes," Bill asked, "or is the skin of that guy a

different color than when we first arrived?"

"There's certainly something strange going on here," Olan declared. Clear patches had formed within the victim's epidermis, allowing more bone structure to show through. The corpse's ears sagged like wilted lettuce. The skin was melting like tar on Front Street in midsummer!

A black, oily substance appeared from under the corpse's shoulders. Olan backed away as the dark liquid crept across the carpet like some outlandish amoebae.

"He's dissolving," Malcolm said, aghast.

"Let's get him contained and transported," Olan said. "And make damn sure you don't get any of that body fluid on you."

"Grab a body bag and that plastic tarp from the ambulance," Bill ordered Malcolm.

Malcolm ran to their vehicle and returned with a body-bag and a ten-foot square of plastic sheeting. Both paramedics slipped on a double pair of latex gloves before checking the integrity of each others jumpsuits.

"Pull the leading edge tight," Bill explained as they unfolded the Nylon-reinforced sheeting. "We'll slip it under this side and work it under him."

Skin on the cadaver's face now oozed into sagging folds. The nose had collapsed into the nasal cavity and the dental gums flowed over brilliant white teeth like molasses.

Working on opposite ends, Bill and Malcolm slid the

plastic sheeting under the body's right side, smearing the black liquid into the carpet as they did so.

"Hold it," Malcolm groaned in disgust. The sheeting had snagged on a belt-loop of the dead man's pants. Tightening his grip on the plastic, Malcolm pulled hard, wanting to get all this over with. His added force shifted the head laterally, ripping open the neck just below the skull. Black fluid that had once been the victim's brain gushed forth.

"Shit," Bill gasped. Sweat rolled down his face.

Malcolm was doing all he could not to vomit.

"You guys need to hurry," Olan prodded the two paramedics. The corpse was dissolving faster now, its clothing saturated in the goo.

"This isn't working," Bill sputtered in frustration.

"Swing the tarp around and try it from the head down," Olan suggested impatiently. "Get those remains contained."

"Dammit Malcolm, come on!" Bill snapped his own frustration.

Malcolm re-positioned himself, gripping tightly his end of the plastic sheet. At Bill's signal the two men slid the sheet under the head and shoulders to the waistline. Upon encountering yet another snag on the pants, they lifted the portion they had.

The cadaver separated at the waist with a wet, sucking slurp. Globs of partially disintegrated internal organs spilled forth within the dark ooze. Both of the body's forearms dropped off at the elbows.

No longer able to hold his gorge, Malcolm let go of the sheeting and staggered back, heaving up his breakfast.

Olan took over for the temporarily incapacitated paramedic. "We need a second body-bag," he said to Malcolm.

Malcolm pushed through the front door.

Olan and Bill dumped the cradled torso into the staged body bag. Corralling the severed forearms against the legs, they captured the lower half in the same manner.

Malcolm returned with the second body-bag into which the lower half of the body was dumped.

"You all right?" Bill asked his partner when the job was complete.

"Yeah," Malcolm said, his face still white as ivory.

"I need you back at the funeral home to get this body ready to ship," Olan said to Malcolm. Malcolm managed the preparations for shipping bodies to New Iberia for autopsies and cremations.

Doff returned. "Doc Martin is on his way," he informed Olan. "As for the claimant, he says he and the others had breakfast at the Waffle House in Simmesport and then came straight here. He said there was nothing out of the ordinary until they arrived here. He never went into the factory."

With the dissolving body stowed in the trunk of his

car and Malcolm riding shotgun, Olan raced to the funeral home where the bagged remains were hauled into the embalming room. Each bag was placed on one of two white-enameled, cast-iron tables set parallel to each other.

Each bag was positioned close to its table's commode-like sink into which blood and body fluids were normally drained.

Olan switched on a fume hood at the end of wall-mounted cabinets containing bottles of vascular and cavity fluids and a fluid pump. Posters of the human arterial/vascular system and internal organs decorated the walls. A dissecting microscope on an adjustable armature was fixed to a counter top. The room held a lingering smell of disinfectant.

"Get a couple of shipping cases ready for transport, one for each bag," Olan told Malcolm and hurried to his office a short distance down a central hallway. Plopping down in his chair, Olan flipped through a telephone directory and found the entry he needed. He quickly punched out the telephone number for Louisiana's Acadiana Forensic Laboratories in New Iberia.

"Hello George, this is Olan."

"Well, good morning Olan," Dr. George Miles boomed. "It's been awhile. What's up?" Olan quickly pictured his longtime friend sitting at his acre-size desk, sipping on a cup of fresh-brewed coffee and reviewing a list of bodies added to his lab's coolers the previous night.

Olan had no time for formalities and got right to the point, explaining the situation at the industrial park and the body in his body preparation room.

"I'll have this body ready to ship to you within the hour," Olan told Dr. Miles. "The victim's driver license and credit cards show this as Arlin Tullis, 220 Red Creek Circle, Natchez, Mississippi. Of course, we'll need positive ID through dental records. Anything you can tell us about the remains will be of great help. Especially what caused tissue destruction."

"And you say there's a second body?"

"That's correct," Olan continued. "Skeletal remains. Found at the rear of the building."

"Are you sending the skeletal remains down also?"

"No. Law enforcement is still securing the site. I felt it imperative to get this first body off to you ASAP."

"What can you tell me about the body you're sending?"

"Not much," Olan admitted. "There's very little left. Just bones and dissolving tissue."

"The entire body?"

"Almost every bit of soft tissue has liquefied."

"Putrefied?"

"No sir, liquefied. There is no sign of putrefaction "Obviously one or more chemicals were involved."

Olan nodded agreement as if his friend were in the

room with him. “But there were no known chemicals in close proximity to the body,” he said. “It took less than thirty minutes from the time I arrived for every trace of tissue, including connective tissue, to dissolve almost completely.”

“That doesn’t make sense.”

“I agree,” Olan said. “What’s even stranger is that the body dissolved from the inside out. It would take a huge amount of any chemical to do that. Much more than anyone could ingest or inhale.”

“Get what’s left of the body down here and I’ll see what we can find out.”

CHAPTER 8

DEPUTY GERALD WILSON FOLLOWED HIS superior into the dark factory. The image of his first DOA had shaken the rookie and the discovery of a second body, a skeleton at that, had further unnerved him. Now he was entering a building that could hold even more horrors. Gerald seriously wondered if he had chosen the right line of work.

Deputy Hebert panned his light across a wide arc in the gloom-filled factory, inspecting each machine coming into view and watchful for the exposed limbs of anyone in hiding or the source of that god-awful sulfurous stench. He quickly appraised the immediate area as clear and motioned Gerald forward. "Stay with me," Justin reiterated to his partner.

Gerald nodded, tensely.

Leading the young rookie across the cluttered floor, Justin advanced toward the first possible point of ambush, a portable cold room. The modular room's single door was open and its textured aluminum walls diffused Justin's prying light. The two deputies approached the compact enclosure with caution. Someone could easily be hiding within.

"Sheriff's department," Justin called from alongside the cold room's doorway. "Step out with your hands over your head." He waited. Nothing happened. He moved forward.

The cold room was clear except for an empty five gallon plastic bucket labeled, *Garlic Powder*. The tinge of sulfur over-powered any residual fragrance of the pungent seasoning. A circular, cold air vent cut from the roof's center was covered with a wire-mesh guard and formed the only other opening. The cooling system and its circulation fan that once perched atop had long ago been stripped off.

Justin turned his attention to the area beyond the cold room.

Police Officer Parker moved toward the opposite end of the building to Justin. Working his light over dilapidated machinery scattered around him, Parker noted an unexpected slope in the floor and ever widening cracks cutting jagged lines into the darkness beyond.

Parker's initial inspection outside the facility had revealed a sinkhole next to the east wall but he had paid little attention to the ground subsidence. After all, the industrial park had been forced to shut down for this very reason. Here though, inside the building, the effect of the depression was considerably worse. He backed away from the sagging concrete and turned his attention to the remainder of the factory. He was looking for civilians, not structural damage.

Red fabric under a car-size machine caught Parker's eye; another body, this one clad in red work overalls. A black, oily fluid crept from the bloated corpse in a narrow rivulet.

"I have another body," Parker called to Justin. "Northeast corner."

"Proceed with caution," Justin responded.

Gerald spotted a shiny object by a pile of machine parts. "Here's a flashlight," he said and reached down to retrieve the torch. He jerked back his hand. "Sir, another skeleton!"

Like the bones outside the factory's rear door, these fully clothed remains appeared to be of a youth, possibly around the same age as the first and bleached just as white. The victim's leather belt had disintegrated wherever it contacted a dark, oily matter in which the skeleton lay.

"Vacate the building," Justin radioed Parker. His team would regroup safely outside and confer with the sheriff once he arrived.

"Ten-four," Officer Parker replied.

Sounds from above caught Parker's attention. He trained his flashlight's beam on movement among the metal trusses. Roosting pigeons, Parker thought. Must be a hundred of them.

As Parker retraced his steps, a high-pitched buzzing broke the near silence.

"What do you have over there?" Justin called to Parker. The sound was of someone twirling a ratcheted wrench.

The creature swooped past Parker's head. Flapping wings tingled the hair on the back of his neck. Parker ducked to one side.

"There's something flying around over here," Parker called out. He worked his light's beam to catch a glimpse of the flying specter.

Parker spotlighted the winged creature when it was nearly upon him. He lurched to one side and blindly swung his twelve-inch Mag-Light like a one-armed baseball batter. The torch connected with the flying apparition, driving it downward and into Parker's stomach. The policeman buckled over from the impact, grimacing when a sharp pain pierced his flesh. Ripping the hard-shelled animal from his abdomen, he slung it away.

Red-hot pain raced through Parker's body. He fumbled for his radio's transmitter and somehow found it. "Help," he said in a shattered voice. Blinding flashes of light exploded in his brain. He collapsed.

Justin and Gerald charged off in the direction of Parker's last known position. An officer in trouble took priority over all else.

They found Parker on his back, shaking violently, his exposed skin crimson. His eyes rolled back in his head.

"Officer down," Justin radioed. "Medical assistance inside, east end of the factory."

The downed officer's eyes bulged. He was no longer breathing. Gerald held his light steady as Justin attempted to clear Parker's airway for CPR but the police officer's grossly swollen tongue sealed closed his throat. He was beginning to look like the first victim they had discovered that morning.

Justin pulled a Buck knife from his utility belt. A tracheotomy was the only way of saving Parker's life. He pressed the makeshift scalpel against skin an inch below the downed officer's larynx and made an incision. Dark plasma oozed from the cut. There was no saving Parker.

A chitinous leg, pencil-thin and studded with short spines, moved into the perimeter of Gerald's light. The creature hooked Parker's pants cuff with a two-clawed foot and levered its body into the circle of illumination.

The impossibly long twelve inch beetle-like creature had an oval abdomen and triangular head ending with an inch long proboscis. Its two eyes had clear cornea and white irises that constricted in the light.

Four jointed legs emerged from the body, two behind its head and two thicker limbs from its abdomen. Unlike the forelegs, these rear appendages had padded toes. A brown exoskeleton protected the body and two wings symmetrically divided its abdomen. From the bug's fleshy posterior protruded a barb-less lance.

The creature had been injured by Parker, its right eye shattered and discharging a colorless substance onto the dusty floor. A milky-white fluid dribbled from the stub of an amputated foreleg and mingled with the eye matter.

The air above stirred. More creatures closed in on the intruders.

"I'm coming in with Bill and Joel," Officer Moore radioed.

"Stay out," Justin responded. "I repeat, no one come in. We're coming out." He and Gerald bolted across the room for the door through which they had entered.

A creature slammed into Gerald's head, knocking off his hat. The deputy went down on all fours. His hat with the huge bug still attached tumbled to the floor alongside him. He pulled his pistol from its holster and fired at point blank range. The bug exploded in a splatter of white matter.

Scrambling to his feet, Gerald caught up with his superior but they were going no further. A swarm of the over-sized insects blocked their exit route leaving them only one sanctuary, the portable cold room.

The two deputies raced across open floor and leaped into the room's musty darkness. Justin wrenched shut the windowed door, the sound of flight seemingly on his shirttail. A hurried inspection of the cold room's cramped interior revealed no creatures had gained entry and the overhead fan guard hopefully was strong enough to keep them out.

"Jack, close the back door," Justin radioed. The hundreds of creatures buzzing about the factory's production area could easily escape from the building.

"What are those things?" Gerald gasped.

"Whatever they are, they don't want us in this factory," Justin replied.

A startled scream, muffled by the cold room's insulated walls, alerted Justin to Jack Moore's presence within the building. Justin radioed his warning for all personnel to stay clear but the silence of his own unit told him the department's five watt radios even though serviced by a four hundred Megahertz transmitting system were not powerful enough to penetrate both the main building and the aluminum walls of the cold room.

Desperate to communicate with his comrades, Justin upended the seasoning bucket and setting the container center stage, mounted the makeshift pedestal. He thrust his radio's stubby, six-inch antenna through the wire covering the overhead circulation vent.

"...going on?" Doff Green's voice crackled over the air. "We heard shots fired. Justin, what is your situation?" The transmission was weak but intelligible.

"Keep all personnel out of the building," Justin radioed in reply. "Do you copy?"

"Repeat." Sheriff Maxwell radioed, now on-site. "Advise your situation."

"Parker's down," Justin reported. "Gerald and I are in a portable cold room. Keep all personnel out of the building."

"Is Moore with you?"

"Negative," Justin said.

"Justin," Sheriff Maxwell radioed, "Can you exit the building?"

"Negative."

"Officer Moore, what's your ten-twenty?" the sheriff radioed.

Again, no reply.

"I'm coming around back," the sheriff radioed. "How many shooters?"

"No shooters," came the transmission.

The sheriff radioed, "Justin, clarify. What's your situation?"

"This place is full of some type of huge insects," Justin transmitted. "Keep all personnel clear of the building and keep that rear door closed."

A half dozen creatures clawed at the cold room's observation window. Others crawled about on the roof jabbing their stingers at the radio's antenna.

"Insects? You mean bees?"

"Giant beetles," Justin reported, "A foot long. They fly and sting."

Bill Moley and Joel Dubonnet ran to the sheriff.

"Moore went inside," Bill stammered. "The place is full of the biggest damn bugs I've ever seen. They were all over Jack. We tried to help him but the bugs attacked us. We barely made it out ourselves."

"What kind of bugs?" Sheriff Maxwell demanded, frustrated he wasn't getting an answer he found straight.

"I've never seen anything like them," Bill said. "They're huge."

The sheriff was certain misunderstanding and exaggeration had led to confusion. He radioed his chief deputy, "Where can we make entry?"

"Don't come into the factory," Justin repeated. "These things will attack anyone coming inside."

"Justin, are you sure about that?" Sheriff Maxwell asked. "What about Parker?"

"Parker's dead. One of these creatures killed him."

"Repeat your situation," the sheriff ordered.

"Gerald and I are secure inside a portable cold room. I can see through a window in the cold room's door. There is a swarm of gigantic bugs in the factory. One of them killed Parker and possibly Moore. Keep that rear door closed. These things can easily escape the building if it is opened."

Justin paused. "And sheriff," he said, "Parker's body was affected the same way as the victim found this morning in the front office."

"Sheriff," Bill said as the sheriff, he and Doff approached the rear door, "when Malcolm and I exited the building, none of the bugs tried to follow us outside before we closed the door. Maybe those things don't like sunlight."

Maxwell made no comment, still uncertain what he would find. The sight of the skeleton beyond the fence didn't help his nerves.

"Where was Moore?" he asked Bill.

"About fifty feet inside," Bill said.

Sheriff Maxwell cracked open the door to see for himself what he found impossible.

"Be damn careful," Bill cautioned. "Those things can fly real fast."

Bright mid-morning sunlight deepened the factory's dark-shrouded interior. Sheriff Maxwell switched on his flashlight and quickly found Moore's bloating body. Repelled at the grisly sight yet intent on finding out exactly what was going on, the sheriff opened the door wider. "Good god," he blurted when his light revealed thousands of the giant bugs clinging to machinery, crawling on the floor and covering the cold room's exterior like a massive cluster of huge bees gathered around their queen.

Some of the beasts took flight to defend the doorway. Sheriff Maxwell slammed the door closed.

Joel radioed, "Sheriff, Doctor Martin's here."

"Tell him to stay put," Maxwell transmitted, then added, "Justin, what can we do to get you two out?"

"Gerald and I are secure," Justin reported.

"We'll work on a plan," the sheriff said.

CHAPTER 9

OLAN HUNG UP HIS TELEPHONE after speaking with Dr. George Miles and joined Malcolm in the embalming room. His assistant was preparing shipping documents. Olan helped Malcolm load the body bags into their individual shipping crates and not wanting to wait, signed the incomplete documentation. "As soon as these have been shipped," he said to Malcolm, "meet me back at the factory."

Returning to the industrial park, Olan was halted by on-lookers and their cars congesting the entrance to Industrial Boulevard. Crowd control personnel guided him through the confusion and he parked behind a police cruiser where Sheriff Maxwell, Doff Green and Joel Dubonnet stood conferring.

"Any more information on the remains behind the factory?" Olan asked when he joined the sheriff and the others, unaware of the most recent developments.

"Parker and Moore are dead," the sheriff said grimly. "They were attacked by some type of bug. Justin and Deputy Wilson are trapped..."

"For Christ sake," Olan cut in. "Larry's allergic to bee

stings. He carries a sting kit." Olan was not aware of Jack Moore's hypersensitivity to insect venom but multiple stings could kill the most resistant of individuals.

"They are not bees," Bill cut in.

"They're a foot long," Joel added.

"Impossible!" Olan said.

"They look like giant beetles," the sheriff told Olan.

"And they sting?"

"Yes," the sheriff said, "and from what Justin says, Larry's body was affected in the same way as the victim found this morning in the front office. I saw Jack fifteen minutes after he was attacked and his body was starting to bloat too."

Doctor Martin joined the team.

Olan's brow furrowed in horror. "My God, what's going on?" he exclaimed.

"That's what I want to know," the sheriff answered and to both Olan and Doctor Martin he said, "Is there anyone we can call?"

Doctor Martin said, "Last year at a medical conference, I met a forensic entomologist from LSU. I have her card. It may be a long shot, but it's worth a try."

"Contact anyone you think can help," Sheriff Maxwell said. "I want to know what the hell we're dealing with and how to kill these things."

Sheriff Maxwell radioed Union Town's dispatcher. "Doris, I need all local emergency-squad personnel on-site here at the industrial park."

"Yes sir," Doris responded.

"What other police personnel are available?" the sheriff asked the dispatcher.

"Just Todd Trudman," Doris said, "but he's on second shift. Steve Zachery is on vacation and won't be back until Sunday."

"Has there been any word from Chief Gallo?"

"No sir and he hasn't answered his pager either."

The sheriff continue, "Contact Stan Wilton. I need the fire department over here."

"Yes sir."

Using the mobile telephone in Tullis' truck, the sheriff dialed his office. "Tanya, I need the phone number for the state police in Baton Rouge."

"Hold on," Tanya said. A moment later she returned to the phone. "Here it is. Are you ready?"

"Go ahead," the sheriff said. He jotted down the number on a piece of paper from the truck's glove box. "Thanks. I also need Gill and Dwight to get to Union Town's industrial park as soon as possible."

"Is everything over there all right?" Tanya asked.

"Not really, no," the sheriff answered with no further explanation.

"If there is anything else I can do," Tanya said, "let me know."

"I'll stay in touch," the sheriff said. He ended the call

and immediately dialed the number Tanya gave him. "Yes, I need to speak with Lieutenant Morty Allain," the sheriff said into the phone. "This is Sheriff Maxwell, Saint Landry Parish. I have an emergency situation. Yes, I can hold."

Joel approached the truck with something to tell the sheriff.

"What is it, Joel," the sheriff asked as he waited for Allain to answer his call.

"Civilians are getting around the cordon," Joel reported. "We don't have enough manpower."

"Grab whoever you can to help out along the outer perimeter," the sheriff replied. "I'm on the phone for additional support personnel."

"Will do," Joel said and hurried off.

"Hello, Lieutenant Allain," the sheriff said into the phone, "this is Sheriff Maxwell…"

The sheriff ended his call to Baton Rouge and hung up the phone.

Doff was next in line. "Sheriff, it might help with identification if we can get some photographs of those bugs," he said. He waved over Gene Lancer, a lanky, twenty-six year old with shoulder-length blonde hair and Mick Jagger lips. Gene was a volunteer Union Town fireman and the town's free-lance camera-buff, available for weddings and birthday parties. He had shown up at the industrial park with a camera sporting a telephoto lens.

"How do you propose to get photos?" the sheriff asked Doff. "We're not opening the back door again and no one else is going into the factory."

"I'm thinking we can unlock the service door leading into the production area," Doff said, "and then create a diversion at the rear door. That might allow Gene to get some shots from the service door."

"What do you think, Gene?" Doff asked.

"I guess I can."

"Out of the question," the sheriff said. "I'm not risking anymore lives."

"From what Bill and Joel said," Doff reminded the sheriff, "it wasn't until Jack and they went inside that the bugs started flying around and even then, none of the bugs followed them outside."

Sheriff Maxwell was not losing sight of their present mission. Two deputies were trapped inside the building by a yet unknown insect and neutralizing the situation as quickly as possible was top priority. This photograph thing just might offer an edge. The photos could be faxed to LSU or anywhere else for fast identification. Surely someone in the world had seen these creatures before and knew how to deal with them.

"Sheriff, what about a camcorder?" Gene asked. "If we can get one inside, we'll have live feed."

"Do you have one?"

"Yes sir, in my car. I also have a tripod."

"What about a monitor?"

"A TV will do," Gene replied, "and I can hook the signal to a VCR so we can record."

"Doff," the sheriff said, "tell Doris to send over a television and a VCR."

Doff stepped aside to radio the police dispatcher.

"We'll need a power source," Gene said.

Sheriff Maxwell hailed over Horace Gail, one of Joel's recruits. Horace was a stocky man with a square head atop a stubby neck. He was a previous member of the town's emergency-squad and owner of 'Union Town Hardware and Electrical Supplies'.

"I need a generator," the sheriff said, "big enough to run a video camera, VCR and whatever lighting we can dig up."

"I've got a hundred and fifty amp unit. That will handle anything you throw at it."

"Lights? For inside the building."

"Got some two hundred watt floodlights."

"Get it all over here as fast as you can."

"Yes sir," Horace said.

"Fetch your stuff from your car," Sheriff Maxwell said to Gene.

Gene hustled to his car, not at all certain why all the fuss for what rumor said was a swarm of bees. Surely Sam Ramey, Union Town's resident beekeeper, was better qualified than anyone present to deal with this problem.

Sheriff Maxwell radioed Justin and explained their plan.

"From this vantage point I can't see either the rear door or the one into the office," Justin cautioned, "but I can let you know if the bugs start moving in one direction or the other."

"That will be a big help," the sheriff said.

"One more thing," Justin said, "None of the keys Doff had fit the service door. It's still locked."

The sheriff grabbed Bill Moley. "Find out if Doris has any more keys to this building on file." he said. "Also, when Horace gets back with his gear, you and Joel take a walkie-talkie to the rear of the building. When I give you the word, crack open the back door just enough to let in some sunlight but not enough to let any of those bugs out. Hopefully we can distract those things long enough to get some photos and set up a video feed."

CHAPTER 10

THE STRANDED DEPUTIES SAT OPPOSITE each other in their secured quarters, a flashlight illuminating the interior. Justin had strapped his radio to the wire mesh guard, its antenna protruding enough to pick up a signal. Dead quiet prevailed.

"How long has your father been in the chicken business?" Justin asked. Their precarious situation had pushed the young rookie toward his limit and getting his mind off their predicament might help him keep control.

"Since before I was born," Gerald said.

"What made you pick law enforcement over chicken farming?" Justin continued.

"I guess I was looking for something more exciting than cleaning up chicken shit," Gerald said. He forced a smile. "I certainly got what I asked for."

"Any brothers or sisters?"

"No sir," Gerald said. "That's why my father wanted me to stay on the farm. He's got a heart condition and can't do heavy work anymore. But I just wasn't happy there."

"Everyone has to find his own way," Justin remarked.

A long silence followed before Gerald spoke, uncertainty creeping back into his voice. "Had you known Larry Parker long?"

"Five years," Justin said, "The first time we met I saved him from an assault charge."

Gerald raised a quizzical brow. "How's that?" he asked.

"It involved the Rumpsin twins," Justin began. "The bodies of Mark and Jacoline were discovered off State Highway 105, just outside Union Town. This happened shortly after Dick Gallo was appointed police chief. When I arrived on the scene, Gallo and Larry were going at it toe to toe. Gallo had instructed his men to haul up the bodies from a ravine so he could have a better look and Larry was refusing to follow orders because the they were beyond the city limits and didn't have jurisdiction." Justin smiled. "Gallo's afraid of snakes. Anyway, had I not shown up when I did, Parker would probably have busted Gallo in the nose and been out of job and in jail."

"Hard to understand why Mayor Brandon would keep someone like Gallo around," Gerald said.

Justin said, "Dick Gallo is a follower, a man sworn to blind loyalty and controlled by petty threats. Mayor Brandon likes to have a 'yes man' and Gallo fills those shoes nicely."

Gerald looked at his watch. "It's pushing noon," he said. "Do you think we'll get out soon?" The four hours they had been incarcerated in this small cell and under constant fear of attack from those hellish creatures seemed like four centuries.

"The sheriff's working on it," Justin assured the rookie. "It shouldn't be much longer."

The flashlight faded, a faint flicker announcing the impending death of its batteries. Justin tapped the lens causing the light to shine more brightly but it would not last. Gerald had his own flashlight in reserve but when its batteries were used up the darkness beyond the cold room walls would crawl inside bringing with it the cover these creatures seemed to prefer.

"Justin, how are you and Gerald?" Sheriff Maxwell was on the radio. "Any change in your situation?"

"No change," Justin responded from his perch. "We're getting pretty thirsty and we can use a pit stop."

"We have the key for the service door," the sheriff said. "We're preparing to set up the camcorder and floodlights."

"Ten-four," Justin replied, adding, "Sheriff, I think what light we're getting from our flashlights is keeping those bugs at bay."

"We've seen the same reaction at the rear door with sunlight," the sheriff admitted. "We just now got the VCR and rest of the equipment so I guess we'll confirm that once the floodlights are in place."

Sheriff Maxwell deployed men and equipment. "Bill,"

he said to the paramedic, "you and Joel get to the rear door. Don't crack it open until I say."

Bill and Joel hurried off.

Horace set up the generator along curbing, linked to two heavy-duty extension cords, one servicing the VCR/monitor and the other, the camcorder and a floodlight.

With everything ready, the sheriff radioed Bill. "Okay, Bill, crack open the door and be damn careful. If any of those bugs gets too close or tries to escape, close it."

Bill pulled open the rear door. Like one mighty beast, the creatures within stirred, hooked claws grating on metal and concrete.

"The door is open," Bill radioed the sheriff.

Maxwell radioed his chief deputy, "Justin, can you see what's going on in there?"

Justin motioned Gerald to man the radio.

"Tell him the bugs are all moving toward the rear door," Justin reported from his position at the cold room's window. "I don't see any flying around."

Gerald repeated Justin's observation.

"What about the area near the office door?" the sheriff asked.

"Tell him they're moving away from that area."

Justin's partner relayed the information.

"Is there any way you and Gerald can make it to the

door into the offices?"

"Negative," Justin replied.

"Does it look clear enough to put the camcorder and lights in place?" the sheriff asked.

"I can't tell from this angle," Justin said, "but it doesn't appear there are any bugs on that side of the room anymore."

The message was transmitted.

Sheriff Maxwell knew he and his team would have to work quickly. Stepping around the black stain left by Tullis' body, he followed a black electrical cable that snaked through the reception area to where Doff and Horace Gail waited at the service door. Within a side office twin floodlights sporting polished reflectors and fitted on extendable stands stood ready for service. Doff held the tripod-mounted camcorder.

The sheriff inserted a key into the doorknob and turned it with slow intent. The knob's internal lock disengaged with a sharp click putting frayed nerves further on edge. Slowly, he pulled the door open just enough to see a halo of light from the factory's open rear door and thousands of creatures carpeting the room, all moving towards Bill's position. Two of the gigantic beetles on the floor fifteen feet from the sheriff crawled in that same direction, unaware of this latest intrusion.

With the door open just wide enough to slip his head inside and alert to all around him, Sheriff Maxwell confirmed the immediate area was indeed clear. Withdrawing, he said, "We have to work damn fast."

The sheriff took the camera from Doff and switched it on. As rehearsed earlier in the front office, he swung the door open and quickly set the tripod-mounted camcorder just within the production area, aimed across the expansive room and taking in a large portion of the portable cold room.

Horace handed him the two floodlights and these were positioned flanking the camera, slightly to the rear. Flipping a common switch, the sheriff instantly brought high noon to the dark interior.

A bug slammed into Sheriff Maxwell's right leg, snagging a claw on his pants and jabbing its stinger at his ankle. The sheriff kicked out and slung the huge beetle against a wall. The over-sized insect was up in an instant and on the attack again. Dozens more turned toward this new threat.

Sheriff Maxwell leaped back through the open doorway and Doff shouldered the door closed, holding it as if it were the lid of Pandora's Box.

Scurrying erupted from above the false ceiling. A water-stained panel in the adjacent office broke through its frame and crashed to the carpeted floor bringing down with it five monstrous bugs. More crawled out of the gaping hole.

"Run!" the sheriff yelled and the crew broke for the

front door.

But not Horace Gail. His split-second hesitation to see for himself what all the fuss was about proved one moment too long.

A creature dropped onto Horace's head. Two more attacked from behind. Their sharp fore-claws dug deep into his back. Shrieking in terror, Horace grabbed the lobster-sized bug from his head and dashed it to the floor. He slammed his back against a wall to dislodge the others.

A barb-less lance pierced into the flesh of Horace's neck. Another invaded his chest. Pain was instant. In a split second, Horace lay writhing in agony on the floor, his blood turning into blackened pulp and his brain into a viscous mass. Stretching out a pain-contorted hand, his mind exploded in a brilliant flash of light.

Sheriff Maxwell had reached the front reception area when the electrician screamed but there was nothing the lawman could do to help the man. Bugs roiled down the hallway in an angry mass of wings, stingers and eyes set on destruction. Doff and the sheriff hurled themselves through the front doorway and Doff heaved the glass-paneled door closed. The creatures circled menacingly within the front room searching for any way outside.

Fearing the giant insects might escape, the sheriff and his support staff backed away from the building, awed by what they witnessed.

"Bill," Sheriff Maxwell radioed, "close the door."

As swiftly as they had attacked, the monstrous bugs retreated from the offices. The crew outside gathered around the monitor. No one spoke as they viewed the scene within.

"Sheriff," Justin's voice broke over the air, "you've really stirred things up in here."

In a stressed voice at having lost another man, the sheriff said, "Ten-four. The camera's in place. We can see what's going on inside now."

"Sheriff, is there a problem?" Justin asked, sensing that there was indeed something wrong.

"No," the sheriff said, aware all eyes were on him. "I believe we're getting a handle on the situation." He intentionally omitted Horace's death. His two deputies had enough to think about without giving them more cause for alarm.

Further disappointment befell the sheriff when he saw that the camera's view was limited to a mere edge of the cold room. Two partially dismantled machines and the opposing corner of the factory area dominated the picture. Dark cracks in the floor formed an irregular pattern into shadows while ceiling struts and braces cut perpendicular lines along the top of the monitor's screen.

More disappointment when it was clear the floodlights were not giving the expected results. Instead of repelling the creatures, the lights attracted them like moths around a porch lamp.

"Are we getting this on tape?" the sheriff asked Gene.

"Yes sir."

"I want a constant monitoring of what's going on in there," the sheriff said.

"Yes sir," Gene replied.

Sheriff Maxwell radioed Justin. "We just proved your flashlights are having no effect on those things," he said.

"I see that," Justin replied. "But why aren't they still trying to get in here?"

"I don't know," the sheriff said. "Maybe they don't see you two as a threat." The sheriff considered his last statement. The ferocity of the attack on Horace was much different from the now almost total disregard shown the two men sitting within these creatures' midst.

The sheriff continued, "We're calling a bug expert at LSU to see if we can find out how to deal with these things."

"And they're going to know what these bugs are?" Justin asked. To him it was obvious any creature this dangerous would have made front-page news wherever they turned up. The fact they hadn't meant no one knew of their existence, until now, or at least weren't saying.

"Do you have any other suggestions?" the sheriff asked.

"I wish I did," Justin replied. The frustration of entrapment was wearing on him and even more so, Gerald, but any attempt at escape would mean certain death.

Justin turned off his flashlight. Luminescence from the flood-lamps found its way through the cold room's window offering ample illumination. Maybe light wasn't keeping those bugs at bay but at least the two deputies could see their attackers.

Andre Loux crossed the weedy yard from the road-block to the sheriff. Andre had a round-face, slumped shoulders and salt and pepper hair. "Sheriff," he said, "there's a pest control guy here from Bunkie. He wants to talk to you. Says he has fumigation gear."

"Bring him over," the sheriff said.

Olan's voice broke over the airwaves for the sheriff.

"What is it?" Maxwell asked.

"Doc Martin and I just spoke with a Doctor Reynolds at LSU," Olan said. "She's that forensic entomologist he mentioned. She's supposed to be the top insect taxonomist in the country."

"Top what?" the sheriff asked, unfamiliar with the term 'taxonomist'.

"Taxonomy, the science of identification," Olan said. He went on, "I gave her a description of those things in the factory and told her what they're capable of. She thinks we're all a little crazy but at least agreed to come take a look. She should be here in a couple hours."

"Olan," Sheriff Maxwell confessed. "This is a lot bigger than I ever imagined. We set a camcorder and lights inside the factory. The place is completely full of whatever these things are."

"Have any of them gotten inside the cold room?"

"No, they're not even trying. But I don't know how much longer Justin and Gerald can hold out. I contacted the state boys for assistance."

"Let's pray this Doctor Reynolds will know what to do," Olan said.

"We may be able to do something now," the sheriff said. "I've got a pest control guy here."

A wiry little man with a mop of black hair and horn-rimmed glasses approached toting a machine nearly four feet long and looking like a ray gun from some Flash Gordon movie.

"You can't use fumigants," Olan said. "Not until Justin and Gerald are safely out."

"There has to be something we can use," the sheriff said.

"I'm going to make a few more phone calls and see if anyone else can help," Olan said. "As soon as Doctor Reynolds gets here, I'll bring her over." He hung up.

"I heard you have a bee problem," the pest controller said to Sheriff Maxwell. His thick-lens glasses gave the man owl eyes. Thrusting out his hand, he said proudly, "Tom Slyger, Tri-Parish Pest Control."

Sheriff Maxwell didn't have time for formalities. He pointed to the monitor. "What are those things?"

"What you have here," Slyger said without hesitation, "is a serious infestation of Coleopterans."

"Infestation of what?" The sheriff was amazed. This guy made it sound as if he dealt with this problem on a regular basis.

"Coleopterans, beetles."

"Beetles?" Sheriff Maxwell said, shocked at the man's instant and totally inaccurate evaluation. "What beetles have you ever seen that are a foot long and lethal?"

Slyger raised a quizzical brow and looked closer at the screen. "Christ have mercy!" he exclaimed when all came into perspective.

"So you don't know what these things are?" the sheriff asked.

"Without a closer look I can't tell but I'm sure I can take care of them with this." Slyger hoisted his ray gun.

"I have two deputies inside," Sheriff Maxwell said. "I've been advised we cannot use fumigants."

"This is a fogger," Slyger explained. "It doesn't fumigate. It produces an oil-based insecticide dispersed in what looks like fog."

"Is it harmful to humans?"

"It has very low toxicity to humans," Slyger said. "The chemicals I use won't harm your deputies but should give a good knockdown ratio for whatever kind of bugs those are. Then your deputies can get out. After that I'll fumigate the building. That will kill everything in there, guaranteed."

Sheriff Maxwell saw a problem. "So the fogger won't kill those bugs?" Sheriff Maxwell asked.

"Not at first," Slyger said, "but it should knock most of them down, paralyze them."

"Does it work fast?"

"Those things have a fairly large body mass," Slyger said. "I may have to fog more than once."

"So there's a possibility some of those bugs could exit the building?"

"If there are any openings, I guess so." Slyger shrugged. "I can plug-up the holes."

Sheriff Maxwell shook his head. At this point, the creatures were not attempting to leave the building and he doubted any amount of sealing would keep them contained if they didn't want to be there, especially if the pesticide didn't kill them instantly. His trapped men were under no immediate threat and Maxwell intended to keep it that way.

"I can mix in an enhancement chemical," Slyger said, "to give it more killing power." Tom Slyger wanted this job. He wanted it bad. Having just started his business six months ago, he saw this as his chance to pick up a badly needed account.

"We've got a bug expert coming from LSU," the sheriff said. "I want another opinion before we use any chemicals."

"Well sir," Tom said, sensing he may be losing this opportunity. "It might be a good idea if I get my equipment set up. Then if we fumigate, we'll have everything ready to go"

"Stage your equipment outside the cordon," the sheriff said. "I'll let you know if I need you."

"Yes sir," Slyger said. This job was in the bag.

CHAPTER 11

DR. JENNIFER REYNOLDS, PHD., TURNED her Ford Explorer from State Highway 105 onto Front Street and an immediate left at Planchard's service station onto Lafayette Street. The town wasn't unfamiliar to her as she had previously visited the area on field trips during graduate school. Still, she found Olan Barnes' directions handy.

Three more blocks and Dr. Reynolds spotted a rusty pipe protruding from the ground and topped with a sign inviting all passers-by to attend Sunday mass at Saint Mathew Catholic Church alerting her that this marked her turn onto Sunset Lane, a newly paved link to the funeral home.

A live oak tree stood proudly next to the funeral home's asphalt parking lot. Dr. Reynolds parked her vehicle within its shade. Slipping from her vehicle, she glanced at her wristwatch. Just after one thirty. She would have only three hours in Union Town if she was to make her evening taxonomy class.

A balding man, fiftyish, rushed out of the building's double doors to meet her, a black case slung over one shoulder. "Doctor Reynolds? I'm Olan Barnes," Olan called as he hurried over to her. "Thank you so much for coming."

"I'm glad I had the time," Dr. Reynolds replied.

"Are you ready to go?" Having expected a much older woman with academic seriousness, Olan was surprised to confront a slender woman of thirty-five years with shapely legs, a pug nose and friendly smile. He could imagine that behind her back male students called her "Doctor Legs", a befitting description.

"Yes, I'm ready," Dr. Reynolds said. "Is it far?"

"A mile or so," Olan said, gesturing in the general direction of the industrial estate.

"I'd like to take my car, if you don't mind," Dr. Reynolds said. "There's no sense transferring all my equipment to another vehicle."

"I'll fill you in on what's happened along the way," Olan said.

Dr. Reynolds was glad she wasn't in for a lengthy jaunt. As she drove, Olan offered a quick overview of the day's events as he knew them.

"And your description of these creatures' size is accurate?" Dr. Reynolds asked with more than a touch of disbelief. "I'm asking because, quite frankly, no stinging Coleopteran has ever been identified and few insect species come close to a foot long. The largest insects known come from the Amazon Rain Forest and they are quite harmless."

"I haven't seen these things myself," Olan confessed, "but from what the sheriff tells me, they are every bit that big. There are three confirmed deaths associated with them and possibly more. A couple of sheriff's deputies have been trapped in the factory by the bugs since this morning."

Olan's remark concerning multiple deaths stunned Dr. Reynolds. "I don't understand," she said. "Severe allergic reactions to bee and wasp stings are extremely rare. They affect less than one percent of the population in America. The odds of having three sensitive people together at the same time is highly improbable."

"Maybe so," Olan said, "but those are the facts."

"We could be dealing with Africanized bees," Dr. Reynolds ventured. "They are a hybrid of the common honeybee. You have probably heard them called, 'killer bees'. They are extremely aggressive and attack unprovoked. They kill by just the sheer number of stings to their victims.

"Quite frankly," Dr. Reynolds continued, "I've never heard of Africanized bees occurring any further north than the panhandle of Texas. Of course, southern Louisiana does fall within the geographical area in which this species could survive."

Dr. Reynolds was still not convinced the information Olan had given was correct. "Can any of the deaths be attributed to anaphylactic shock?" she asked.

"One could," Olan said. "A police officer who I know was allergic to bee stings but this is not simple anaphylactic shock. I've shipped one of the victims' remains to the forensics lab in New Iberia. The toxins we are dealing with are far more potent than any common insect venom. I assure you, none of this is an exaggeration."

Olan instructed Dr. Reynolds to turn left onto Old Simmesport Highway. Heat from the August sun shimmered on the macadam surface and washed color from thick brambles and a distant stand of pines.

"I'm not saying anyone is exaggerating," Dr. Reynolds said, "but perhaps there's misinterpretation of the facts. I've seen a swarm of bees take on the appearance of a few hundred large individuals grouped together and not a congregation of fifty thousand smaller ones."

Olan made no reply. He and Dr. Reynolds would see for themselves. The industrial park was right up ahead.

Approaching Industrial Boulevard, Dr. Reynolds slowed her car to make her way through on-lookers. A television news crew from WATC, Lafayette, was busy setting up gear atop their van while the station's anchor newsman attempted to talk his way past a bevy of law enforcement personnel. Lonnie Nethero, a tall, lanky, twenty-three year old with a rescue squad badge dangling from around his neck recognized Olan and flagged him and Dr. Reynolds through.

As she parked behind an emergency vehicle, Dr. Reynolds spotted two red cylinders of fumigants and assorted gear piled up next to a pest control truck. “Someone called in the cavalry,” she commented. Alighting from the car, she pulled on a tattered ball cap emblazoned with – “Insects Rule”.

Olan led her to a knot of people gathered at a television set resting on a metal, folding chair. Cables from the TV ran to a VCR, across the lawn and under the building’s front door where it snaked down the hall. A tarp had been erected for shade.

“Sheriff Maxwell,” Olan said, “this is Doctor Reynolds.”

“We’ve been waiting for you,” the sheriff said.

“Any luck with that?” Dr. Reynolds motioned to Tom Slyger’s fogger set in the grass.

“We haven’t tried it yet,” the sheriff said.

“Where are the problem bees?” Dr. Reynolds asked. It wouldn’t take long to identify the species and if they were indeed an Africanized breed she would let the pest control operator do his job. A local beekeeper would be called if they turned out to be the domesticated variety.

“See for yourself,” the sheriff said, indicating the monitor. The team looked on.

“Was this prerecorded?” Dr. Reynolds asked, studying the bland, colorless picture.

“That’s live,” the sheriff said. “We’re recording on the

VCR."

Like Tom Slyger, it took Dr. Reynolds a moment to put into perspective what she was witnessing. When all came clear, her mouth gaped in astonishment.

"Can we tighten up this shot," Dr. Reynolds asked. None of the insects were within close proximity of the camera and she couldn't tell much about them, only that they weren't bees and they were huge.

"I'm afraid not," Sheriff Maxwell said. "Someone would have to go inside the building and I've already lost one man getting the camera set up." Looking at Dr. Reynolds he said, "You do know these bugs have killed six people, including two police officers?"

"Six?" Dr. Reynolds asked, astonished.

"And I've got two deputies trapped inside."

Dr. Reynolds studied the screen, unnerved at the rising body count.

"And these things sting?" Dr. Reynolds said.

"Let me show you something," the sheriff said. He led Dr. Reynolds to the glass-pane front door. "That black oily substance on the floor at the back of the hallway is the hand of a sting victim. He was stung less than three hours ago."

Dr. Reynolds' face blanched. "My God," she stammered. What she saw resembled a large mushroom, oozing rot. The thought of what the rest of the body might look like made her feel ill. And what the hell were those things inside the building? She and the sheriff returned to the monitor. "I just don't understand, she said, "there are no known insects in the world that can do this."

"There are now," the sheriff commented.

"Can these things escape the building?" Dr. Reynolds asked.

Sheriff Maxwell explained how the backdoor had been open during the initial search by his deputies, the attacks on Officers Parker and Moore and how the creatures had not attempted to exit. He also described how the bugs had reacted when Bill opened the door as a diversion.

The sheriff pointed to the apex of the building's roof and three equally-spaced exhaust stacks that looked like metal tree stumps topped with rain guards. "Those chimneys open directly into the factory and those warehouse bay doors have gaps big enough to put your hand through. If those bugs wanted to get out, they would."

Dr. Reynolds took a long moment to digest what she had been told. "Are these organisms in any of the other buildings in this area?" she asked.

"We've made a thorough search of the entire industrial park," the sheriff explained. "This seems to be the only structure affected."

"Which means only one thing," Dr. Reynolds said.

"These bugs, as you call them, are here, in this building, because they want to be. That's good. It buys us time."

"How much time does it buy my deputies?" Sheriff Maxwell asked.

"I don't know," Dr. Reynolds said, "but from what Mister Barnes and you have told me, these organisms are apparently social." Consulting the monitor once again, she added, "This is evident by the way they react to stimuli and are congregated in one particular area."

"And that's good?" Sheriff Maxwell asked.

"Yes it is. It indicates these organisms attack only when threatened, like most species of bees, wasps and hornets. They also are likely to have a distinct social order; a queen, drones and workers."

"And how does that help us?" the sheriff asked.

Dr. Reynolds went on. "It gives us some insight into what we are dealing with, what factors provoke attack and from what you've told me, that provocation is disturbing their nest. No doubt, species preservation and self-preservation."

Tom Slyger had managed to get close enough to hear the conversation. "I got a good look at one on the monitor," he declared with the authority he felt was his. He added, showing off his knowledge of insect anatomy, "Their front wings are hard, no veins. No cerci either. Definitely Coleoptera."

Dr. Reynolds regarded Tom's magnified eyes, amazed

the man could see anything at all. “Coleopterans are not social,” she reminded him, “and they don’t sting.”

Tom shrugged his lack of comprehension. “Go figure,” he commented.

“So you’re saying these things are some type of bee or wasp?” the sheriff asked Dr. Reynolds.

“At this stage, I have to believe they are in some way related to them.”

The sheriff alerted, “There’s one moving into the picture.”

All attention returned to the monitor.

The bug crawled on the floor, ten feet from the camera’s tripod. With movements smooth and alert, it crept across the screen in full view of those outside watching.

“It’s missing a pair of legs,” Dr. Reynolds observed as she considered what she was seeing. Except for its gait, the creature did have characteristics of Coleoptera beyond size but something was not quite right.

The creature moved out of the camera’s view. “Can you play that back?” Dr. Reynolds asked when it was clear the bug would not offer a repeat performance.

Gene rewound the tape and switched it to play. The screen flickered showing the factory’s colorless interior a minute before. Then from a lower corner, the creature retraced its original steps.

“Stop, there,” Dr. Reynolds said to Gene.

Gene hit the pause button.

Amazement filled Dr. Reynolds' voice when she said, "That thing isn't missing any legs. It only has four!"

Gene ran the footage a moment longer. In growing fascination Dr. Reynolds said, puzzled, "The origin of the posterior legs is from the abdomen, not the thorax." Looking more closely she added, "In fact, it doesn't have a thorax."

"What does all that mean?" Sheriff Maxwell asked.

"These things aren't insects," Dr. Reynolds said, barely believing her own words. "Insects have three body segments – a head, thorax and abdomen, also six legs."

She nodded Gene to continue the replay.

"Look!" Dr. Reynolds gasped. "The eyes."

Gene hit pause again.

"Those eyes aren't compound," Dr. Reynolds stammered. "They have pupils! This thing has binocular vision."

"And how does that get my men out?" Sheriff Maxwell asked.

"Sheriff, I don't know," Dr. Reynolds admitted. "This is way out of my league."

"Can we use any of this pest control equipment?" Sheriff Maxwell asked.

Tom Slyger stepped closer to the monitor. "I reckon if we plug all the holes in the building along with those exhaust stacks, we can fog real good," he said with confidence. "Then the two deputies inside can get out.

After that, I'll fill the place with methyl bromide. That will kill everything in there, three times over." Tom planned to make certain everything in the factory was stone-cold dead before passing out his business cards.

"At this point," Dr. Reynolds caution, "I wouldn't attempt using poisons. We don't know how this organism will react to conventional pesticides. We need more information before trying anything like that." She made no mention that live specimens would need to be collected before attempting any type of extermination. This find was just too important to act hastily.

"If there's no other way of getting my men out," the sheriff said, "then I have no choice." He turned back to Tom. "How soon can you have your fogger machine ready?"

"All I have to do is crank it up," Tom said.

"Sheriff, these things are not insects," Dr. Reynolds reiterated. "You could be making a bad situation much worse. Like I said, we don't know how these creatures will react to conventional pesticides, even something as toxic as methyl bromide. You could be endangering many more lives."

"Then what do you suggest?" the sheriff asked.

"Let me contact someone I know in New Orleans," Dr. Reynolds said. "If anyone can help us, he can."

"I'm not wasting anymore time," the sheriff said. "If your contact doesn't know what these things are or how to deal with them, we'll be back to square one."

"We're way past square one," Dr. Reynolds pointed out. "We know a lot about what we are dealing with. The inside of this factory is the nest. I'm certain of that. These organisms are territorial and will only attack if threatened and as long as your two deputies do not pose that threat, there should be no reason for worry. But if you create a threatening situation, these creatures could go on the defensive. That could prompt them to attack your deputies or even leave the factory."

"If there is no other way," Sheriff Maxwell said, "then I am willing to take that chance. My men have been trapped nearly seven hours with no food or water. The factory's interior is getting hotter and the longer this situation goes on the less chance they have of getting out safely."

"Sheriff, there's something you need to see," Gene said. "Take a look between these two machines, at the back of the factory." He pointed out the twin hulks of equipment as viewed on the TV monitor. "Do you see down here on the floor?"

The sheriff and Dr. Reynolds looked closely at the image. The creatures were moving underground in what was clearly the exposed edge of a large hole through the floor.

"That very well could be the entrance to the main part of their nest," Dr. Reynolds said.

Joel approached the group at the monitor. "Sheriff," he said, "Mister Linderson, the high school biology teacher, is here. Wants to know if there is anything he can do to help."

"Have him come over," the sheriff said.

Joel waved over Linderson.

"Mister Linderson," the sheriff said, "whatever is discussed here or anything you see is not to be revealed to anyone outside of this group. Is that clear?"

"Yes sir," Linderson replied, "and please, call me Phil."

The sheriff introduced Dr. Reynolds and then showed the biology teacher the scene on the TV monitor. "Last school year, do you recall any of your students talking about unusual things happening in Union Town?" the sheriff asked. "Anything at all?"

"No sir," Linderson said. "Summer school ended two weeks ago and I heard nothing then nor anything during the school year. The only unusual thing I can think of is there being no gulls or crows at the landfill, that's all." He took a longer look at the monitor's screen. "Those things only have four legs, don't they?" he asked Dr. Reynolds. "And claws. Are they some type of arthropod?"

"We don't know yet what they are," Dr. Reynolds said. "About the landfill, is it close to here?"

"From here, about three and half miles, on the other side of town," the sheriff said.

"I dropped off some stuff out there this morning and noticed there were no birds," Linderson said. "That's unusual. In fact, the only animal I saw was a raccoon."

"Phil," the sheriff said, "I need you to report to me anything you see or hear that could pertain to these bugs. Also, I'd like you to remain available, should I need your input. And remember, nothing to anyone outside this group."

"I understand," Linderson replied. "Do you need my phone number?"

"Joel will get that from you," the sheriff said. "Thanks for your cooperation."

CHAPTER 12

MAYOR BILL BRANDON GAZED OVER the scene at Number Two Industrial Boulevard from inside his car. He frowned. "Maxwell, I'm going to bury your ass," he snarled. He glanced in the rear view mirror as a Union Town police car rolled up behind him, Dick Gallo at the wheel. The police chief stayed put.

Lonnie Nethero pushed his way to Brandon's car. He leaned in the open window.

"What's the latest?" Brandon asked.

"Phil Linderson and some bug expert are here," Lonnie replied. "The expert is supposed to know all about whatever is inside the factory."

He paused.

"I guess you know about Larry and Jack."

"You're damn right I know," the mayor growled. "Are Maxwell's deputies out of the building yet?"

"No sir," Lonnie said.

"Turn-about is fair play," Brandon muttered. "Thanks. Keep me posted."

The mayor turned his car onto Industrial Boulevard and parked alongside emergency vehicles. Chief Gallo obediently followed. The two men got out of their vehicles. "You keep your mouth shut," the mayor told his chief of police.

"Yes, sir," Chief Gallo replied.

Mayor Brandon slipped under the cordon and marched across the factory's front yard tailed by his one-man entourage. He scowled at Linderson as their paths crossed. "Maxwell," Brandon blustered, pushing through ranks. "What the hell's going on here?"

The town's executive was not someone the sheriff wanted to see just then. "Mayor Brandon," he said, "are you aware of our situation?"

Brandon harrumphed. "You're damn right I'm aware. Your department got two of my police officers killed."

"Larry Parker and Jack Moore were good men," Chief Gallo piped up. "And you got them killed."

The mayor's searing glance sent the police chief back pedaling.

The sheriff said, "Mister Mayor, I've got enough on my hands right now. If you're not offering anything constructive, move back behind the cordon."

The mayor's eyes narrowed. "I'm not going anywhere until I know exactly what's going on," he stated.

"We're having a problem with some unknown bugs in the factory," the sheriff said. "Deputies Hebert and Wilson are trapped inside. We're working on getting them out."

"And my men?" the mayor asked. "What happened to them?"

"They were victims of the bugs," the sheriff said.

"Bugs?" the mayor bleated. "How the hell did bugs kill two of my officers?"

Sheriff Maxwell showed Brandon the television monitor.

"This is ridiculous," the mayor said, unfazed. "Just fumigate the damn place. Or is that too difficult for you?"

"Mister Mayor, please," Sheriff Maxwell said irritably. "Step behind the cordon."

Brandon stood his ground. "I want to know how you plan on resolving this," he demanded. "And who's your girlfriend?" He was referring to Dr. Reynolds. His stare encompassed her trim figure.

"This is Doctor Reynolds," the sheriff said, "a professor of entomology from LSU. She's helping us identify those things."

The mayor nodded a curt greeting to Dr. Reynolds. "So you're the expert on bugs, are you?" he asked. "Just what kind of bugs are we dealing with?"

"They're not insects," Dr. Reynolds said, having no desire to get dragged into the middle of whatever problems the mayor and the sheriff seemed to have.

"What do you mean, not insects?" the mayor scoffed. "That's what the sheriff says they are." Brandon looked at the monitor again. "They sure look like bugs to me."

"I've seen some behavioral traits associated with the Class Hymenoptera," Dr. Reynolds stated dryly, "and they do have some morphological traits associated with Coleoptera but as far as I can tell, they are not a known species. Physiologically, I need more data."

Mayor Brandon frowned. "You can see what happens when the sheriff won't step up and take charge," he said loudly to anyone listening. "A lot of babble and nothing gets done."

"That's right," Police Chief Gallo piped up. "You can see exactly what happens."

To the sheriff, Brandon said, "If I were you…".

The sheriff cut him off. "Mayor Brandon, move back behind the cordon, now."

"I hope you see what's going on here," Brandon said to those around him as he stormed off.

"Incompetence, that's what it is," Chief Gallo said of the sheriff, scurrying after his boss.

Sheriff Maxwell disregarded the interruption. He called over Doff. "When you rechecked the factory's perimeter," the sheriff asked, "did you notice any other openings in the building?"

"No sir," Doff said. "Just a sink hole along the east wall."

At any other time Sheriff Maxwell would not have found this fact strange but now a warning pinged in his head. The industrial estate was plagued with sinkholes but the east wall of Cajun Snacks' facility was the same wall behind which the apparent entrance to the creatures' nest was located. "I need you to take a look at a sinkhole," the sheriff said to Dr. Reynolds. "Doff, come with us."

✕

"EXCUSE ME, MAYOR BRANDON?" TOM Slyger said as he sidled up to the mayor outside the cordon. He handed the mayor his business card. "Slyger's the name and pest control is my game."

"Pest control?"

"Yes sir. Tri-Parish Pest Control, out of Bunkie."

"Can you clean up this mess?" the mayor asked.

"I can take care of this and any other pest problem Union Town may have," Tom bragged, unable to restrain a smile. A contract with Union Town was all but a sure thing. "When do you want me to get started?" he asked.

Brandon regarded Sheriff Maxwell and that professor of bugology as they made their way to the far side of the building. Maxwell's department had already botched this situation and with a little nudge, he just might go over the top.

"As far as I'm concerned," Brandon replied, "you can start right now."

Tom's eyes gleamed.

✕

SHERIFF MAXWELL, DR. REYNOLDS AND Doff inspected the six foot wide sinkhole. Doff knelt down and pressed his ear to the ground. "I can hear them," he said. "Sounds like they're digging."

"Very likely enlarging the nest," Dr. Reynolds said, "an indication the colony is still growing, if they are similar to ground-nesting Vespids, yellow-jackets and the like. If so, then there will be one egg-laying queen. The workers will all be infertile females. There will also be cycles in the year when fertile males and females are produced. That cycle begins when nest expansion is complete, when the digging stops."

"And when will that be?" the sheriff asked.

"It's imperative we find out," Dr. Reynolds said, "because that's when individuals are likely to leave this nest to start new colonies."

The sheriff radioed Justin. "How are you guys holding out?" he asked.

"We need water," Justin replied in a drained voice.

"We're doing all we can to get you out," the sheriff said. "I have Doctor Reynolds with me, that insect expert from LSU. She has something to tell you."

The sheriff instructed Dr. Reynolds how to use the radio. "The deputy's name is Justin Hebert," he told her.

"Deputy Hebert," Dr. Reynolds said. "Those organisms in the factory are not insects. I don't know what they are. That's why we're moving cautiously. It could be disastrous if we do the wrong thing. Do you understand?"

"Yes, I do," Justin responded. Even with his and Gerald's immediate need for water, he was glad a healthy dose of discretion was being employed in tackling this problem.

"We do know," Dr. Reynolds continued, "that these organisms behave like social insects. They all react in a similar way to the same stimuli."

"Will that bit of knowledge get us out of here any faster?" Justin asked.

"It will certainly help," Dr. Reynolds answered. "The predictability factor of how these creatures behave increases a hundred fold."

"You also need to know," Dr. Reynolds said, "from all indications you and the other deputy are sitting directly over the main part of the nest."

"That makes my day," Justin joked.

"There's one other thing," Dr. Reynolds added, "and that is, you probably will not be attacked as long as the creatures don't see you as a threat."

Justin had already figured that much out himself.

Sheriff Maxwell took back the radio. "Justin," he transmitted, "can you see the two big pieces of machinery by the east wall?"

"Ten-four," Justin said. The east wall was the only

portion of the building's interior he could view in its entirety.

"And can you see the dark area in the floor between those machines?" the sheriff asked.

"I see a lot of activity over there."

"There is a hole there," the sheriff said. "Doctor Reynolds believes it leads into the nest."

"We'll wait for your instructions," came Justin's stoic reply.

Olan's voice crackled over the radio. "Sheriff, you better get back here," he reported. "That pest control guy went up on the roof."

CHAPTER 13

"DOFF, GET SLYGER OFF THE damn roof," the sheriff ordered the policeman. Sheriff Maxwell had no doubt who had authorized the pest controller to go atop the building.

Mayor Brandon stood beyond the cordon speaking to Chief Gallo when Sheriff Maxwell confronted the town official. "Something you need, sheriff?" the mayor chided the lawman. "If so, stand in line."

The sheriff's nostrils flared. His hands trembled with anger at the mayor's arrogance. "Mister Mayor, leave immediately or I'll have you placed under arrest."

The mayor's eyes widened in surprise, caught off guard at Sheriff Maxwell's dictate but just as quickly a smug smile replaced shock. "You should know," he said, "I'm bringing you up on criminal charges. Accessory to murder. I'm going to fry your ass." He glared disdain at the sheriff, spun on his heels and stomped away with Chief Gallo in tow.

×

DOFF MARCHED TO THE BUILDING'S service ladder, ticked off that the mayor's own actions were sending him up on the roof during the hottest part of the day. Doff planned to get this over quickly and make certain Mr. Tom Slyger would be no further problem.

Reaching the ladder's top rung, Doff slipped on his sunglasses against the mid-afternoon glare. Radiant heat from the metal roof was stifling. The three exhaust stacks sprouted from the back side of the roof's low peak. Black residue from overheated cooking oil dribbled down their sides in unsightly streaks. Slyger was busy unfastening the rain guard on the center stack, the shortest of the three, an open toolbox at his feet.

"Off the roof," Doff called from his position, hopeful he wouldn't have to go any further.

"I have authorization from the mayor," Tom called back. He continued working.

Doff's dander rose as fast as the sweat soaking his shirt. Wanting an end to this here and now, he stepped onto the roof and shuffled along perpendicular avenues of bolts marking the location of underlying support beams. With each step the roof's aluminum sheeting popped under his weight. He wondered how the bugs would react to the sound of footsteps on the roof. He focused on his mission.

Doff was in no mood to reason or argue. Twenty feet from Tom, just past the first stack and out of sight from those below, Doff did the only thing he felt would get the little man's fast and immediate attention. He pulled his pistol from its shoulder holster. "If you don't get off this roof now, I'll throw your dead body off," he threatened.

Tom's owl eyes grew incredibly large. "Don't point that thing at me!"

"Off the roof. Now!"

"All right, already," Tom stammered. He wiped sweat from his face with a rag slung over his shoulder. Stowing his wrench, he picked up his toolbox and squeezed past Doff back to the ladder. "The mayor will hear about this," he grumbled.

"Big deal," Doff snorted.

A fresh breeze moved stagnant air, brushing aside the unmerciful heat and cooling Doff's temper. He moved to the roof's peak to take full advantage of the refreshing breeze. From his new position he took in a grand view of The Swamp's tangled brambles wedged between the industrial park and Union Town. The levee along the Atchafalaya River and Old Simmesport Highway cut a line due north, becoming lost among moss shrouded oaks, tall pines and afternoon haze. On the front side of the building, members of the town's emergency-squad kept crowds of curiosity seekers at bay.

KATC's television crew had been joined by a CNN van. Both crews were busy filming while their correspondents bickered with authorized personnel for statements.

From the front lawn, Bill and Olan watched the goings-on topside. The funeral home director gave a thumb's up to Doff for a job well done. Doff signaled he himself was coming down.

Doff moved back over the roof's peak and started for the ladder. As long as the air continued to move, he reckoned he wouldn't completely melt away.

An eerie sense of being watched seized Doff. It wasn't Olan or anyone down below observing his progress. Someone else was on the roof. He could feel it in his bones. It crawled on his skin. He halted and looked behind him. No one. Still, the feeling lingered.

And then, Doff froze. His first thought was how Mr. Tullis had looked a half hour after his death. That mental picture still sickened him but even more so now for Doff was staring down death's throat.

One of the gigantic bugs had partially crawled from the first stack. Bright light constricted its white irises to tiny black pupils and those pupils were fixed on Doff.

Sweat burned Doff's eyes and blurred his vision. He forced himself not to blink, not to move a muscle. The slightest twitch could be his last.

Doff was painfully aware he could not remain in the intense heat much longer. Moisture was being sucked from every pore of his body and heat exhaustion threatened, but to move was to die.

Doff struggled for a plan, anything to get out of this alive. Sprinting down the roof's slope and taking his chances with gravity came to mind but these bugs were fast and he would never make it past the first step before the creature was on him.

With agonizing slowness, his heart beating like a racehorse at full bolt, Doff slid out one foot and then the other. Roofing bolts creaked under his weight as he crab-walked in slow-motion never looking away from the dark creature and never imagining he would make it one more inch.

The farther Doff edged from the creature, the more his hopes of escape grew for he realized his fate might not be sealed. The bug was not watching him after all, only staring at some distant point.

Heartfelt relief flooded Doff when he grabbed the ladder's handrails and swung down onto the first rung. He took a final look across the roof to the bug's dark shape camouflaged by streaks of grease. The bug had obviously been there when Slyger and then he had come up on the roof and it was equally obvious something had killed it.

Doff hurried to the factory's front. "One of those creatures is up there." Doff said to Sheriff Maxwell and Dr. Reynolds. "I looks dead."

"If it is dead," the sheriff said to the bug expert, "what killed it?"

"Possibly the heat," Dr. Reynolds replied. "If these things have a thin cuticle it would lead to rapid dehydration."

"Then heat might be the answer we're looking for," the sheriff commented. He motioned to the television monitor. "Gene noticed there are fewer bugs in the factory now. The rising heat inside could be driving them underground."

"Good observation," Dr. Reynolds said. "It certainly makes sense. These organisms are no doubt cold-blooded which means they can't regulate their body temperatures. They are returning underground to stay cool."

"So if it gets real hot in there they'll all go underground?" the sheriff asked.

"It's only an assumption based on limited observation," Dr. Reynolds said.

"Limited or not," the sheriff said, "we are going to give it a try." He called over Joel. "Where can we get some space heaters?" he asked.

"There should be some at the hardware store," the emergency-squad member said, purposefully omitting the shop's late owner's name.

"Get whatever is there," the sheriff ordered.

Joel hurried off.

The sheriff was hopeful this heat thing would finally gain his two deputies' freedom. After that they would obliterate the nest and every creature in it.

Three state police cruisers arrived with five troopers. Sheriff Maxwell met Police Sergeant Blare Benoit halfway across the front yard. Benoit was a tall, man with tan skin and a square chin.

"Afternoon sheriff," the trooper said. "I'm Sergeant Blare Benoit. Lieutenant Allain sent me. I understand you need support. What's the problem?"

"Sergeant, thanks for coming," the sheriff said. He motioned for Dr. Reynolds to join them. "Sergeant Benoit, this is Doctor Reynolds, from LSU. She's advising us on how to proceed."

Maxwell, Reynolds and Benoit moved to the video monitor. "It's difficult to get a perspective from here," the sheriff told the new arrival, "but the factory is infested with some type of bug that killed two Union Town police officers and at least four civilians."

"Do we know what kind of bug it is?" the sergeant asked.

"We don't have sufficient information at this point," Dr. Reynolds stated, "but it's actually not a bug or any form of insect. It has traits associated with at least two classes of arthropods and two Phyla."

"What is… oh, never mind," Sergeant Benoit said. "What assistance can my men and I provide, sheriff?"

"I need you to organize an hourly inspection of the

other factories," Sheriff Maxwell said. "I'll have someone familiar with these creatures go with you. I'd like all other troopers to assist with maintaining the cordon."

CHAPTER 14

"I WOULD LIKE TO GO up on the roof and collect that dead specimen," Dr. Reynolds said to the sheriff. She, Doff and Sheriff Maxwell stood at the curbing along Industrial Boulevard taking in a grand view of the factory's sloped roof and exhaust stacks.

"What do you think, Doff?" the sheriff asked.

Doff regarded the wavering lines of radiant heat dancing on the roof's metal surface.

"I think it's safe," Doff said. "I'll go up with her."

"Make sure that thing is stone cold dead before you get too close," the sheriff said to Dr. Reynolds.

From her car, Dr. Reynolds retrieved large forceps, a plastic tray with lid and from her pocketbook, a mirror. She followed her escort to the access ladder.

Doff ascended the ladder first, specimen box in hand. Dr. Reynolds shoved the forceps and mirror into a pants pocket and started up. She accepted a hand-up from the police officer at the top. The reflected heat was dreadful.

"Follow the anchor bolts," Doff advised. He led the way up the slope. The continuing breeze made this return trip more tolerable but the nearer he drew to that bug, the slower his progress. Even if the creature was indeed dead, just being on the roof with it again gave him the willies.

Doff shifted to a lower row of bolts allowing Dr. Reynolds passage. He drew his pistol and positioned himself where he could get a clear shot. One twitch from that overgrown beetle and he would blow it to smithereens.

Dr. Reynolds moved closer to the lifeless creature and like Doff, paid full attention on the slightest movement. Now was not the time to find out how good a marksman Officer Green might be.

"Is it dead?" Doff asked. Dr. Reynolds was taking an awfully long time getting on with her work and he had no desire to remain on the roof any longer than absolutely necessary.

"It appears to be," Dr. Reynolds replied, wiping perspiration from her forehead. Her scientific curiosity overcoming her fear, she leaned in closer, looking deep into the creature's lifeless eyes. The fact its eyes faced forward meant this creature would have full frontal vision with limited peripheral capability. Visual perception would be increased if the eyes were articulated, certainly not something found in the insect world.

Dr. Reynolds slipped the forceps from her pocket. Painfully slow, she extended her arm and poked the creature's front leg. No response. The creature's pinpoint pupils remained fixed on the distance. She tapped its stubby antennae. Touching this sensory organ should have elicited a response. Nothing.

“Get the specimen box ready,” Dr. Reynolds said to Doff. As far as she could tell this creature was indeed dead.

Dr. Reynolds retrieved the mirror from her pocket and slid her foot alongside the smoke stack. Positioning the looking-glass over the vent’s orifice, she adjusted its angle to reveal thick, greasy residue coating the stack’s internal walls like rivulets of black lacquer. Darkness funneled into an emptiness accessible only with the mirror’s reflected light. There were no signs of other creatures.

Slipping the forceps around the dead bug’s girth and applying just enough pressure to maintain her grip, Dr. Reynolds lifted the beast up and out. Rigor mortis held the bug’s appendages motionless. It was heavier than Dr. Reynolds expected, maybe a pound.

Dr. Reynolds laid the lifeless body into the specimen tray held by Doff and delicately touched the forceps to the bug’s right eye. A hard, clear cornea covered an underlying white, granular iris. Unable to lift the elytra, the hard, outer wing of the creature’s exoskeleton, the entomologist rolled the specimen onto its back, confirming her original video observation. The odd bug indeed had only two body segments; a cephalothorax and abdomen, traits found in arachnids, like spiders and scorpions. Yet this creature could fly. The only flying arthropods are insects and unlike arachnids, they have three body parts; head, thorax and abdomen.

Of its four legs, the creature's two rear appendages attached directly to its abdomen. In arachnids, all eight legs connect to the cephalothorax while the six legs of insects, to the thorax. Probing further with the forceps, Dr. Reynolds located within this odd bug's soft belly a ring of rigid tissue to which its rear appendages were connected. The abdomen was covered with half-inch long tactile hairs but was not segmented and the entomologist was not surprised when she failed to locate openings through which it would breathe, neither book lungs as in arachnids nor spiracles as in insects. This seemed to confirm the two openings on its short proboscis were nostrils.

"Can you check that thing after we get down," Doff suggested. Sweat once again streaked his shirt.

"Sure," Dr. Reynolds said, still engrossed in her work. "Just a moment."

Dr. Reynolds prized open the bug's mouth. Greenish tissue surrounded two plates of chitinous teeth set on a maxilla and mandible. The gullet was closed.

The creature's inch long, distended stinger was a barb-less protuberance that within the insect world meant it could sting once and survive to sting another day. Dr. Reynolds found no exterior reproductive organs.

Doff's radio crackled with a short transmission between Justin and Sheriff Maxwell. The trapped deputy reported he saw only a few bugs remaining in the building and the sheriff confirmed this from his view on the monitor.

"We have two space heaters on site," the sheriff radioed his chief deputy. "We're setting them up now inside the building, through the back door. Let me know if you see any movement in that direction."

"Ten-four," Justin replied.

"Sorry, Doctor Reynolds," Doff said, "but we have to get off the roof."

"Oh, yeah," the entomologist replied. Returning the forceps and mirror into her pocket, she secured the tray's lid and she and Doff shuffled back to the ladder.

"You first," Doff instructed, taking the tray. "I'll hand it down to you."

Dr. Reynolds descended the ladder three steps and braced herself against the security frame before reaching up for the tray.

Doff lowered the makeshift coffin into her waiting hands. As the transfer was made, the tray's lid struck the ladder, knocking it askew.

Struggling to maintain her balance and that of the tray, the entomologist inadvertently tilted the container to a more severe angle and causing the tray's lid to fall away. She gasped as the lifeless creature tumbled out. One of its rear legs snagged her blouse, it's stinger inches from her face.

"Hold on!" Doff yelled. He knelt down and carefully extracted the creature with thumb and forefinger.

"Don't drop it," Dr. Reynolds panted, her heart racing from the ordeal. She adjusted the tray's position and Doff laid the monster bug inside.

Bill and Joel waited at the bottom of the ladder after having installed the space heaters, two jet engine-looking units with powerful fans. When Dr. Reynolds and Doff were safely on the ground, they returned together to the building's front.

"I'm going to make that phone call," Dr. Reynolds said to the sheriff. "We need help."

CHAPTER 15

"AND THIS IS FROM THE New Jersey site?" retired Professor Irving Potter asked his guest and long-time colleague and geology professor, Mike Jenkins. The two men were meeting in Dr. Potter's house in New Orleans.

Adjusting his magnifying glass, Potter refocused on a fly embedded in a thumb-size globule of honey-colored amber. Unlike most amber he had seen from the New Jersey site, this rare specimen was beautifully transparent, containing only a trace of inclusive debris and allowing a clear view of the tiny insect trapped within. He nodded approval of the sample's quality.

"It's not the largest piece I've received," Dr. Jenkins said, "but its clarity makes it by far the best."

Jenkins had had a recent run of good luck when amateur fossil-hounds stumbled upon a rich deposit of Upper Cretaceous succinite in a Central New Jersey sandpit. The site was yielding some of the oldest insects, flowers and arachnids ever found in amber.

"I believe what we have here is a Simuliidae," Dr. Potter said with a touch of excitement. "A black fly."

The four-millimeter insect featured the typical humped thorax of present day black flies but its mouth parts were markedly different, much more robust. No doubt, Dr. Potter thought, for biting through tough dinosaur skin.

"I'll take it," Jenkins said, "it's a keeper."

"I should say so," Potter remarked. As a leading entomologist in the country, he had been identifying insect inclusions in amber for Jenkins for nearly twenty years; midges, mosquitoes, an occasional millipede and a wide variety of beetles, but this specimen was the first Cretaceous black fly he had seen. A rare find, indeed.

Upstairs the telephone rang shrilly, audible throughout the entire split-level house.

"It's for you," Potter's wife, Mattie, called down a moment later from atop the stairs.

Dr. Potter laid the amber globule in a box containing other samples he had already examined and took the nearby receiver off the hook. "Good afternoon, this is Irving Potter."

"I'm sorry to disturb you," the female caller said. "This is Jennifer Reynolds."

"Jenny! What a lovely surprise. How are you?" Dr. Potter exclaimed when he heard his ex-student's voice. They hadn't spoken to each other for quite some time. "Are you in town?"

"No sir, I'm not," Dr. Reynolds replied, calling from

Tullis' mobile phone. "I'm calling from Union Town."

"A field trip?" Dr. Potter asked. That area had been his favorite place for taking entomology students, the marshes and bayous being prolific breeding grounds for insects.

"I guess you could call it that," Dr. Reynolds responded. "An unexpected one."

"Anything wrong?"

"Well sir, right now, yes," Dr. Reynolds confessed, "but I'm hoping you can change that." She took a deep breath and said slowly and clearly, "I have a dead specimen with traits of both arthropods and arachnids. Its sting is lethal. Body length, about twelve inches, two body segments..."

"How many points on this test?" Dr. Potter cut in with a chuckle. His own exams had often been salted with trick questions on taxonomy that kept even the brightest students searching the classification keys with no chance of positive identification. His ex-student was apparently pulling the same stunt on him.

"Doctor Potter," Dr. Reynolds said with continued seriousness, "I wish I were kidding but I'm not. There's an organism here in Union Town that I've never seen nor heard of before. It's killed at least six people and doesn't fit any key: exoskeleton, four legs, elytra, clavate antennae and binocular eyes and a venom more hemolytic than all the brown recluse spiders in Louisiana."

"Four legs? It's poisonous? With binocular eyes? And it has an exoskeleton?"

"Yes sir, with two body segments," Dr. Reynolds repeated, "and a twelve inch body length."

"You're serious, aren't you?"

"Dead serious."

"Tell me more." Dr. Potter picked up a ballpoint pen and notepad from his desk.

Dr. Reynolds started from the beginning, describing the events as she knew them.

"And you're saying they have killed six people?" Dr. Potter asked. "How?"

"The venom. It's injected with a barb-less, retractable stinger," Dr. Reynolds said. "And there could be more than six deaths. I don't believe law enforcement knows exactly how many bodies are in the factory where these organisms appear to be nesting."

"A nest?" Dr. Potter asked. "How many individuals are we talking about?" He gave Mike Jenkins a quizzical look.

"Possibly thousands," Dr. Reynolds said.

"Jenny, I don't have to tell you what the implications of this are," Dr. Potter stated, excitement and envy in his voice. "It appears you might have stumbled upon a completely new Phylum. It's the opportunity of a lifetime."

"Yes it is," Dr. Reynolds agreed but with her

knowledge of what these bugs could do, not sharing her ex-professor's zeal. She was afraid. "Doctor Potter, this is not like identifying a new species of Homoptera. I have a dead specimen and want so much to capture live ones but these organisms are extremely dangerous. I don't know how to handle them." Hesitating, her voice wavering, she said, "I've seen what destruction they cause."

"Jenny, I'm coming up there," Potter said. "I can be in Union Town in a few hours." He wasn't about to let such a unique experience pass him by.

"I would appreciate that," Dr. Reynolds replied, relieved at getting Dr. Potter's help. One mistake, one oversight could spell disaster and she wasn't up to that responsibility. The late Horace Gail's liquefied, blackened hand convinced her of that.

"What about other nests?" Dr. Potter asked.

"I haven't heard of any other nests here or anywhere else," Dr. Reynolds said. "And as for this one, I believe the colony is still growing." She described the subterranean activity.

"It would be nice if their colony cycle is indeed similar to Vespids," Dr. Potter said cautiously. "If that were the case, they won't have started producing breeding stock yet. But I don't know how reliable such a comparison will be, considering the uniqueness of these creatures."

"I don't know what other criteria to use," Dr. Reynolds said.

"Nor do I," Dr. Potter agreed.

"The behavior I noted inside the factory, on the video monitor," Dr. Reynolds said, "is similar to the Vespula species: social and fiercely protective of their nest."

"Any indication if they are diurnal or nocturnal?" Dr. Potter asked.

"At this point, we don't know," Dr. Reynolds said. "It does appear that they are highly sensitive to heat. It was noticed that as the factory's interior heated up individuals began migrating into the underground portion of the nest. Since then, authorities here have inserted a couple of space heaters inside to make it even hotter."

"Interesting about the heat," Dr. Potter mused. "We'll need live specimens."

"Yes sir, we will but it was sheer luck I got this dead one," Dr. Reynolds said. "I don't know how we can isolate and capture live individuals. They are just too dangerous."

"Besides heat, do you see any other method of control?"

"The only obvious way is with fumigants," Dr. Reynolds said. "There's a pest control operator here. It doesn't appear to be a big operation but he has a marginal quantity of methyl bromide and hydrogen cyanide."

"And we don't know how big the nest is, right?" Potter asked.

"That's correct. Nor do we know how these organisms will react to fumigants."

"I think we're pretty safe with methyl bromide and hydrogen cyanide," Potter said. "It's not knowing the nest size that is a worry."

"You're not suggesting fumigation, are you?"

"I think at this point we need to be prepared for any contingency," Dr. Potter said, "but capturing live specimens is imperative and must be done first."

"What about involving the CDC?" Dr. Reynolds said.

"I'd like to see these things for myself before bringing in the Feds," Potter replied. "You know how things can get overly complicated when they are involved."

"Yes sir."

"Mike Jenkins is coming with me," Dr. Potter said.

Jenkins nodded with a thumbs-up.

"Good," Dr. Reynolds said and added, "Doctor Potter, I'm scared. What if we are unable to contain all of the individuals in this colony? What if some escape? Even if we clear all the people from the area there is no way we can know what these organisms might do under stress. I have seen a sting victim, at least his hand, and I have heard descriptions of what happens to the body. The venom is so potent it kills a human in less than a minute and dissolves every bit of soft tissue down to bone."

Dr. Potter fell silent.

"Doctor Potter, are you still there?"

No answer.

"Doctor Potter?"

"Bleached white bones," Dr. Potter said as if answering a question on a freshman biology exam. "All that remains are bleached white bones and a dark viscous matter."

"Are you familiar with this organism?" Dr. Reynolds said, amazed.

"Jenny, can you hold on a moment?"

"Yes sir." Dr. Reynolds said. She wasn't going anywhere until she had an answer.

Dr. Potter pulled open the top drawer of a gray file cabinet set beside a stack of assorted magazines tied with heavy twine. He dug behind a rack of dog-eared manila folders and extracted a tattered journal and pint-size glass specimen jar sealed with a black lid. He closed the drawer and returned to his desk.

To Dr. Jenkins, Potter said, "I think we're about to have a long overdue answer to a lingering question."

The ancient journal's binding crackled when Dr. Potter opened it. The penned entries were smudged with dirt and faded with time. Skimming over one page, he skipped a dozen more, scanned another entry and moved on. When he found what he was looking for, he hurried back to the phone.

"I want you to listen to what I'm about to read," Dr. Potter told his former student, sounding to her as if the word of God were to be spoken. "This is from notes I kept while on a field trip in the Venezuelan jungle." He looked at the year jotted at the top of the page and continued. "1956. I was a graduate student with a team of entomologists and geologists. Doctor Jenkins was on that trip also."

> *"November 16, 1956,"* Dr. Potter began solemnly. *"Very unsettling day. Member of Doctor Fowler's geology team found a human skeleton not a hundred yards from our camp. Frightening sight. From clothing, individual was native Indian. Been there a long time. Bones picked clean and white. Remaining tissues decomposed to a black residue. No explanation why not found earlier. We have all been studying area nearly every day – biologically sterile: no invertebrate or vertebrate life forms and no explanations why. Fowler's team luckier. Found a meteorite fragment in a washed out ravine. Supposedly rare type. All very excited."*

Dr. Potter flipped more pages. "There's one other note I remember," he said. "Here it is."

> *"November 18. Today Indians in camp. Juan (our guide) contacted Yanomami tribe – a mile south. Indians indicated remains are of one of their warriors. Recognized his blowgun. Burned bones and*

gathered up ashes. Indians claimed Heckura (sp.) spirits killed him and ate flesh. Said he was on hunting trip with three others. Now missing. Left village two days ago. This obviously not one of those men. Body here much longer. Hope missing warriors turn up. PS: Interesting to note that skeletal remains articulated and not disturbed by scavengers."

"My god," Dr. Reynolds exclaimed. "That was in 1956? In Venezuela?"

"Does this describe the victims in Union Town?" Dr. Potter asked.

"Precisely." Dr. Reynolds was aghast.

Dr. Potter lifted up the specimen jar to view a single curved claw, a quarter inch long and half as wide at its base, tapering to a sharp point. He recalled plucking it off the jungle floor near to where the skeleton had been found over forty years before. No one he had shown it to was ever able to identify its origin and he had eventually stuck it in the back of his file cabinet and forgotten about it, until this day.

"Do these organisms have claws?" Dr. Potter asked.

"Yes," Dr. Reynolds said. "Two on each foreleg."

"Describe them to me."

Her description matched perfectly the specimen in his hand.

Whether originally from the Venezuelan jungle where they were considered spirits or a transplant from some other location on the globe, this bizarre creature had somehow remained isolated from major human populations since their evolutionary birth. This find in Union Town proved these organisms were now posing a definite threat to larger human populations.

"Our priority must be for safety," Dr. Potter said, "but we must capture live specimens."

"The sheriff here is insisting on extermination," Dr. Reynolds said.

"This discovery is a lot bigger than any sheriff," Dr. Potter asserted. "I need you to make certain nothing drastic is done until I get there. On second thought, I believe I will call the CDC. It doesn't sound like we can handle this ourselves."

"Please hurry," Dr. Reynolds said.

"I'll get there as fast as I can," Dr. Potter told her. "And one more thing, in case we do need to fumigate, how big an area is the factory?"

"About seventy-five thousand square feet," Dr. Reynolds said, "forty-foot ceiling at the peak. It's an abandoned food factory."

"How is it constructed?"

"Pre-fab, aluminum-sided building with a concrete floor."

"Does the pest controller there have a tent large

enough?" Dr. Potter asked, referring to the vinyl-coated, nylon enclosure used to shroud larger structures.

"It's a pretty small operation," Dr. Reynolds said. "He certainly doesn't have an enclosure here."

"No problem," Dr. Potter said. "I'm going to contact a friend of mine, Allen Derbigby. He owns a commodities fumigation company here in New Orleans. I'll get him to come up with us. He'll have a much larger arsenal of fumigants and gear than the guy from Bunkie and I prefer to use someone I feel certain is fully capable of handling this situation."

"Should we at least tape and seal?" Dr. Reynolds asked.

"Yes, if it can be done safely. That will put us a bit ahead of the game."

"Any other preparations?"

"No, stay safe and do nothing more."

Dr. Potter hung up his phone. "Are you up for a ride to Union Town?" he asked Dr. Jenkins.

"Sounds like Jenny has more than a bit of a problem," Jenkins observed. He motion toward the jar and added, "And that thing came from a bug?"

"I'll fill you in on the way up there."

Dr. Potter lifted up his phone's handset once again and dialed a number in Atlanta.

"Frank, Irving Potter here," the entomologist said. "I've got an interesting situation for you."

Potter finished his call and went to the upstairs den where Mattie would be, folding promotional fliers for their church's annual cake sale.

"I have to drive up to Union Town," Potter told his wife. "I may be gone a couple of days."

"What on earth for?" Mattie asked.

"That was Jenny Reynolds who just called," he explained. "She has a problem with some sort of stinging bug and needs my help. Mike's going with me."

"You let Mike do the driving," Mattie said.

"I'll call you when we get to Union Town."

Mattie made the two men a thermos of coffee while her husband packed clothes in an overnight bag. They kissed and he and Jenkins were out of the door. They would link up with Allen Derbigby before heading north.

CHAPTER 16

FOUR O'CLOCK IN THE AFTERNOON made it eight hours since Justin and Gerald had taken refuge in their aluminum-clad cocoon. The cold room's observation window allowed only a limited view of the factory interior and Justin's radio had maintained communications with the sheriff, so the two trapped lawmen had not been totally isolated, but hot stagnant air within the insulated room had drained them of moisture. The resulting headaches and raging thirst were now giving way to dizziness and nausea.

Justin had not spent much airtime on his radio. Sheriff Maxwell was doing all he could to get them out and a lot of questions would just add to his work. When the sheriff had something significant to tell Justin, he would, and Justin had no problem with that.

Through these intermittent communications the two deputies were aware a bug expert from LSU, a Dr. Reynolds, had arrived, as well as a pest control operator. Justin hoped whatever decisions the experts made would not rile these creatures again. Being in the middle of the frenzy was an awesome and frightening sight and while he felt the wire-mesh guard would hold, he didn't want to test it again.

"The space heaters are driving more of the bugs underground," Justin said to Gerald.

Gerald joined his supervisor at the observation window for a quick scan into the cavernous room. The situation beyond the door was indeed improving.

Scratching from above alerted the two deputies of a lone bug staring at them through the cooling vent.

"Do you think it's cooler in here?" Gerald asked the creature, his hand on his gun. "Just try to get in and I'll make sure you have a third eye socket."

As if in defiance to Gerald's threat, the creature stepped onto the fan guard. It hooked a front claw around a wire strand and pulled, as if testing the wire's strength. When the strand flexed, the beast attacked it with greater determination, tearing at the covering with both front claws.

A single creature was not going to pull apart the steel mesh but this bug's actions were attracting others and Justin was concerned the guard might not hold under a concerted attack.

Drawing his pistol, Justin reached up and poked the bug with its barrel. The creature drew back, hissing like an angry cat but quickly returned to yanking at the wires.

"Blow its head off," Gerald urged.

"Take it easy," Justin said to his unnerved partner. He

stood on the overturned bucket and blew hard into the bug's face.

The bug jerked back, its eyes instantly glazing over with a white, opaque film. It rolled its eyes to clear the purulence and pounced on the wire guard again, jabbing its stinger at the radio's antenna.

Justin countered with another powerful exhalation. Again, the giant bug lurched backward, the pus-like matter again blurring its vision. It warily circled the hole, keeping well out of reach.

When a second bug sprang onto the vent, Gerald's nerves raced toward their breaking point. The enraged creature was doing all it could to gain entrance and Justin's tactics were proving little more than an irritation. Something else had to be done. More bugs had appeared outside the vent.

Running his thirst-swollen tongue along the bottom of his mouth, Gerald worked up a wad of spittle with what felt like the last trace of moisture in his body. He corralled the dab of saliva on his tongue and worked it into position. Tilting his head back, he pursed his lips and let go an oblong wad with prize-winning accuracy. Through the wire guard the spit sailed, striking the offending bug in its right eye.

The bug reared back as if hit by a powerful force. Like a reined-in horse, it moved in tight circles, clawing at the shimmering dribble. Alerted to their nest-mate's plight, a half dozen other creatures ripped at the cold room's metal skin.

The distressed bug scampered frantically across the vent, scattering its nest mates, wings fluttering and its body motions labored and erratic. It tumbled from the roof onto the floor in front of the cold room and in clear view of Justin and Gerald.

Bugs flitted about their stricken companion as it cut circular patterns on the floor. The impaired bug attempted to fly but only spun on its head smearing a tattoo of spittle onto the dusty floor. Completely disoriented and no longer able to coordinate leg movement, the creature's pupils dilated and it stopped moving.

"We're ready to open the rear door anytime you say," the sheriff radioed Justin.

"Wait," Justin replied. "One of the bugs just fell off the cold room. I think it's dead."

"Good," the sheriff radioed. "The heat must be working. Let me know when you want to make a break for it."

The other bugs abandoned their dead comrade and retreated into the entrance hole.

"It looks clear," Justin radioed. He didn't expect the situation to get any better than now.

"Justin, when you exit the cold room head for the rear door," the sheriff said. "We don't know if there are any creatures still holed up in the front offices." He purposely didn't mention Horace Gail's body, or what was left of it.

"Roger. We're coming out now," Justin radioed.

Nerves tense, Justin and Gerald prepared themselves to leave their tiny sanctuary. They were both dehydrated and exhausted but neither had lost his will to live.

"Where do you think Jack's body is?" Gerald asked Justin. Their imminent departure had Gerald's thoughts on the dead police officer. Gerald dreaded seeing the fallen lawman's body after all these hours since his death.

"Keep your eyes locked on the rear doorway," Justin coaxed. "And whatever you see, don't stop.

Late afternoon sunlight filled the big room when the rear door was swung open. Hurried shadows danced across walls as the heaters were moved aside.

Gerald flexed his fingers and bounced on jittery legs like an anxious athlete on deck. Spitting was impossible. His mouth was bone dry.

"Are you ready?" Justin asked the rookie.

A quick, 'yeah', was all Gerald could muster.

Justin levered out the cold-room's internal handle. The latch disengaged with an audible click. When he saw no bug movement, he swung the door open. Desert-hot air flooded in.

"You first," Justin said to his partner. The person bringing up the rear would have the greater risk of being attacked and Justin intended to be that person.

Gerald's breath caught in his throat upon seeing the vast room without benefit of protective glass. "What if…," he stammered.

There was no time for discussion. No time for a pep talk. Every second counted. "Go!"

Nervous sweat boiled from Gerald's skin. He charged from the aluminum box, hitting the concrete floor running. Everything around him was a blur. He bounded straight for the blinding tattoo of sunlight where safety waited on the other side.

Pure adrenaline charged through Gerald's veins. One long stride and then another brought him closer to the door, closer to freedom. He pulled in ragged breaths, running without conscious thought, his every fiber bent on escape.

Gerald's stomach leaped into his throat when he felt a sickening wetness underfoot. In another instant the floor skidded out from under him. He crashed heavily down, dashing the wind from him. He rolled onto his side, staring into the empty eye sockets of the late Jack Moore. Gerald forced his lungs to draw in air. Black, wet matter smeared on his right arm, burning as if he had been splashed with acid.

Justin's strong hand jerked the young deputy to his feet by his shirt collar and propelled him forwards. The rookie somehow found his footing again and broke from Justin's grip, scrambling into blinding light and cool, fresh air.

Bill Moley reached Gerald first.

"Get if off," Gerald pleaded, holding out his arm, his face twisted in agony.

Bill flushed away the dark matter from Gerald's arm with a bottle of water. Doff cut free Gerald's shirt with surgical scissors, careful not to touch the shimmering black goo smeared on cuff and sleeve. Once free of his contaminated garment, the deputy was rushed to an awaiting ambulance, barely conscious.

"Justin, are you all right?" the sheriff asked as Bill gave the deputy quick inspection.

"I think so, just really thirsty," Justin said.

"You're clean," Bill announced.

The sheriff and his team returned to the facility's forecourt where someone handed Justin a quart of Gatorade and a ham sandwich brought in from Coleman's Diner.

The sheriff assigned Doff and Dr. Martin to process the skeletal remains behind the factory and Olan returned to the funeral home to follow up on the shipment to New Iberia.

Waving over Dr. Reynolds, the sheriff said, "Justin, I'd like you to meet Doctor Reynolds." Justin and Dr. Reynolds shook hands.

Sheriff Maxwell was called away.

"Thank God you made it out all right," Dr. Reynolds said.

Justin nodded his appreciation. "Any idea yet what

those things in the factory are?" he asked.

"Still nothing," Dr. Reynolds said. "A colleague of mine, one of my ex-professors, is coming up from New Orleans. He may have more information. From what we do know, this bug, as you call it, has never before been identified. They are extraordinary organisms."

Justin wasn't sharing the entomologist's scientific fascination. "Has anyone figured out how to kill them?" he asked.

"We're not going to kill them," the sheriff said as he rejoined the two. "I just spoke with Governor Phillips' office. The Feds have gotten involved and we are to secure the building. They'll take over once on-site."

"So, we just sit and wait?" Justin asked.

"The factory's interior heat should keep the creatures underground for the time being," Dr. Reynolds said. "That will give us more time to determine the best way forward."

"It also gives those creatures more time to escape from underground," Justin said.

"With no further threat to their nest," Dr. Reynolds said, "they should remain below ground. In fact, these creatures could be diurnal, meaning they are only active during the day. If indeed they are diurnal, then they will remain underground during the night, with or without heat."

Dr. Reynolds turned to the sheriff. "I need a secure location where I can further examine the specimen from the roof."

"The funeral home might be the best place," the sheriff said.

"It's going on five o'clock," Dr. Reynolds said. "My colleague, Doctor Potter, is on his way here. I expect him to arrive in an hour or so. That gives me time to get some preliminary work done."

"Do you remember the way back to the funeral home?" the sheriff asked.

"I'm sure I can find it," Dr. Reynolds said.

"I can take you," Justin offered. "I want to go by the hospital to see how Gerald's doing. The funeral home is on the way."

"That will be fine," Dr. Reynolds said. "I'll get the specimen from my car."

"Oh, by the way," Dr. Reynolds added, remembering Potter's instructions and figuring this would still be needed in the light of the new information, "Doctor Potter would like the entire factory taped and sealed, initial preparation for fumigation."

The sheriff requested Slyger to join them and the entomologist explained to the exterminator what was needed.

"I'll need tape, a lot of it, and at least four helpers," Slyger said.

"I'll give you three," the sheriff said.

Tom started to say something, thought twice about it and nodded agreement. "That's fine," he said.

CHAPTER 17

JUSTIN GULPED DOWN THE LAST of his Gatorade as he walked to his cruiser, feeling revived after replacing lost body fluids and putting food in his stomach. Even so, as he waited for Dr. Reynolds, he thought a juicy Coleman Burger with an order of home fries still sounded good.

Dr. Reynolds opened her vehicle's tailgate. The auto's interior was oven hot. She retrieved her trayed specimen along with some equipment she would need and hurried over to Justin's vehicle. The tray was placed on the cruiser's backseat.

Justin cranked his car's engine and switched on the air-conditioner. He adjusted the vent, relishing the cooled air blowing on his face. "I take it you don't see a bug like this every day," he commented as he pulled out onto Industrial Boulevard. Dr. Reynolds's profile was highlighted against the side window, an attractive woman with exceptionally smooth skin. A ray of late afternoon sunlight caught her hair and set it aglow in auburn brilliance.

"This bug will write a new chapter in the books," Dr.

Reynolds said. She was conscious of Justin's appreciative glance and found she liked the attention.

A fleet-footed reporter brandishing a microphone rushed in front of Justin's car at the intersection of Old Simmesport Highway. The deputy braked and thanks to a state trooper latching onto the news-hound's arm and snatching him back, Justin narrowly missed the overly intrepid newsman.

Dr. Reynolds checked the boxed creature through the cruiser's Plexiglas security screen. The tray's lid had slid off when Justin avoided collision with the reporter but the tray was still set firmly on the seat.

"Where do you think these things came from?" Justin asked.

"That's the sixty-four thousand dollar question," Dr. Reynolds commented. "They have certainly never been identified before."

"Does that mean Union Town, Louisiana, is the only place in the world they exist?"

"It would be nice to think so," Dr. Reynolds said, "considering how deadly they are, but there's evidence that at least one other colony existed in Venezuela about forty years ago."

"And now there's a colony here," Justin commented.

"We don't know if the colony in Venezuela is still active but it may be that individuals in the nest here are originally from South America."

"Which means they are spreading," Justin remarked.

"Yes," Dr. Reynolds said. "That is why it is imperative we capture live specimens before any attempt at extermination. Everything we learn here can be applied elsewhere."

"How did you get involved with bugs?" Justin asked, wanting to move on to a lighter subject.

Dr. Reynolds smiled, a distant, thoughtful look. "A boyfriend set me on the road to this profession," she said. "My first love in undergraduate school." Shaking her head dreamily, she continued. "He was in biology. I was in art. We decided to share some classes. One of those classes was invertebrate zoology. After that semester, I was hooked on Class Insecta."

Justin turned right onto Front Street. "From art to ants," he said. "Interesting."

"I'm still into art," Dr. Reynolds said. "Insects offer very colorful subject matter."

"What happened to your boyfriend?" Justin asked. "Is he now a world famous artist?"

"We got engaged in our senior year," Dr. Reynolds answered. "Then, just after we graduated in '71, he received a commission in the army through ROTC, went to Viet Nam and was killed." No emotion stirred her voice when she made this statement, as if telling another person's life story. "It seems like another lifetime ago."

Pausing she asked, "And you? How did you get into

law enforcement?"

"Pat Corey, a friend," Justin said. "He didn't want to go through the police academy by himself and talked me into signing up with him."

"Where was that?"

"New Orleans. We were both patrol officers with the city for six years. The Gruesome Twosome, they called us."

Justin gave his own reflective smile. "Did you ever read *The Onion Fields* by Joseph Wambaugh?" he asked.

"Yes, I did."

"Well, we had our own version of Choir Practice," Justin explained. "We called ourselves the HCD's, 'Hard Core Drunks'. Our motto was – 'We'll drink anything, with anybody, at anytime, anywhere, and for any reason.'"

Giving a regretful shake of his head at these unexpected recollections, Justin continued, "There were seven of us and we were all crazy, only Pat and I more so. Then one morning we got off the night shift and Pat went home, put a gun to his head and pulled the trigger. That was my wake-up call about what the stress from policing in a big city can do. I resigned from the department a couple of weeks later and headed north. Opelousas was as far as I got."

"Why Opelousas?"

"The sheriff there at the time, Ben Valez, had been an

instructor at the academy when Pat and I went through. He retired a couple years after we graduated and moved to Opelousas, where he hailed from originally. He was elected sheriff the following year and when I resigned from the force in New Orleans, I dropped in to pay him a visit. I was offered a job on the spot. That was fifteen years ago."

"So you've been in Opelousas ever since?"

"No," Justin said. "Ben was diagnosed with cancer and resigned his position and a guy named George Brandon was elected sheriff. You already met his brother, Mayor Brandon. Between them, they controlled the gambling and moon-shining in Saint Landry Parish. I didn't fit in too well so I moved to Baton Rouge and joined the sheriff's department there. When Maxwell was elected sheriff, I moved back to Opelousas."

"You must like living in small towns," Dr. Reynolds said.

Justin turned left onto Sunset Lane. "I do," he said. "It's quieter than the city. People are friendly, the air is clean and it doesn't have all the bright lights. A great place to hunt for comets."

Dr. Reynolds looked at Justin in some surprise. She had never picked a sheriff's deputy as someone interested in studying the heavens. "You mean, astronomy?" she asked, expecting him to subscribe to something less scientific.

Justin nodded. "I have a Coulter 10-inch Dobsonian reflector telescope set up on my back porch. Astronomy has always interested me and when I moved back to Opelousas I figured it was time to do something about it."

"And you search for comets?"

"Comets and asteroids."

"Have you ever found one?"

"Actually, I did," Justin admitted with a wry grin. "But I was a few days too late. A guy named David Levy reported it first."

"Not Comet Levy, the one that passed by earth a couple years ago?"

"The one and only," Justin said.

"Comet Hebert," Dr. Reynolds said. She found the subject matter interesting and the person telling it even more so.

Dr. Reynolds added, "It's funny how we can end up where we never expected."

"Yeah," Justin agreed. Nothing more could be added to that.

Justin pulled his cruiser into the funeral home's black-topped parking lot and stopped alongside Olan's Chevy Impala.

Dr. Reynolds glanced back through the protective screen. The color fled her face. "It's still alive," she gasped.

"Don't move," Justin said. "It's on the floor. Next to

your left foot." The creature's head protruded from under the forward seat, its clear eyes fixed on Dr. Reynolds leg.

"Turn the air-conditioner off," Dr. Reynolds whispered in a strained voice. "Then turn on the heater. Don't make any sudden moves."

Justin nudged the appropriate switches on the dashboard. The air-conditioner compressor went dead and a mechanical thump indicated the heater vent cover had opened. He adjusted the fan to a faster speed. Immediately the car's interior became stuffy. "What now?" he asked.

"Unlock the doors."

Justin tapped a switch on his door's panel. The door latches sprung up with a sharp click. The creature adjusted its antennae in response to the sound.

As the temperature inside the car steadily increased, Dr. Reynolds considered what she had already learned of this organism's behavior. Her observations on the video monitor outside the factory indicated little difference between this creature's reactions to environmental stimuli and those of all other living complex creatures, innate behavioral traits designed to protect its nest and ultimately, itself. The fact it had not already attacked meant it did not feel threatened, at least not yet. Like a bee far from its hive, only provocation would cause aggression, an assumption on Dr. Reynolds' part but still a comforting thought. She wondered if this life form had capabilities beyond basic, instinctive behavior. Its morphology certainly pointed in this direction. She hoped her current hypothesis concerning its reaction to temperature variations would prove correct.

The sun's fiery ball rested atop spindly pines, painting the surrounding landscape pastel pink as cooler evening temperatures stole across the land.

Within the police cruiser, hot, stagnant air drew beads of sweat from Justin and Dr. Reynolds. Just the atmosphere the entomologist wanted.

"When I say 'go', get out as fast as you can. Keep the heater on."

The bug's eyes constricted.

"Go!"

CHAPTER 18

"I DIDN'T EXPECT YOU TO call so soon," Olan spoke into the phone to Dr. Miles, calling from Louisiana's forensic laboratories in New Iberia.

"I just want to let you know that I received dental records of Arlin Patrick Tullis, faxed over this afternoon from Natchez, Mississippi," Dr. Miles said. "The results confirm what you had expected. This was your man."

Olan flipped through his notebook and scribbled entries on a page he had made earlier. He circled Arlin Tullis' name and wrote above it, "CONFIRMED".

"As for the victim's tissue breakdown," Dr. Miles continued, "preliminaries indicate the body's soft tissue reacted with an extremely strong agent, possibly an enzyme. We sieved the liquid portion and got out some plant fiber, no doubt from the gut, and a gall stone."

He paused as if checking his notes. "Your report stated that tissue breakdown initially involved internal organs and then the epidermis."

"That's correct," Olan said. "Internal organ destruction appeared to be nearly complete before the epidermis was affected."

"Which indicates to me," Dr. Miles concluded, "the victim's internal tissues were infused with the agent, possibly through ingestion."

"And you believe it to be an enzyme?" Olan asked.

"That is what preliminary tests indicate."

Olan made another note in his book. The forensic expert was confirming what he had already suspected concerning a chemical agent but there was an important fact his colleague was missing.

"The agent you're speaking of is a venom," Olan said, "possibly similar to spider venom. It was introduced into the victim's body by an insect-like creature before his death."

"Impossible," Dr. Miles snorted. Miles had seen enough unusual cases during his twenty-five years in forensics to refrain him from using this particular word but for this case he made an exception. No venom could do such massive tissue destruction unless introduced in unbelievably large quantities.

"I should be able to identify the substance used but unfortunately from my end, it'll be impossible to tell exactly how it was administered or when. Law enforcement up there will have to sort all that out."

Olan said, "George, I know this all sounds like science fiction, but these bugs, or whatever they are, do exist, I have seen them. They have killed at least five other people."

There was a long silence before Dr. Miles spoke. "Olan, what the hell's going on up there? Are you holding back information?" Not giving Olan time to respond, he went on. "Has there been a chemical accident that's not being reported?"

"I saw video footage of the creatures in the factory where all the deaths have occurred," Olan said. "Two of the most recent deaths were police officers and both were killed by these bugs."

"I don't understand what insects have to do with this victim," Dr. Miles said, referring to Arlin Tullis. "We're not talking about anaphylactic shock."

"I don't even know if they are insects," Olan said. "They have four legs, eyes like a human and are a foot long."

"Olan, are you sure of that?"

"The head of LSU's entomology department is here," Olan said, "and even she doesn't know what they are."

"Olan," Dr. Miles said, "you know the situation up there better than I do but it sounds to me as if this thing is out of control. Has the problem been isolated?"

"Law officials are doing all anyone can," Olan said. "They appear to have the problem contained and I heard just before you called that Dr. Reynolds, the entomologist from LSU, has a dead specimen. She's bringing it over here for dissection. We should know a lot more after that."

"Jennifer Reynolds?"

"Yes, that's correct."

"I know her through some forensic entomology work she's done for us. Very competent."

"That's good to know."

"Look Olan," Miles said, "it's not that I don't believe you. It's just that the facts don't add up; giant bugs and an agent that reduces human bodies to a black soup. The deaths you've mentioned may not even be related."

"Law enforcement is convinced they are," Olan said.

"Could this be a case of hysteria?" Dr. Miles asked. "I'm sure you remember that incident a few years ago at Riverside Hospital, in Los Angeles, when the hospital's emergency room medical staff claimed they had been overcome by unidentified noxious fumes from a patient's blood. Their over-reaction led to hysteria in a number of hospitals across the country."

"I remember the case," Olan said, "but this is far from hysteria."

"Well then," Dr. Miles said, "I'll see what further information I can get from the samples we have. I would appreciate you keeping me abreast of any updates."

"I will," Olan said. He hung up the phone, conscious of his own rising doubts about the facts and events surrounding them. He had seen Arlin Tullis' body as well as skeletal remains and what was supposed to be Horace Gail's hand. Those were facts. He had also seen the creatures on the camcorder monitor with Dr. Reynolds, another fact, but he had not witnessed any of the victims actually being attacked. Maybe, Olan thought, Dr. Miles was right and somehow he and the others were somehow hysterically feeding each other into some sort of mass delusion.

A digital clock mounted in a pen-holder showed Olan the late hour, five thirty P.M. Sheriff Maxwell had radioed a half hour earlier to say Dr. Reynolds and Justin were on their way over but the two had yet to show up.

Olan was about to take further notes when Malcolm stuck his head through Olan's office doorway. "Mister Barnes, Deputy Hebert and some lady are outside in a patrol car," he announced.

"Great," Olan said, anxious to get a close-up look at the beast she had brought over. "She can use the embalming room for her work."

Olan went to the back door with his assistant. Both the deputy and the entomologist sat perfectly still within the car. The car's front doors suddenly burst open and its occupants spilled out from opposite sides, soaked in sweat. They slammed their doors shut, their attention on something within the car.

"What's going on?" Olan called. He crossed the blacktop to the cruiser.

"We have one of those bugs," Justin said, "and it's not dead."

The bug had not moved from its position under the front seat.

Olan peered through a window. "Amazing, look at those eyes."

"I was convinced it had died from hyperthermia and dehydration," Dr. Reynolds explained. With a shudder, she recalled how the specimen had fallen from the tray and caught on her blouse. That recollection chilled her when she considered they were dealing with an undetermined number of these creatures.

"You know," Justin said suspiciously, "the way this bug is reacting to the heat is a lot different from a bug I saw die in the factory. That bug acted like a poisoned cockroach, crawling around in circles on the floor, flapping its wings, totally disoriented. And then, it just stopped moving." Pointing to the creature in the car he said, "This guy is calmly drifting off to sleep."

"The individual you saw in the factory," Dr. Reynolds said, "might have died from other causes, excessive dehydration, disease or injury. There's a lot we don't yet know about these organisms."

Within the car, the captured bug's irises constricted to a fine white point.

"One other thing," Justin said. "The eyes of the bug in the factory didn't constrict, they dilated."

"And you're sure of that?" Reynolds asked.

"Positive."

"Well then," Dr. Reynolds said, "let's get our little friend inside and see what else we can learn." To Olan, Dr. Reynolds said, "I need a sturdy container with a good lid."

"Get one of the large glass specimen jars," Olan said to Malcolm.

Malcolm hustled off and quickly returned with a circular container of thick glass, eighteen inches in diameter and a foot in depth. The jar had a lid of equally thick glass with an inset rubber gasket to seal the vessel tightly.

"I'll get the bug out," Justin said, seeing no one else would. "Olan, take the door. If that thing even twitches, I'll jump out of the way and you slam the door closed."

Justin opened the car's front passenger door and placed the jar on the seat above the motionless bug. He pulled out a rag kept in the car's glove-box and wrapped the cloth around his hand for whatever protection it might offer. Gently, he lifted up the creature by a foreleg and laid it inside the glass container. He quickly replaced the lid.

"Let's get it inside," Dr. Reynolds said.

CHAPTER 19

BUCK GREELY APPROACHED A STATE trooper and said in his deep voice, "I have a message for Sheriff Maxwell."

"What is it? I'll pass on to him."

"I'm supposed to give it to him in person."

"Only authorized personnel within the cordon," the trooper stated.

Unperturbed by the trooper's refusal, Buck said, "The message is from the police dispatcher." Doris was Buck's mother and he figured this gave him all the authority he needed.

"Then she can call it in," the trooper said.

"Hey Buck," Lonnie Nethero stepped up, a walkie-talkie strapped to his side. He showed the trooper his emergency squad badge. "I'll escort him to the sheriff," Lonnie said.

The trooper lifted the cordon. "Fine," he said, glad to be rid of the distraction. The number of curious on-lookers had increased with folks arriving from towns as far away as Bayou Current.

"Thanks Lonnie," Buck said as they made their way

across the front lawn. Buck was surprised at Lonnie's amenability. He and Lonnie had never liked each other and rarely spoke. Adversity seemed to be making for short memories.

"Is there a problem?" Lonnie asked, walking briskly to keep up with Buck's long stride.

"That's for the sheriff to figure out," Buck said.

"Come on," Lonnie pressed, "I got you through the cordon, didn't I? We're all on the same team."

Buck's instructions had been clear, tell only the sheriff but Lonnie had indeed helped him and, Buck thought, maybe he wasn't such a grade-A butt-hole after all. "Nothing much to tell," Buck said. "Just something Amory Planchard's boys found at Maurice Dubois' house."

"It's not any more of those bugs, is it?" Lonnie asked. Buck told him nothing more.

Buck confronted the sheriff and modifying his powerful voice to a whisper, he said, "Mom just got a phone call from Sammy Planchard. He says he and his brother found human bones in a hole at the Dubois farm."

"Thanks," the sheriff said, realizing the implication of this news. Calling over Doff, he said, "I have to check on something across town. If there's any renewed activity here, let me know immediately." He instructed Joel and Lonnie to patrol the factory's perimeter and report anything unusual to Doff.

"Sheriff, what about the press?" Doff asked. "They're really putting up a stink about not getting more information."

"No one is to provide any information beyond a large swarm of bees being in the factory. Is that clear?"

"Yes sir," Doff replied.

The sheriff radioed Justin. "What's your ten-twenty?"

"At the funeral home with Doctor Reynolds," Justin responded. "I am just now heading over to the hospital to check on Gerald."

"That will have to wait," the sheriff said. "Meet me at the police station in ten minutes and bring Doctor Reynolds."

"Ten-four," Justin said. He returned to the embalming room where Dr. Reynolds was seated, notepad in hand and full attention on the jarred specimen set before her on a table.

"What's the bug doing?" Justin asked the entomologist.

"So far, nothing," Dr. Reynolds answered. "It's coherent again but hasn't moved."

Justin informed her of the sheriff's orders.

"I can't leave," Dr. Reynolds insisted. "This specimen just now revived."

"You have no other choice," Justin said.

"Where is he sending us?" Dr. Reynolds asked, unhappy at this unexpected interruption.

"He didn't say," Justin replied, "but apparently it's important enough to involve you."

Five minutes later Justin and Dr. Reynolds arrived at Union Town's police station, a wooden structure with a wrap-around porch and set on the town's southwest corner.

Doris Greely sat behind a black radio console in the dispatcher's office. "Justin," she shouted, "thank the Lord you're all right. I've been on the edge of my seat listening to the goings on. Half the town's called to find out what's happening. Father Morris stopped by a little while ago to see if he could be of help."

She paused.

"Now, I told everyone exactly what Sheriff Maxwell told me to say about bees. Lord only knows where Chief Gallo is."

"Doris", Justin cut in, "has the sheriff been here yet?"

"No, he hasn't," Doris replied, not having intended to carry on so.

Justin introduced Dr. Reynolds.

Doris nodded softly then said in a strained voice, "I just can't believe it about Larry and Jack."

"Any idea what the sheriff has going?" Justin asked the dispatcher, purposely omitting mention of the two dead police officers. Their deaths were something the town would have to get over later.

"I'll tell you on the way," said Sheriff Maxwell as he

strode in the door.

"Lord have mercy," Doris said. "Ya'll be careful."

The trio piled into the sheriff's Ford Explorer as the last trace of daylight faded into a thin line on the western horizon.

"Amory Planchard's oldest son, Sammy, reported human bones in a hole on Maurice Dubois' property," the sheriff told his two companions.

"What kind of hole?" Justin asked.

"Sammy didn't say," the sheriff replied. He looked at Dr. Reynolds' reflection in the rear view mirror. "Are we dealing with another nest or an extension of the one at the industrial park?"

"Where are we talking about?" Dr. Reynolds said.

"Two miles south of town," the sheriff said.

Dr. Reynolds said, "I can't believe it's the same nest. Seems too far from the factory site."

"So our problem is spreading?" the sheriff asked.

"If this is indeed a second nest," Dr. Reynolds said, "it is possible one of the two colonies has produced fertile females at least once."

"What does that mean?" the sheriff asked.

Dr. Reynolds explained, "In known species of ground-nesting wasps, a foundress lays eggs in an empty rodent hole or other underground cavity. The eggs hatch into larvae that mature into sterile females that forage for food and build the nest. They are also the defenders of the nest."

"And fertile females?" the sheriff asked.

"By late fall or early winter nest-building stops and both fertile females and males are produced. They mate and the mated females leave the nest to found new colonies."

Sheriff Maxwell switched on his vehicle's headlights. "Does anyone know where these things came from?" he asked Dr. Reynolds.

"Doctor Potter indicated they may have originated from the Venezuelan jungle."

"Venezuela?" Sheriff Maxwell said. "How did they get all the way up here?"

"How did the foundress get all the way up here," Dr. Reynolds corrected. "It is highly unlikely an entire nest of individuals could migrate thousands of miles without being observed. As for a single foundress, it is quite possible she flew north and eventually located a suitable nest site, if indeed this colony was actually established by an individual from South America."

The sheriff fixed his eyes on the crumbling road illuminated by his car's headlights. "If you confirm this is another nest," he said, "what do you plan to do?"

"I don't know," Dr. Reynolds remarked. "I think it best to wait for Doctor Potter and government officials."

The sheriff's vehicle bounced from the two-lane onto Maurice's rutted driveway, a dirt track cut through tall sage grass. Stubby pines leaned in from both sides. Passing through a narrow gap between two ancient oak trees, the car broke into an open, weedy yard.

Maurice's home stood center-stage, a run-down, two-story structure with a sagging front porch and windows blocked from the inside by sundry boxes and mounds of electrical parts. Paint peeled in unsightly patches from the structure's exterior and the front door's screen panels had long since gone missing.

An older model pick-up truck was parked on a barren patch to one side of the building. Pulling alongside the scratched and dented vehicle, the Ford Explorer's headlights illuminated two boys standing on the far side of a fence separating side yard from field. The lads looked to be eight and ten years old. The elder held a flashlight, the younger, a mason jar.

Exiting their vehicle, Sheriff Maxwell, Justin and Dr. Reynolds approached loose dirt piled next to a hole. A shovel lay nearby.

No one had to tell the boys to stay back. They were too scared to do anything else.

"Somebody dug this hole," Justin observed, calming his fears that this was a second nest. He moved to the opening. Sheriff Maxwell and Dr. Reynolds came in from separate angles. Flashlights illuminated the interior.

"There's a ladder down there," Dr. Reynolds exclaimed. The extent of the excavation was suddenly revealed to all.

"Ya see him?" Sammy called from his position. He was a tall lanky kid with red hair grown long in the back, ponytail length.

A clothed skeleton lay at the foot of the ladder and like the remains at Cajun's Snax's abandoned facility, these bones appeared bleached white on bare earth stained black. Metal glinted at the mid-line between pants and blue workman's shirt.

"That was Maurice," the sheriff said to his two companions. "I'd know that over-sized belt buckle anywhere."

"Why would he go down there?" Dr. Reynolds asked of no one in particular.

Justin stooped down and played his light over a canine skeleton deeper in the excavation. "He must have gone after his dog," Justin said, adding, "This tunnel appears to run north and south."

Sheriff Maxwell asked Dr. Reynolds, "We have another nest, don't we?"

The entomologist studied the underground structure. "Yes we do," she said, "but I'm not convinced it's active."

"Then how do you account for what happened to Maurice and his dog?" Justin asked. He stepped away from the hole, having seen enough to persuade him those creatures were still lurking about.

"That, I don't know," Dr. Reynolds said, "but if this were an active colony, I would expect sentries."

“So, where is the nest?” the sheriff asked.

“These creatures seem to prefer to build their nests under structures, like the factory site, so it’s likely this nest is under Maurice’s house but I’m convinced it has been abandoned.”

The trio walked to the fence. “You boys all right?” the sheriff asked.

“Yes sir,” Sammy said. His younger brother nodded.

“When did you find this hole?” the sheriff asked Sammy.

“This afternoon,” Sammy said. “I come down to git Seth. Pa would skin ’im alive if he know’d he come down here by hisself.”

“Where’s your father now?” the sheriff asked.

“Down at the auction.” That would be the same monthly auction that Todd Trudman attended.

“And your mother?”

“She’s got a touch of the sickness,” Sammy said. “We ain’t to bother her unless the house is burning down.”

The sheriff was aware Mrs. Planchard suffered from Crohn’s Disease and was confined to her bed when it flared up. His department had ferried her to the hospital on several occasions when she suffered severe bouts and her husband was off pursuing other interests.

“Why did you come down here?” the sheriff asked Seth.

The younger boy gave a timid glance at his brother

but said nothing.

"Have you seen anything unusual around here?" Sheriff Maxwell figured he would change tack and see if he could get some answers.

"No sir," Sammy replied. "Weren't nothing here but that there hole and them bones."

"You didn't see anything around this hole?"

"No sir," Sammy piped up, elbowing his younger brother.

"No sir," Seth mumbled.

"I'm going to take you boys back home and I want you to stay there," the sheriff told the lads. He looked from one to the other. "You boys were very brave to report what you found. If either of you sees or hears anything strange, call the police department again."

"Mister Sheriff," Seth spoke up with a worried voice, "what about them big ants?"

"Seth, you be quiet," Sammy snapped.

Sheriff Maxwell knelt down and took Seth by his shoulders. Looking deep into the boy's brown eyes, the Ford Explorer's headlights illuminating the youngster's pudgy cheeks, he asked gently, "What big ants?"

Seth lowered his eyes, scared to even look at his brother.

"Sammy, do you know what your brother is talking about?"

"Pa'll whoop us again for lying," Sammy said.

"Lying about what?"

Sammy didn't respond.

"Sammy, look at me." Sheriff Maxwell waited until he had gained the boy's full attention. "Something bad happened here. It's very important that you tell me everything you know."

"It's Seth that says he's seen 'em." Sammy jabbed his brother's leg with the toe of his shoe. "You tell 'im."

Seth shifted his eyes to the sheriff.

"Seth?" the sheriff asked with an encouraging nod and a smile, "Maybe they are the same ants I saw."

"You saw 'em too?" Seth's eyes lit up.

"I sure did," the sheriff said with mock amazement. He held his open hands a foot apart, palms facing each other. "They were this big."

"And they can fly," Seth said, his eyes as round as saucers as he tracked a finger in the air as if following one in flight.

"When did you see them?"

"Now or before?"

"Before."

"When ma took us shopping."

"Where was that?"

"Big Dot. I got new shoes." He held up one foot to show off his now dirty off-brand sneakers.

"Did you see them around Big Dot?"

"No sir," Seth said. "They was flying over the weeds."

"You mean The Swamp?"

Seth nodded. "Uh huh."

Sheriff Maxwell looked up at Dr. Reynolds. "The Swamp is the scrub-land between town and the industrial park," he said. "Big Dot Market butts up against The Swamp's southern edge."

"Did you see any of the big ants here, on Mister Dubois' property?" the sheriff asked Seth.

"Uh huh." The lad held up the jar. "I come down here to catch one and show pa. He thinks I was lying' when I told him about the other ones."

"I saw 'em too," Sammy spoke up, not about to let his little brother get all the glory. "I keep one under my bed. Ya wanna see?"

"Not right now," the sheriff said, suppressing a grin. "I'll take you boys home. Don't forget, call the police station if you see any more of those ants."

"Ya won't say nothing to pa, will ya?" Sammy asked the sheriff. "If he finds out we come down here he'll put the strap to us."

"Not a word," Sheriff Maxwell promised.

The service radios crackled. "Sheriff, do you copy?" It was Officer Green.

"Go ahead, Doff," the sheriff said.

"The mayor's back."

"I'm on my way," Sheriff Maxwell said in a tired voice.

Sammy and Seth climbed through the fence and they all marched to the Ford Explorer. The two boys were delivered to their home where Sheriff Maxwell waited until both lads were safely inside before backing out of the short driveway and speeding away toward town.

"I'll drop you two off at the police station," the sheriff said to Justin and Dr. Reynolds. "I need to get back to the factory before the honorable mayor creates further problems." He added for Dr. Reynolds' benefit, "As soon as Doctor Potter or the Feds arrive, I want them out at the industrial park." And to Justin, he said, "After you check on Gerald, get some rest. You deserve it."

"I'm fine." Justin replied. He had no intention of walking away from this situation before witnessing its conclusion.

CHAPTER 20

THE IMAGE ON THE VIDEO monitor was little more than a still shot, a gray and black picture of irregular angles set against corrugated walls and peaked roof. The monitor's sound had been turned off eliminating the steady drone of the twin heaters.

Low in the eastern sky a thin crescent moon struggled for recognition among stars stretching from horizon to horizon, like diamond dust poured across black satin. A perfect night for dreamers, a perfect night for lovers, but Mayor Brandon had no interest in either. The only heavenly bodies he watched were in his collection of XXX-rated movies and his only dream was getting rich and moving out of this flea-bag town to greater opportunities elsewhere. To this end little was sacred, especially when it came to a tin-buckle sheriff.

Mayor Brandon stood silently in front of the video monitor, a stance he had taken up since arriving a half hour before. Detective Green had informed the city executive where the supposed nest entrance was located but the mayor had yet to see it among the dead machines and refuse piled on the floor. In Mayor Brandon's opinion it was just a ploy to stall for time while the sheriff was off with his white sweetheart.

A smile crept about the corners of the mayor's mouth when he thought of the reporters corralled outside the cordoned perimeter. He had not been able to get the media past state police but that had not stopped him from giving the news hounds his own assessment of the situation. This tune was turning out to be a very merry melody.

Police Chief Dick Gallo sidled over to the monitor. "Mister Mayor, the sheriff is here," he said.

The mayor didn't bother to look around, an action for the anxious or the curious. He wanted to display neither of these conditions. Sheriff Maxwell, the reporters and everyone else watching would see an elected official more concerned with a still unresolved problem than this two-bit sheriff.

Chief Gallo stepped back from the impending confrontation while reveling in whatever the mayor had up his sleeve.

"Mayor Brandon, I want a word with you," Sheriff Maxwell said brusquely.

The mayor looked around. "What was that?"

"Now!" Sheriff Maxwell said. Livid and in no mood for games, he grabbed the mayor by an arm and unceremoniously pulled him off to one side. All those nearby, including Chief Gallo, prudently drifted away.

"You've been talking to the media," the sheriff said.

"The last time I looked we are in a free country," the mayor said, his smile oozing contempt.

"Mayor Brandon," the sheriff said, exasperated, "you are doing nothing but fueling the fires of fear."

Brandon's eyes narrowed. "This is my town and the people of Union Town have a right to know about these bugs and everything that's going on here or should I say, isn't going on."

Sheriff Maxwell looked the mayor straight in the eye and not wanting to waste any more time, said the only thing he felt would keep the city official at bay, "Mayor, this is a secured area. I'm arresting you for unauthorized entry to a crime scene."

The mayor's eyes flashed daggers. "You wouldn't dare," he said.

The sheriff waved over Sergeant Benoit. "Do you have anyone available to transport Mayor Brandon to Opelousas? I've just placed him under arrest."

Benoit frowned at the mayor. "About the best we can do is detain him here, on-site," he said to the sheriff. "I don't have the personnel to spare right now."

"I have an obligation to protect the people of my town," Brandon bellowed in protest.

"Yes you do," Sheriff Maxwell said, "but you are interfering with official law enforcement and stirring up the press. That's protecting no one." He gestured toward the town. “For now, if I even hear of you being anywhere near this industrial park, you’ll be handcuffed and I’ll personally drive you to Opelousas. Is that clear?”

“You’re making a big mistake,” the mayor hissed, inwardly vowing to avenge. He stormed off at this defeat.

Doff approached the sheriff after having checked on Slyger’s progress. “You all right?” he asked the lawman. Maxwell looked ready to bust.

“Nothing a thirty-eight caliber slug won’t fix,” the sheriff growled.

“Slyger needs more duct tape,” Doff said. “I sent Joel to get some.”

“Where’s Slyger now?” the sheriff asked. The front of the building showed no evidence that sealing had begun.

“Around back, says he’ll have the building sealed before midnight.”

“I don’t want anyone to touch the east wall,” the sheriff ordered. “We can’t take chances of a cave-in.”

“I’ll pass on the word,” Doff said. “By the way, what’s up at Maurice’s place?”

“We have another nest,” the sheriff said. “Doctor Reynolds believes it’s abandoned.”

“If it’s abandoned,” Doff asked, “where did the creatures go?”

“Hopefully here,” the sheriff said. “Seth Planchard said he saw some of the bugs flying over The Swamp earlier this week. They might have come out of the factory or, God forbid, from a third nest. At first light tomorrow morning, I want you to check The Swamp."

Returning to the monitor, the sheriff asked Gene, "Any activity inside the factory?"

"No sir," Gene replied, "not a thing."

Sheriff Maxwell tried to smile but failed. This situation was far from being under control. He would be much happier when these creatures had been gassed off the face of the earth. He wondered what the hell was keeping Dr. Potter and the Feds.

CHAPTER 21

MAYOR BRANDON BARGED THROUGH THE front door of his house and slammed his car keys onto a foyer table. “Damn that Maxwell!” he boomed. He stormed into the living room and swung around, stabbing a demanding finger at his chief of police. “I want his ass in a sling. Do you understand me?”

“Yes sir,” Gallo said meekly, not even daring a salute lest it be misread. Being on the wrong side of Mayor Brandon’s wrath was not something the police chief could afford.

“Yes sir, yes sir,” the mayor mocked. Eyes narrowing, face red, Brandon shouted, “Then for once in your useless life, do something! You’re the damn chief of police in *my* town. If you can’t handle this, I’ll find someone who can. Is that clear?”

Anxiety knotted Gallo’s stomach. “Yes sir, Mister Mayor,” he said and with what little conviction he could muster, he added, “I’ll come up with a plan.”

“You do that,” the mayor hissed, his ire continuing to climb. “I want Maxwell on his knees.”

Pacing back and forth across the carpeted floor,

Brandon shook his head knowing full well whatever the scheme, he himself would have to devise it. Gallo's usefulness lay not in any ability for originality but in his blind loyalty to his patron. This devotion could be exploited without question and that, the mayor reminded himself, was why he had hired the man.

In mock concentration, Gallo bowed his head, one arm across his chest, chin cradled in his other hand, all the while trying to think of a plan that didn't lead to the end of his career. Returning to a vocation as a security guard would not make his father proud nor silence his pushing mother. Mayor Brandon was pissed and if he, Gallo, didn't come up with something, his boss just might follow through with his threat.

"There's got to be a way of getting rid of Maxwell once and for all," Brandon pondered out loud. "He may think he can saunter into my town and take over but…"

"And getting two of my officers killed," Gallo reminded the mayor. "Christ, that's half my police force."

Brandon plopped onto an over-stuffed sofa.

"Maybe you could get one of those bugs will sting Maxwell," Gallo idly tossed out. "That would be the end of him, for sure."

Brandon's eyes opened wide in revelation. "What did you say?" he asked.

"It was just a thought," Gallo said, certain he was about to get fired.

A sinister smile edged the mayor's lips. "That would indeed get rid of our sheriff, once and for all," he said. He looked Gallo in the eye and asked, "Can you handle that?"

"Sir?" Gallo said, perplexed.

"You're going to make sure Maxwell gets a little too close to one of those bugs," Brandon stated.

Gallo was aghast. "How am I supposed to do that?"

"Don't worry," Brandon chided. "You'll have help." He picked up a telephone on an end table.

"I need to get back over to the industrial park and see what's happening," Gallo suggested as the mayor punched out a phone number. Gallo knew that look in his boss's eyes and he didn't want any part of what the mayor had cooking. Going down to New Orleans to buy pornographic material for him was one thing, but Mayor Brandon was now talking murder. And the man was dead serious.

The mayor covered the telephone's mouthpiece. "You're not going anywhere," he said.

"But I've got men there," Gallo said, ready now to assume his responsibilities.

Brandon held up a quieting hand and leaned back. "This is Brandon," he said. "I need you to get over to my place, now. If you see Lonnie, tell him to call me at home. I need him to do something."

CHAPTER 22

With Dr. Reynolds delivered back to Union Town Funeral Home, Justin started for the town's hospital to check on his injured partner. A television news crew setting up in a parking lot wedged between the courthouse and police headquarters spotted Justin as he passed by and signaled him to stop.

Disregarding the journalists, Justin arrived at the hospital and parked in the rear lot of the single story, brick building. Following procedure, he radioed his location to dispatch as he entered the hospital through its emergency doors.

This night, Nurse Laura Daniels manned her usual station at the admittance counter of the Spartan emergency room. A heavy-set woman, middle-aged, with short, curly blonde hair and flabby arms, she had an equally flabby chin.

Nurse Daniels looked up from her *McCall's* Magazine when Justin entered. Having expected someone from the sheriff's department ever since Gerald Wilson had been brought in, she was relieved to see Justin. "Is it true what I heard about Larry and Jack?" she asked Justin.

"I'm afraid it is," Justin said.

"It's hard to believe," Nurse Daniels said shaking her head. "Patty, Larry's 'ex' is my best friend, you know."

Too involved personally to be able to offer any support, Justin moved on. "I'm here to see my deputy," he said.

"Of course," Daniels said. "Oh, just one more thing. Is it safe to go outside? I mean, the problem with the bees and all."

The exterior doors flew open and the television crew barged in.

"Deputy," one reporter asked, "how many people has the swarm of bees killed?"

"You'll need to speak with the sheriff about that," Justin stated.

"Are they African killer bees?" another reporter asked.

"I have no information on that," Justin responded.

"Is it safe for the people of Union Town to go outside?" another reporter quickly added.

"I am unable to answer your questions."

"Are you saying it's not safe to be out-of-doors?" the first reporter cut in.

"Justin," Nurse Daniels said in her most imposing voice. She rose and waddled from her station. "He's in room eight. His parents and Miss Neumann are with him." When the reporters attempted to follow, Nurse

Daniels solidly blocked their passage. "Authorized personnel only," she announced in her 'I'm the nurse here, not you' voice. The reporters protested but complied.

Within room number eight, four equally spaced beds, each surrounded by an aqua-colored nylon curtain hung from overhead tracking, lined a bare wall. The room smelled of disinfectant and floor wax.

Cindy Neumann rose from her chair set beside Gerald's bed. Glen and Wylene Wilson were seated on a sofa. "Can you please tell us what's going on," Cindy pleaded to Justin.

"There's not much I can tell you at this time," Justin confessed.

"You can't tell us or you won't," Mr. Wilson declared, his deep voice contrasting with his small, lean frame. He got to his feet. "We've been trying to get answers all evening and no one from the police or sheriff's department has been forthcoming with information. The only person who seems to care is the mayor and he doesn't know much because law enforcement isn't cooperating. I want to know what happened to my son. What's this about bees? Why hasn't law enforcement been more open?"

"The sheriff regrets not being able to come here himself," Justin continued, not authorized to field questions in great detail but knowing Cindy and the Wilsons had a right to more than vague explanations.

"Gerald and I were on an emergency call this morning at the industrial park," Justin began. "We entered one of the factories and were attacked by some type of flying bug. They're not bees. In fact, a bug expert from LSU doesn't know what they are."

"How does that explain my son's injuries?" Mr. Wilson demanded.

"We were trapped in the building for several hours and when we made a break to get out," Justin said, "Gerald slipped and fell in a liquid that might have contained poison from the creatures."

Mr. Wilson went red in the face. "Poison?" he snapped. "From a bug?" His eyes narrowed, nostrils flaring. "The doctor says my son's injuries were caused by some type of strong chemical. You people know what's going on. Why aren't you telling us? Don't think for one minute…" He gasped for air and clutched his chest, looking very old.

"Glen!" Mrs. Wilson grabbed her husband's arm. Justin helped her seat him and she slipped a nitroglycerin tablet under her husband's tongue.

Cindy dropped onto her chair, sobbing.

When her husband responded to the medication, Mrs. Wilson turned back to the deputy. "We don't want to blame you or the sheriff's department for what happened," she said with regained composure. "It's just that no one has been able to answer our questions. Doctor Holloway says Gerald has chemical burns."

"I know you are all worried," Justin said, "but all I know is the poison from one of the bugs likely caused the burns. A sample has been sent off for testing." Looking from Mrs. Wilson, to Cindy and back again he added, "The moment we have more details I'll let you know. In the meantime, please keep what I told you confidential."

"We will," Mrs. Wilson promised.

Cindy nodded affirmation, then said, "If you happen to see my father, tell him I'm here at the hospital. I've called home all evening but he doesn't answer."

"I'll swing by the depot when I leave here," Justin said. Spencer Neumann occasionally took a few hours after work to clean up the parish's garbage truck while killing a six pack of beer.

Justin turned his attention to his partner.

Gerald lay on his stomach, his head turned to one side. His right arm was splayed at a ninety-degree angle from his body and supported by a stainless steel table covered with towels. Skin below the deputy's shoulder to the base of his fingers was swollen as if seared by heat. Below his right ear a quarter-size ulcer oozed clear plasma. He was heavily sedated.

Dr. Ron Holloway, MD, stepped into the room.

"How's he doing?" Justin asked Dr. Holloway.

"Your deputy has some serious injuries," Dr. Holloway stated. Holloway was a large man with short, salt and pepper hair and weak chin. "I was told about the problem at the industrial park but quite frankly, I don't understand what any animal could have had to do with this man's injuries."

"There's not much more I can tell you," Justin said.

"Someone needs to identify the chemical," Dr. Holloway remarked. "This is extremely serious. We have been unable to stop tissue necrosis and there's not much more we can do here. We're preparing to transport him to Baton Rouge but unless someone can identify the chemical we're dealing with, he might not get much help there either."

"Talk to Olan Barnes," Justin said. "He sent off samples of whatever this stuff is for analysis."

A young, petite nurse slipped up to the bed holding a plastic bottle marked, 'Sterile Saline'. Gently squeezing the container, she flushed the raw skin on Gerald's outstretched arm. The cleansing water ran into already soaked towels and dribbled into a collection bucket through the table's drain hole.

"I already spoke to Olan and the paramedics," Dr. Holloway said, "and they told me essentially what you have. It's just difficult to believe insect venom can cause such extensive tissue damage."

"We're doing all we can," Justin said.

Dr. Holloway nodded. "Then all we can do is wait for the test results from Olan and pray a treatment can be found soon."

CHAPTER 23

JUSTIN STOOD OUTSIDE THE EMERGENCY room's double doors. An ambulance's red trip-lights flashed rhythmically over the asphalt parking lot and nearby trees as it sped away. Cindy was visible through a rear window, her attention firmly fixed on Gerald laid out on a gurney. A car carrying Glen and Wylene Wilson followed obediently behind. Mr. Wilson rode shotgun, still looking very tired.

Justin radioed Sheriff Maxwell from his cruiser.

"The situation here hasn't changed," the sheriff reported.

"Has Doctor Reynolds' associate or any government folks shown up yet?" Justin asked. He looked at his watch. It was nine thirty P.M.

"I just spoke to Doctor Reynolds," the sheriff said. "She doesn't know what is taking her colleague so long but says he should be here any time now. We expect the Feds in the morning."

"Ten-four," Justin said. "I'm going to swing by Coleman's. Can I bring anything for you guys?"

"Marge Devlin just brought over a stack of sandwiches," the sheriff replied. "There's plenty to go around."

"A burger and fries sounds better," Justin said.

Justin drove to the town's service depot. The compound's front gate was open with Spencer's pick-up and Calvin's motorcycle parked within the dimly lit yard.

Justin radioed Union Town's police dispatcher. "Doris," he said, "can you relay a message to Cindy Neumann? Let her know that her father hasn't returned from work." He gave Doris the pertinent information on the ambulance and its destination.

Justin continued through town to Coleman's Diner, a local eatery in a double-wide trailer set in a lot cut from pines. Coleman's Diner was far from the fanciest restaurant in Saint Landry Parish but in Union Town, if you didn't want to cook for yourself, Coleman's was the only show in town.

Justin parked between two other vehicles. Climbing from his cruiser, he mounted a short, wooden flight of stairs to the diner's front door and strode in. The restaurant's interior was austere but adequate; a dozen Formica tables with aluminum-framed chairs, a rear door leading to a storage area and a standard kitchen set behind a counter lined with well-worn stools. Water stains dotted the paneled ceiling and photographs of successful deer hunts adorned the walls.

Justin took a seat at a wobbly table decorated with an open-faced napkin dispenser and three dog-eared menus wedged between a squeeze bottle of catsup and a saltshaker.

Dick Driskoll stood behind the counter, an overweight man with brown teeth and a swollen nose laced with blood vessels. Dick had bought the diner from Milly Coleman shortly after her husband's death a year ago and was barely keeping the place afloat.

Kathy Flores, the diner's only waitress, was there too, wearing stretch-pants that accentuated every roll of cellulite on her ample thighs. A low-cut blouse exposed a tattoo of a motorcycle on her left breast. Long, black hair fell over her shoulders and bright red lipstick adorned her lips.

Kathy sauntered to Justin's table with order pad in hand. "What can I do for you, Justin?" she asked, smiling at her only customer.

"A burger, fries and a large coffee," Justin said. He looked as tired as he felt.

"A rough day?" Kathy asked. "How about one of my special massages?" She gave him a wink.

"The food will do fine," Justin dryly replied. Kathy's come on was more than he could handle right then.

"I hear ya'll are having trouble at the industrial park," Dick stated from across the counter. He opened a tin of snuff, loaded a fresh pinch in his mouth and returned the can to a hip pocket. "Some folks supposed to have been killed or something." Working the dip into place between cheek and gum, he took the order from Kathy and turned to throw a frozen meat patty on the grill.

"The situation is under control," Justin said, wanting only to eat in silence and hurry back to the industrial park.

"You haven't seen anything of that bastard stepson of mine, have you?" Dick asked over his shoulder. "He snuck out of the house last night and hasn't had the decency to come home. His mother's worried sick."

"I'll keep my eyes out for him," Justin said, still unaware Rod's remains had been those he himself had discovered behind the factory.

Kathy brought Justin his coffee. "Are you sure there's nothing else I can do for you?" she asked with a hopeful smile.

"Not a thing," Justin said. Kathy was laying it on heavy tonight.

"Such a waste," Kathy sighed.

"Hey, Miss Flirt," Dick called to his waitress. He spit a dollop of snuff-blackened saliva into an economy-size coffee can he kept under the counter for just such a purpose. "Go clean up the damn store room like I told you."

Kathy sneered back at him and whispered to Justin, "As soon as I find another job, I'm out of here."

"Did you hear me?" Dick yelled. "Get to work."

Kathy gave him the finger when he wasn't looking

and flounced away.

Dick put the finishing touches to the meal; lettuce, tomato and a thick slice of onion, just the way the deputy liked his burgers.

"You better make that to go," Justin said to the cook. He'd rather be facing down those creatures in the factory again than listening to any more squabbling.

A horrific scream from the back room rattled the compact building. Kathy hit the doorway at full tilt, nearly tripping over a chair. She dashed behind the counter looking as if she had just seen a ghost. "Jesus Christ," she wailed on the verge of panic. "There's a cockroach back there the size of a freakin' rat!"

Justin was on his feet immediately.

"What!?" Dick snapped. "You scared the living hell out of me. It's just a damn bug."

"Well you go back there," Kathy challenged.

Justin moved to the storage room's doorway. "You stay in here," he ordered Dick. "Where is it, Kathy?"

"It's a freakin' bug," Dick exclaimed, throwing up his hands in mock surrender. "Women!"

"In the corner, by the freezer," Kathy said.

Justin drew his pistol. He peered inside. The walls of the eight by ten foot room were lined with shelving overfilled with boxes of Styrofoam cups, man-size jars of condiments and stacks of paper napkins. The floor was in desperate need of mopping. To the left a collection of corrugated boxes were stacked on floor-mounted cabinets and to the right, a top-loading freezer butted up to a stainless steel sink. A plastic garbage barrel held a position near a back door. The room smelled strongly of mildew and rot.

"It's over by the sink, behind the garbage can," Kathy said from a safe position behind the deputy.

Dick marched through the doorway armed with a can of bug spray. "This is ridiculous," he declared.

Justin grabbed the man's arm. "Stay back," he ordered.

Giving the deputy a baffled look at the firmness of his grip, Dick complied readily enough.

Justin moved cautiously forward. The musty smell grew stronger with each step. With great caution, he hooked his pistol's barrel over the garbage bin's edge and tilted it forward, just enough to peer inside. The bin was half full of wastepaper and table scraps.

Between garbage can and sink Justin saw the butt end of an overturned coffee can. A grainy black liquid had spilled from the container forming a thick puddle that had soaked into plywood flooring. Fruit flies buzzed about. Justin slid the garbage bin to one side, streaking the black matter across the floor.

Fear leaped into Justin's throat. Sweat beaded his forehead and his heart thundered in his ears. From the overturned coffee can protruded the posterior end of a creature sickeningly like those at the factory. The big bug lay on its back, one wing partially open and covered in the black, syrupy matter.

Justin carefully inspected the remaining area but found no other creatures. Turning his attention back to the bug on the floor, he observed a tiny white maggot emerge from a borehole in a leg joint. The insect larva crawled a short distance before it rolled off into the pooled black substance. Squirming and struggling, it had no chance of escaping the same fate as countless other hatch-mates floating in the black goo.

Justin nudged the can with his pistol. The creature didn't move.

"Mister Driskoll, come in here, please," Justin called.

The cook stepped in. Kathy remained safely back.

"Damn, that's a big roach," Dick blurted upon seeing the creature.

"I told you," Kathy piped up.

Gingerly, Justin gripped the can's bottom rim between thumb and forefinger and dumped out the lifeless bug. A mass of maggots spilled from its open mouth. More larvae wriggled within the corneal domes of its eyes.

"That's not a roach," Dick said. "What the hell is it?"

"Do you know what this black stuff is?" Justin asked the cook. Unlike the black goo originating from the human bodies, this thick substance had a grainy texture and an overpowering musty stench.

Dick's eyes narrowed. Turning to Kathy, he said with cold authority, "You were supposed to throw that out."

"I told you I wasn't touching it," Kathy snapped. "It's disgusting."

"What is it?" Justin ordered, having had all he could take of these two.

"It's his snuff-spit," Kathy said, curling up her nose. "He uses coffee cans as spittoons and expects me to clean up after him." Looking at her boss, she said, "I left that one for you, Dick."

"How long has it been in here," Justin asked Kathy before her boss could get in his two cents worth.

"A couple days," Kathy replied.

"Is there any place where this bug could have entered this room?" Justin asked. Unless the back door had been left open, he saw no other point of entry.

Dick stepped to the back wall and pushed aside a wooden plank covering a fist-size hole in the floor. "Probably through this rat hole," he said. Then with a sudden look of concern, he added, "You won't tell the health department, will you? I just haven't had a chance to repair it."

Justin grabbed an empty, corrugated carton and using a wad of napkins for protection, picked up the dead bug by a back leg and laid it into the box. "You will have to close your diner," he told Dick.

"Close?" Dick laughed. "Because of a few rats and one damn bug? Get real. A little elbow grease is all this place needs."

Justin carried the strange cadaver into the diner's service area, closing the storage room's door behind him when Dick and Kathy were out. He picked up his meal and laid a ten-dollar bill on the counter. Law enforcement officials ate for half price at Coleman's but Justin figured full payment would make what he was about to say a little easier for Mr. Driskoll to swallow.

"I don't have authority to close your diner," Justin said. He walked to the front door and turning toward Dick, added, "but the health department will be notified first thing in the morning if you don't close up. And I'll make sure they come down hard on you." Justin wanted to leave no doubt of his intentions. Something in this building had attracted this bug and could attract others.

"For Christ's sake," Dick pleaded. "I have a business to run. I'm barely keeping things afloat as it is."

The deputy was unimpressed.

"I'll give up dipping snuff, if that's what you want," Dick said, as if upping the ante would win him the bet.

"Someone will be over to cordon off the area," Justin said. "It's only temporary."

Justin walked to his cruiser and set the creature's boxed corpse in the trunk. He slipped in behind the steering wheel and rolled down the front windows, letting a cool southerly breeze caress his face. A nameless dirt track stretched out before him, disappearing into low scrub-land and pines and eventually ending at a clearing where every November hunters gathered for the start of deer season.

Unwrapping his hamburger, Justin was fully aware how drained he felt. The nap Sheriff Maxwell had suggested sounded good to him right then but Justin knew he couldn't sleep, not until he at least learned what Dr. Reynolds' colleague had to say.

Raised voices drew Justin's attention back to the diner. Kathy and Dick were going at it again, hammer and tongs, the diner's owner no doubt accusing his waitress of causing his business' closure. Kathy was a tough one and wasn't standing for any of that. She appeared at a window, yelled something at her boss, picked up a squeeze bottle of catsup and threw it across the room. Her angry voice shrieked over Dick's cursing.

Justin considered how fortunate the three of them had been to survive the encounter in the storage room. Things might have turned out much different had this one bug been alive or had there been live creatures lurking about.

As Justin ate he mulled over the evidence at the scene, sensing there was something significant about this bug's death, something he had yet to fully comprehend. He delved deeper into his sleep-weary mind, searching nooks and crannies for answers, anything on which he might hang more than a hunch. Slowly, as hazy images cleared, like morning mists lifting from over The Swamp, he once again saw the events of the day, in particular, one incident when he and Gerald were trapped inside the cold room. At the time, it had seemed insignificant, but now Justin's tired mind patched the jumbled information into a new sequence, a whole new perspective.

Justin cranked the cruiser's engine and sped off toward the funeral home. Dr. Reynolds would most certainly be interested in this revelation.

CHAPTER 24

SOFT LUMINESCENCE FROM A FLORESCENT street lamp cast long shadows across the funeral home's parking lot as Justin parked his cruiser.

He pushed through the building's rear door with boxed specimen in hand, acutely aware of an uneasy silence within. He entered the embalming room where Dr. Reynolds had previously been working. He found no one. He checked Olan's office. Deserted.

Justin set the boxed corpse on Olan's desk and searched further, confirming the four viewing rooms were also empty. He hustled to the funeral home's tiny chapel. No one.

Justin radioed Sheriff Maxwell. "Are Doctor Reynolds and Olan with you?" he asked. "I'm at the funeral home and no one is here."

"I haven't seen Olan since he left for his office, hours ago," the sheriff said. "And the last time I saw Doctor Reynolds was when I dropped you both off at the police station."

"I brought her back to the funeral home" Justin said, "before visiting Gerald at the hospital." He looked about the tomb-quiet chapel, painfully aware the live creature from atop the factory could be loose and Olan and Dr. Reynolds might have become the latest victims.

"I'll send back-up," the sheriff said.

"Ten-four," Justin answered before adding, "There's something else, sheriff. I found a dead bug at Coleman's"

"Another nest?" Sheriff Maxwell asked, alarmed at the thought.

"I don't know," the deputy replied. "There was just one bug and it's been dead awhile."

"What do you suggest?" the sheriff asked.

"I had Driskoll close up," Justin said. "I don't see much more that we can do there until daylight. I have the dead bug with me. Hopefully it will be of some use to Doctor Reynolds."

"Keep me posted."

Unable to bring himself to wait for his back up, Justin went against his better judgment and proceeded cautiously from the chapel, down a hallway to the embalming room where the live specimen had originally been sequestered.

Entering the windowless room, he took in all around him; the closed cabinet doors, secured drawers and the neatly folded shrouds on the tables. No sign of a struggle. Nothing out of place.

Fear's cold breath chilled Justin. From somewhere close, there came a nauseating sound of a low timbre of a human voice, sounding very much like a moan. Moving to the wall behind a portable surgical cabinet, he focused on the sound.

Justin finally realized from where the muffled noises came. In his initial concern, he had forgotten about a cubbyhole storage room behind this wall and with a door into Olan's office.

Voices from the hallway alerted Justin his back-up had arrived. The chief deputy quickly explained the situation to the two state troopers. One was to stand watch outside the embalming room and the other, to accompany Justin. Nothing more needed to be said as both officers understood how dangerous these creatures were.

Justin led the one state policeman forward, pistols drawn and ever watchful for any sign of the freed bug.

Holding up a halting hand when they reached the storage room door, Justin called, "Olan, Doctor Reynolds?"

The storage room's door flew open. "What the..." Olan exclaimed, taken aback at the sight of two handguns leveled at his chest.

The weapons were lowered. "Are you all right?" Justin asked the mortician. "Is Doctor Reynolds with you?"

Dr. Reynolds stepped out. "I'm right here," she said.

"We're fine," Olan said. "What's got you spooked?"

"I thought our bug had managed to escape," Justin

said.

"Our specimen is safe and sound," Dr. Reynolds assured him. "We have it in here, more secure than the larger rooms."

"You guys head on back to the industrial park," a relieved Justin said to his back-up. "Let the sheriff know all is well here."

Justin retrieved his box from Olan's desk and joined Dr. Reynolds and Olan in the storage room. The narrow room held assorted supplies stacked neatly on shelving and in cabinets. A coffee maker gurgled hot brew with its enticing aroma alongside a dated Frigid-Air refrigerator/freezer. A Bunsen burner protruded from the opposing end of a slate-topped counter fitted with a stainless steel sink. The heavy-glass jar containing the creature sat next to this.

"How is your deputy?" Dr. Reynolds asked Justin.

"That bug venom burned him pretty badly," Justin said. "He has been transported to Baton Rouge for more advanced medical treatment." Turning to Olan he said, "Any word from forensics?"

"Not yet," Olan replied, "but Doctor Miles and his staff are putting in overtime. They sent samples to the CDC."

"And Malcolm?"

"He's gone to pick up some burgers," Olan said.

"Coleman's is closed," Justin stated.

"Since when does Dick miss out on the second shift folks from the hospital?" Olan asked.

"Since I found this in the diner's storage room," Justin said. He set the boxed corpse on the counter and lifted its lid.

Dr. Reynolds peered inside, raising a quizzical brow at the sight of fruit fly maggots before realizing what she was looking at.

"You got this at Coleman's?" Olan asked.

Justin nodded and explained for Dr. Reynolds' benefit, "Coleman's Diner is about a half mile from here."

"I'd like to clean it up," Dr. Reynolds said, referring to the maggoty remains.

Olan pulled a stainless steel tray from a cabinet. Dr. Reynolds donned latex gloves and lifting up the specimen, laid it on the tray.

The entomologist made a mental note there were no fly pupae and instead of the sharp, pungent odor of decomposing flesh, she detected the distinct smell of rotting vegetation.

She turned the creature onto its back. "What's this black liquid?" she asked, fearing the bug had been found in association with yet another sting victim.

"It's Dick Driskoll's snuff spittle," Justin said. He explained the events related to the find.

"That explains the fruit fly larvae and smell," Dr. Reynolds said. "Fruit flies are attracted to decomposing plant matter."

"Could there be another nest somewhere around the diner?" Olan asked Justin.

"The area will be checked in daylight but I don't think so," replied Justin. "There have been no reports of anything unusual out there, until now."

"So what was this bug doing there?" Olan asked.

"It might have been foraging for food or nest building material," Dr. Reynolds commented. She probed the creature's body with forceps, working from a mental picture of standard dissecting procedure. Perhaps enough of the stomach contents remained to reveal what made up this animal's diet. That would give her a better idea where these creatures might be feeding.

Of both men the entomologist asked, "The big question is, what killed it?"

"It probably fell into the spittoon and drowned," Olan offered.

"I don't believe so," Justin said. He expounded on the evidence.

"The waitress might have unknowingly tipped the can over before the bug got into the room," Dr. Reynolds said with a shrug.

"That's certainly possible," Justin agreed, "but how could the bug drown if the can was already on its side?"

"Go on," Olan said, interested to see where this was leading.

"The maggots were all over the remains, from head to tail," Justin said. "If the bug had fallen head first into the can, the maggots couldn't have reached the head."

"It might have died of natural causes," Dr. Reynolds said, "or maybe it drowned first and the can was knocked over sometime later."

"If that last statement were true," Justin added, "the can had to have been knocked over after the creature died. From what I saw, the liquid had soaked into the wooden flooring which means the can was knocked on its side just after it was put there, a couple days before."

To Dr. Reynolds, Olan asked, "How long does it take fruit fly eggs to hatch?"

"In summer temperatures and humidity like we're having, the eggs hatch out about eight to ten hours after being laid. The maggots become fully grown in about two days and pupate within five." She motioned to the smelly remains. "The fact there are no pupae on this corpse and the larvae are in their first instar, the first of two stages prior to pupating, indicates these eggs hatched between one and two days ago. That certainly fits in with your time frame, Justin, but I still don't see the significance."

"Maybe the bug was allergic to snuff," Olan jested.

Justin said to the coroner, "You might be right."

"That snuff killed it?" Olan asked.

"Not snuff," Justin said. He paused, knowing what he was about to say would sound absurd. "At one point, when Gerald and I were trapped in the cold room," he went on, "Gerald spit on a bug through an overhead cooling vent. I didn't think anything about it at the time, but it was the same bug that fell off the roof and died."

Dr. Reynolds said, "I believe what you saw was heat induced dormancy. We saw that in your car and I've reconfirmed that here in the lab."

"The bug I saw didn't go dormant," Justin insisted. "It died."

Dr. Reynolds listened.

"When this bug goes into a dormant state, what happens?" Justin asked.

"The irises constrict and it stops moving. You saw that in the car," Dr. Reynolds said.

"Exactly," Justin said, making the point, "but the irises of the bug Gerald spat on didn't constrict. They dilated."

Her nod urged him on.

"When this bug overheated in the car it became progressively more lethargic before its irises constricted and it stopped moving, right? But the bug in the factory acted totally different. It hopped around like a poisoned cockroach, flapping its wings and too disoriented to fly. Then it started quivering and stopped moving. That's when its eyes dilated."

"And you are certain of that?"

"Positive," Justin answered. "I have no doubt now

that Gerald's saliva killed the creature in the factory. And now we have a second dead creature in association with saliva."

Olan said, "Justin, saliva contains nothing more toxic than Alpha-amylase, an enzyme that breaks down starch and lysozyme, an enzyme that kills bacteria."

"Olan is right," Dr. Reynolds said. "We know this is a very unusual organism, unlike anything ever identified, but we can be certain its physiology falls within known parameters. I assure you those parameters tell us spitting on a creature this large does not kill it."

Justin acknowledged a score of scenarios were possible and these two deaths might not be related to saliva but he could not totally discount what his eyes had seen and his instincts told him.

Looking at a wall clock, Justin said, "It's nearly ten o'clock. I need to get back to the factory." No reason to continue this line of conversation until he had more evidence to back up his assumption.

"We'll be out to the factory as soon as Doctor Potter arrives," Dr. Reynolds said. "He called a while ago and said he was running late. I told him about our captured bug."

CHAPTER 25

DR. POTTER'S LATE-MODEL OLDSMOBILE PULLED into Union Town Funeral Home's parking lot, followed by a white, extended-body Econoline van and twin-cab truck towing a supply trailer. The sides of the multi-seater and trailer were decorated with a depiction of a baseball bat KO'ing an animated cockroach and the name 'Louisiana Slugger – Pest Control'. Headlights swept the building as the vehicles pulled under a colonnade.

The van's driver, Allen Derbigby, climbed out. A lanky man of fifty-seven years, Derbigby sported red hair and a magnificent handlebar mustache.

"You guys wait here," Derbigby told Reg Vaughn and Franklin Delano Johnson, as his two employees exited the twin-cab to stretch their legs.

Drs. Potter and Jenkins joined Derbigby.

Dr. Reynolds and Olan emerged from the funeral home and introductions were quickly made.

"Where's your specimen?" Potter asked. His anxiousness for a firsthand look at the captive bug showed on him like a child.

Olan led the group inside while Dr. Reynolds offered

the newcomers a review of this day's events, including the decomposed specimen Justin had discovered. They entered the embalming room where the over-sized jar holding the bug had been relocated.

"Oh my! Oh my!" Dr. Potter managed, overwhelmed with amazement at the sight of the motionless creature within its glass prison. Leaning closer to the jar, he gawked, "Oh my."

"And there are hundreds of these things?" Jenkins questioned Dr. Reynolds, equally amazed.

"There could be thousands," Reynolds answered. "We don't yet know how large the colony is."

"What have you found out about our little friend?" Dr. Potter asked. He moved his hand closer to the jar, noting the creature's eyes followed his every motion. "This is remarkable," he exclaimed excitedly. "Articulated eyes!"

Picking up a pencil from the table for use as a pointer, Dr. Reynolds stated in scientific discourse, "Aside from the obvious, the specimen breathes through nostrils, not spiracles." She moved the pencil along the outside of the big jar from the lateral line of the creature's abdomen, where the breath-holes of insects are located, to the bug's anterior proboscis. "The mouth is a simple mandible and maxilla with no specialized mouth parts. Also, you can see it has one characteristic of arachnids, two body segments; cephalothorax and abdomen.

"Now we get to its two most striking features, its legs and eyes." Pointing again with the pencil, she went on as if teaching a freshman biology class. "There are no known arthropods with less than six legs. This organism has only four, and as you can see, four leg parts; femur, tibia, tarsus and pretarsus. As for its binocular eyes, this is a trait seen only in more highly developed animals from cephalopods, octopus and squid, up to humans."

"Anything more than instinctive behavior?" Dr. Potter asked.

"Nothing that I've seen," Dr. Reynolds said. "But then again, we have had only limited observation. The only movement from this individual since being placed in the jar has been its eyes. It has excellent visual perception. The only time it does not respond to stimuli is when ambient temperature is above one hundred five degrees Fahrenheit." She indicated a bulb-thermometer hanging from the underside of the jar's lid and showing an internal temperature of seventy-eight degrees.

"Tell me more about this heat factor," Dr. Potter said.

"We noticed this phenomenon when I retrieved this specimen from the factory roof," Dr. Reynolds said. "High temperatures force these creatures into a dormant state, reverse hibernation if you will."

She motioned to a handheld hair dryer lying on the second embalming table. "I used the hair dryer to slowly heat the jar and the air inside. At exactly one hundred five degrees 'F' the creature's irises constrict and it no longer responds to visual stimuli.

"Once the ambient temperature falls below one hundred five degrees for a few minutes, the creature regains consciousness and is fully alert."

"And it hasn't moved since you put it in the jar?" Dr. Potter asked.

"Only when the jar was shifted from one location to another or the lid was tampered with," Dr. Reynolds said.

"But not at temperatures above one hundred five," Dr. Potter stated, puzzled.

"That's correct, there's no movement at all. But when placed in the freezer and with the jar's internal temperature below freezing, the specimen is totally alert, eyes clear and responsive to all external movements."

"Very unusual, indeed," Dr. Potter said. "A dormant state should occur at lower temperatures and greater activity at higher temperatures. Of course, this is going by our knowledge of arthropods and other cold-blooded organisms." Looking at his former student, he asked, "Are we dealing with a warm-blooded animal?"

"With this creature, anything is possible," Dr. Reynolds admitted.

"A missing link on the evolutionary tree," Dr. Potter pondered out loud. "Traits represented in nearly every phyla in Invertabrata and Vertabrata." Once again he drew closer to the jar, his own eyes magnified through the convex glass. "It obviously has an advanced nervous system," he commented. "Well-developed ocular nerves and no doubt, an equally developed brain." Turning to Dr. Reynolds, his face boyish in amazement, he added, "I wonder if it *is* capable of cognitive thought."

"What I've noted thus far indicates behavior more instinctive than cognitive," Dr. Reynolds said. "Of course, it will take many more behavioral studies to determine that."

"Do we know what it eats?" Derbigby asked. "And what about its life cycle? Gradual or complete metamorphosis?"

"We don't have those answers yet," Dr. Reynolds said. "The only things we do know are; these organisms behave similarly to Vespids, their venom is highly necrotic and this colony appears to have gone through at least one mating cycle."

Dr. Potter's eyes widened. He looked to Dr. Reynolds for further explanation.

"Earlier this evening we found what appears to be an abandoned nest some three miles south of the factory site," Dr. Reynolds said.

"The original nest?" Dr. Potter asked.

"Possibly," Dr. Reynolds replied. "A man and his dog were killed there and a neighbor's son saw airborne individuals a few days ago so we know it hasn't been inactive long."

"And you are sure it's abandoned?" Dr. Potter asked.

"As far as we can tell," Dr. Reynolds said. "The man who was killed dug into the tunnel and actually went inside."

"Have you found that nest entrance?" Potter asked.

"It was too dark at the time," Dr. Reynolds responded.

"We'll have to locate it," Dr. Potter said. "Further live specimens must be retrieved."

"What about the CDC?" Dr. Reynolds asked.

"From what I understand, there is some mix-up between the CDC, NASA and the military as to jurisdiction but someone from the Feds should be here by tomorrow," Potter said.

"Can we fumigate?" Olan asked.

"Mister Derbigby brought an arsenal of fumigants," Dr. Potter said, "but the Feds will decide if we use them."

"Are we ready to go out to the factory site?" Dr. Reynolds said.

"Most certainly," Dr. Potter replied.

CHAPTER 26

"HAVE ANY OF THE OTHER buildings in this area been affected?" Allen Derbigby asked Sheriff Maxwell. Derbigby, Drs. Reynolds, Potter and Jenkins, along with the sheriff, had completed an exterior inspection of Cajun Snax's facility and now stood in the middle of Industrial Boulevard taking in a grand view of the building's floodlit frontage. The night-shrouded silhouettes of the eight other factories formed broken canyon walls extending to a near horizon of tangled vegetation.

Before them, Cajun Snax's own facade had been decorated with Tom Slyger's handiwork; silver lengths of duct tape and blue plastic sheeting framing wall seams, the row of warehouse bay doors and its service door and the front office door.

"The interiors and exteriors of every building have been inspected on the hour since this afternoon," the sheriff replied to Derbigby's query. "This building is the only structure affected. I have orders from Governor Phillips not to fumigate but that doesn't mean we can't get things set up, just in case."

"Sheriff, fumigating this building alone will do nothing," Derbigby said. "The bugs have retreated underground which requires the fumigant to be injected into the nest as well as this building. We know nothing about the total subterranean area in question nor do we know how deep underground the nest is. Without knowing any of this, there is not much more I can do, fumigation-wise."

Sheriff Maxwell frowned. "Is there no way of determining the size and depth of the nest?" he asked.

"Beyond actually going inside, no," Derbigby said.

"Sheriff, I'd like to retrieve the bug your deputy saw die." Dr. Potter said. "We already have a live specimen for observing behavioral traits and if I can dissect an intact creatures, we will be even better equipped for dealing with the other individuals."

"Fine," the sheriff said, relieved there was at least one thing they could do. "Get in there, get the dead bug and get out."

"While Doctor Potter is collecting his specimen," Derbigby said, "I can stage some fumigation equipment inside the factory. If we are able to inject fumigant into the underground part of the nest, we will also need a lethal concentration in the factory should any of the creatures exit from underground."

"And you brought enough fumigant?" the sheriff asked.

Derbigby motioned toward the sidewalk where Tom Slyger was assisting Franklin and Reg Vaughn to organize red cylinders of compressed gas, sheets of tenting material and related extermination paraphernalia.

"I brought methyl bromide, a highly lethal, broad spectrum fumigant that will kill anything," Derbigby said. "With what I brought and what Mister Slyger has, we have enough to fumigate half the buildings in this industrial park."

"How long will it take you to get set up?" the sheriff asked.

"A half hour," Derbigby said.

"If I order you out, you vacate immediately," the sheriff said.

"Of course," Derbigby replied.

"And the other nest, on the Dubois farm?" the sheriff asked. "What can we do there?"

"We have to find the entrance first," Dr. Reynolds noted, "and that's too dangerous to do at night. If that nest is indeed still inhabited there could be sentries."

"Sheriff, there's one other thing," Derbigby said. "As soon as the Dubois entrance is found, I suggest we relocate some of the fumigant to that site. If and when we initiate fumigation here, we'll need a lethal atmosphere in all potential exit points."

"Let's get things set up here," the sheriff said.

"Excuse me," Phil Linderson said. The high school

biology teacher joined the others, uncertain if he should say more in front of the new arrivals.

"Yes Phil," the sheriff said. "What is it?"

"I don't know what significance it is but after I left here earlier I started thinking. There is something else that may or may not mean anything. When I was out at the landfill this morning, one of the workers showed me a geode he found there. I didn't think anything of it but it has a chipped end that exposes a crystalline core with an inclusion of a similar shape to the claws on those bugs."

"What do you think?" the sheriff asked Dr. Reynolds.

"Where is the landfill?" the entomologist asked.

"About three and half miles from here," the sheriff said.

"I'm not sure what a geode has to do with these creatures," the entomologist said, "but a visit to the landfill might be in order."

"We'll go at daylight," the sheriff said. "Phil, I'd like you to go with us."

"Sure," Linderson said. "Where should I meet you and at what time?"

"Be here at the factory, five thirty," the sheriff said.

CHAPTER 27

DANK AIR PRESSED DOWN ON him like a heavy cloak, filling him with fear and refusing to yield. Taking an uncertain step, he halted, drew an anxious breath, wheezed and coughed. The sulfur-laced air was stifling. It burned his nostrils and permeated his every pore as if his blood had turned to fetid ocher and now encased the hard knot of panic writhing deep in his belly.

Tight-throated, Wreckerman attempted to swallow. He exhaled and listened for a long moment before taking his next reluctant breath. The silence was as heavy as the stench surrounding him, nothing but his own heartbeat pounding in his quickly sobering mind. He touched his cheek with clammy hands, fully aware now he was not dreaming. He held his hand an inch in front of his face and wiggled his fingers. Even with his eyes wide open, he perceived no movement, no shapes, nothing at all, only cold clay beneath his feet and a mile deep blackness that told him he was below ground.

Wreckerman didn't know how long he had been underground, didn't even remember how he had come to be there. He recalled the events leading up to his blackout, the half-gallon of bourbon he had shared with Pete and the last remaining bit he had greedily finished off after his sometime-partner returned to his flop.

Wreckerman remembered that final, delicious gulp and the satisfaction he had felt at copping a great buzz on such quality liquor. Tossing the emptied bottle into the weeds, he had gone for a pee in his usual spot behind a clump of withering sage grass but after that, things were hazy. Closing his eyes, as if that might help, Wreckerman managed to recollect getting into position, wobbling unsteadily and fumbling with his zipper. Then, in an instant, the ground under his feet gave way. One moment he was looking up at evening's twilight, his bladder ready to burst and the next, the surrounding foliage leaped to the sky and he was falling.

Exactly what had happened to him, Wreckerman didn't know, but he had come to in eternal darkness with a goose egg welt on his head, a splitting headache, urine-wet pants and no idea where he now was. And that horrible rotten egg smell. He tried to swallow again, realizing how thirsty he was. The very air seemed to be sucking him dry.

By feeling about, Wreckerman had discovered this foul tomb was a horizontal shaft with a level floor that sloped upward on the sides forming curved walls dappled with tiny depressions. The ceiling was beyond his reach, even on tiptoes, but the walls' curvature indicated the excavation was perfectly symmetrical. Maybe, Wreckerman thought, he had fallen into a long forgotten gold mine or part of an ancient sewer system. It certainly smelled like one.

When Wreckerman had first regained consciousness he had heard chirping crickets and an old hootie-owl, but in his attempt to find a way out the noises had faded. Retracing his steps like a chicken along a fence line, he failed to find those familiar sounds again and finally, completely disoriented and desperate to escape, Wreckerman had walked on in one direction, warily testing each step for some unseen precipice and praying to any god who might listen for a ray of light.

Wreckerman could not calculate how far he had already walked in this unlikely passage. It seemed to him like miles and he had yet to find the slightest variation in his surroundings to indicate he was making progress. Hopelessly lost, he was terrified to take another step into the abysmal blackness.

There were lights, phantom points that floated across Wreckerman's vision with every blink. He concentrated on one particular pinprick of illumination hovering at a great distance down the tunnel but when he blinked once more, his rising hope was dashed as the glowing speck drifted upward to vanish under his eyelids.

An unnerving image took shape in Wreckerman's mind, a picture he had seen in a National Geographic

Magazine. The photo had always intrigued him but now it filled him with horror. The snap shot showed the mummified remains of a native Indian who, hundreds of years ago, had become lost deep in the maze of caverns now known as Mammoth Cave, in Kentucky. With all hope for escape exhausted the young warrior had curled up as if once again in his mother's womb and succumbed to dehydration and hypothermia.

Wreckerman struggled to control a fear that crept closer to panic. His heart hammered his chest and tears of self-pity welled in his eyes, certain he faced a similar fate as that Indian of long ago.

Unwilling to accept this fate for himself, Wreckerman banished the photo from his mind, conjuring up another familiar image, one that ignited a spark of hope, the celluloid hero, John Rambo. In Wreckerman's favorite movie, 'First Blood', Rambo had been in the same situation as Wreckerman was now and the Hollywood tough guy had outwitted a posse of sheriff's deputies, defying the impossible to break free from an underground labyrinth and kick ass for the remainder of the movie.

Wreckerman clenched his fists with resolve, filled with conviction that he was just as tough as the John Rambo character. If some hole in the ground failed to hold this unrelenting hero, then by god, it couldn't hold Wreckerman either. Like his fellow warrior, whose iron will and fearlessness could pull him through the most unbelievable plights, Wreckerman felt determined to live to tell the tale.

Taking a long, restorative breath, Wreckerman pondered more clearly his dilemma. This tunnel had an access point to the surface, that he was certain. After all, someone had dug the damn thing so there was surely a way in and out.

With his newfound confidence strengthening his fear-weakened knees, Wreckerman slid one cautious foot in front of the other, crab-walking ever deeper into the tunnel and counting each step as he went, insurance for returning to the position he had just abandoned. That unseen spot may not have been any different than the rest of the tunnel but it was comforting to have a safe point from which to reconnoiter.

On his ninety-ninth step Wreckerman halted in the raven-black gloom, aware he was now standing on more level ground. He moved laterally, arms outstretched but the slope of his companion wall had vanished. His confidence shaken, Wreckerman backed up and turning about-face, counted backwards, retracing his footsteps to familiar ground.

A blunt edge of cold earth stubbed into Wreckerman's probing fingers. Tracing the increasingly wide formation, he realized it was a corner where two tunnels intersected.

A tantalizing whiff of fresh air wafted past Wreckerman's nose. Sniffing anxiously, he found another taste of the sweet fragrance borne on the slightest breeze from the left-hand corridor. The welcome scent raised his hope of escape to new heights.

Wreckerman moved toward the tempting smell, alarmed when the floor within this new tunnel began sloping downward. Going deeper underground had not been his expectation but, if that is what it would take to get out of this black Hell, he would walk to the center of the earth and through to the other side. He was tired but most of all, he had a raging thirst that clamped his throat.

Fifty feet below its upper portion the tunnel's floor leveled off. Cleaner air carried only the slightest hint of the foul odors Wreckerman had left behind. Somewhere nearby was an opening to the outside world and he would let nothing stop him from finding it.

Wreckerman found a spot where cool air drifted down from overhead. Reaching up on tiptoes, he found the ceiling was still too high to touch, even when he jumped straight up, arms extended.

Wreckerman tried to crawl up the wall's slope but was unable to get sufficient purchase. In desperation, he probed the floor with his fingers for a root, a stick, anything that might give him a boost up. But there was nothing, nothing but the cold earth and hellish darkness.

Tired from his struggle with gravity and giving in to

rising hopelessness, Wreckerman fell against the wall and slid to the floor. He was trapped and he knew it.

Wreckerman's foot struck something solid. His pulse quickened. Reaching out a cautious hand, he picked up what felt like a discarded sardine can. A delicate tang of mustard and fish played in his nose. Tossing aside the useless tin, he patted the dappled earth with his hand, finding more trash but nothing he could use to determine the location of the hole above.

His fingers brushed cloth. Uncertain what he had found, Wreckerman explored more cautiously. The material covered a pile of sticks soaked in an oily residue. Tearing at the cloth to get at a sturdy limb, he came up with a melon-size stone surprisingly lightweight. The smooth sphere had three large holes on one side. And teeth!

"Jesus!" Wreckerman shrieked in horror. He threw the skull down and fled madly into the eternal blackness. He had to get away from those bones and free of this Hell.

Wreckerman tripped and crashed to the floor where he lay, gasping for air, heart racing. His skin was clammy, every joint icy cool and his entire body shivered with more than fear. The cold tomb had been drawing more from him than just moisture. It had been sucking away precious body heat and though he didn't realize it, Wreckerman was experiencing the first signs of hypothermia.

Pulling himself to his feet, Wreckerman was conscious now of his uncontrollable shivering. Fear squeezed tighter his throat. All visions of the brave, bare-chested John Rambo character had vanished and in their place appeared ghostly shapes that danced before his eyes.

Wreckerman could no longer hold back his tears. He was going to die. He was…

Noises slithered into Wreckerman's range of hearing. Faint at first, the slow, rhythmic thumps and scrapes emanated from the direction he had just come and were growing louder, ever closer.

The approaching sounds pushed Wreckerman's nerves to their brink. Into the impenetrable blackness he blundered certain the skeleton he had discovered was dragging its bare bones through the tunnel, groping for him in the darkness. No longer concerned with what unseen dangers lay at his feet or the specters that danced around his head, Wreckerman knew he had to get out of this dank netherworld or go stark raving mad.

Wreckerman found himself treading on debris strewn over the tunnel's floor. He tripped on uneven footing and went down again, scattering the swirling imagines around him in a burst of star-haze. He quickly realized the debris was discarded bottles and ceramic chard. Struggling to his feet, he bounded away as the evil sounds swelled behind him.

Another spirit-shape materialized from nothingness before him but this apparition had not risen from Wreckerman's tortured mind. Like a single star in a moonless night sky, this fairy-ray of light remained steady, beckoning from fifty yards ahead.

Wreckerman lurched toward the pale light, scattered trash crunching underfoot and the rustling sounds behind threatening to overtake him.

Diffused light dusted the littered floor and outlined the tunnel's perfect symmetry, guiding Wreckerman the final hundred feet to the exit from the dank passageway. Breaking free of the stinking darkness into light, he sucked in ragged breaths, guffawing disbelief at his good fortune.

The tunnel had become a vast, circular cavern two hundred feet across and thirty feet deep. The excavation's clay walls and floor were constructed with the same flawless symmetry as the tunnel but capped with a gigantic concrete slab supported by concrete pilings. Illumination came from a round hole chiseled from the far side of the sagging concrete ceiling.

Wreckerman scampered to a position directly below the cleft. Through a crisscrossed mesh of reinforcing steel bars he saw a trussed ceiling high overhead and heard what sounded like the faint drone of jet engines.

Crawling simian-fashion up the slope to the interface of concrete and clay, Wreckerman took hold of a steel bar. It would be a tight fit through the mesh but that was not going to stop him. Movement in the shadows below caught his eye. Death had arrived.

CHAPTER 28

GENE LANCER STARED AT THE video monitor's screen, his eyes fixed on its bluish glow and its unchanging picture. Yawning, he took a long drag on his last cigarette and flicked it away. The spent butt struck the sidewalk and burst into a fiery sparkler.

It was two A.M. and Gene was fighting heavy eyelids. In a couple of hours his body would kick into its "day" mode and he would feel more coherent but that didn't help his fatigue now. He hoped there was enough coffee to last until then.

Gene's thoughts drifted to Donna and Shirley Forrest, twins he had met at a wedding party in Palmetto, six months earlier. The sisters liked to pose in the buff and Gene, being the semi-professional photographer he was, accommodated their every desire. His last session with the girls ended with all three of them in bed. Shirley liked…

"Mister Lancer!" Dr. Jenkins called, pulling Gene from his self-induced trance.

Gene looked up. A state trooper was passing out cups of coffee. Dr. Jenkins held a cup aloft in friendly offering.

Gene waved appreciation. He could use a cup of coffee. In fact, he could go for the whole pot. He turned back to the screen and his vigil.

"Black, with sugar, right?" Dr. Jenkins said. He held out Gene's java.

"Thanks," Gene said. He took a sip, savoring the coffee's strong flavor.

"Do you want me to spell you?" Dr. Jenkins asked.

"I'm good for now," Gene replied.

Sheriff Maxwell joined them. "Any activity?" he asked, referring to the factory's interior.

"Not a thing," Gene replied. "How soon before Doctor Potter and Mister Derbigby go inside?"

"They should be about ready," the sheriff said. "I'm going around back to check on their progress. Remember, if you see any movement at the entrance hole, anything at all, radio me immediately."

The sheriff left.

Gene set the empty cup next to the video recorder. Rummaging through his camera case for a cigarette he knew he didn't have, he glanced up at the still-life image on the monitor's screen. Dr. Potter appeared on the right of the picture. Allen Derbigby and Franklin Johnson followed. They all averted their eyes and made a wide berth around something outside the camera's view, no doubt Officer Jack Moore's remains.

"So far, so good," Dr. Jenkins commented to Gene as

they watched the monitor.

Armed with a collection tray, Potter made a beeline for the cold room while the other two men fed out three clear, half-inch fumigation hoses. Heavy sweat glistened on Franklin's black skin, speaking of the heat within the structure.

"How are we looking?" the sheriff radioed Gene.

"All cl...." Gene halted. "There's a bug moving around at the hole!"

"Everyone out," the sheriff called through the factory's open rear door. "Let's go. Move it!"

With the trayed specimen, Potter bustled across the floor and out of the door, Derbigby and Franklin close behind. The door was slammed closed.

Gene and Dr. Jenkins leaned in closer to the monitor's screen, jaws agape in disbelief as a human arm reached out of the entrance hole. A moment later a head topped with tousled hair and rimmed by a scruffy beard emerged, followed by broad shoulders set atop a bear-sized torso.

"Son-of-a-bitch!" Gene stammered. He got on the radio. "Sheriff, Billy Nagle's inside the factory."

"Who's where?" Sheriff Maxwell asked.

Wreckerman popped through the steel bar mesh like a champagne cork from its bottle. He crawled away from the gaping entrance on his hands and knees, his saucer eyes wild and desperate. Taking hold of the first machine he came to, he levered himself to his feet and staggered into the flood-lamps' bright light.

"It's Billy Nagle," Gene repeated. "He's inside the factory. He just came out of the bug hole!"

"Inside *this* building?"

"Yes."

Wreckerman was frantic, having no idea where he now stood. Upon seeing the chasm through which he had just escaped, he reeled backwards as if the dark abyss would swallow him again. He scuttled across the floor toward the flood-lamps and camera.

Sheriff Maxwell wrenched open the rear door. "Billy, this way," he shouted over the roaring heaters.

Wreckerman screeched in terror at the unexpected sound of a human voice. He spun about, his body wracked with fear. Pressing his hands over his ears, he shrieked, "Leave me alone!"

Sheriff Maxwell didn't wait to find out with whom Wreckerman was conversing. Those bugs might swarm at any moment. Bolting across the factory floor, the sheriff grabbed Wreckerman's arm. Wreckerman let out a howl of horror before recognition flashed across his panic-stricken face.

"Is there someone else with you?" the sheriff asked.

"He's coming," Wreckerman wailed, trembling so hard his teeth chattered.

"Who's coming?" the sheriff queried.

Wreckerman was sobbing, too frightened to speak. The sheriff urged him past the heaters and outside into cool, early morning air.

"Gene," the sheriff radioed. "Do you see anyone else?"

"Negative," came Deputy Herbert's voice. He and a party of state police had just returned from another uneventful inspection of the other factory buildings. "We see no further movement on the monitor."

The rear door was shut. Sheriff Maxwell led Wreckerman to the factory's front.

Wreckerman's clothes were filthy. He smelled of stale urine and sulfur. Someone handed the haggard man a bottle of mineral water which he scarfed down along with four chocolate-covered doughnuts.

"Billy, how did you get into this building?" the sheriff asked. Gene had to have been mistaken about Wreckerman actually coming up out of the nest. No one could possibly enter that hole and come out alive.

Wreckerman chomped through his last doughnut, his brow furrowing as he brought together the shattered fragments of his nightmare. "I don't know," he said in a shaky voice. "The ground gave way and I fell into some sort of tunnel."

Wreckerman's gaze wandered across the front yard to the gathering of official vehicles and silent factories. Enlightenment dawned when he realized where he was.

"Was anyone with you?"

"Pete Baxter. He left before I fell in."

"Where did you fall into the tunnel?" Sheriff Maxwell asked. He wondered if Wreckerman had somehow entered the factory and indeed ended up inside the nest.

"Behind Red Dot Grocery, in The Swamp." Wreckerman didn't care anymore who knew about his hideout. He was just glad to be alive.

"You fell into a hole behind Red Dot Grocery and wound up here?" The sheriff was stunned. "How the hell did you do that? You're talking almost a half mile." Any other time Sheriff Maxwell would not have believed anything Wreckerman told him. The guy told the tallest tales in the state, but at this moment the sheriff had no choice but to take seriously every word the big man uttered.

"I guess it's an old mine," Wreckerman said.

Knowing the only mining in and around Union Town had been sulfur extraction which used superheated water injected into sulfur deposits and not mines, Sheriff Maxwell turned to Dr. Reynolds. "We don't have two separate nests, do we?" he said.

"I can't believe a single nest could be that large," Dr. Reynolds said.

Sheriff Maxwell considered the ramifications, aware one important question had yet to be answered. "Did you see or hear anything while you were down there?" he asked Wreckerman.

"Oh man," Wreckerman cried with a shudder, "there's a freakin' skeleton."

"A human skeleton?" the sheriff asked.

Wreckerman's anguish returned in a rush. "It was after me," he cried, still hearing the bony ghoul's rattling bones as it crawled ever closer.

"Billy, calm down," the sheriff said. "You're safe now."

"Oh man, oh man," was all Wreckerman could manage.

"Doff, as soon as it's light enough, get a state trooper and check the area behind Red Dot," the sheriff ordered the police officer.

"I'll check with Pete too," Doff said. "He might have seen something."

"What's on your clothes?" Dr. Reynolds asked Wreckerman. A dark substance tattooed his pants.

"Man, it's from the bones," Wreckerman groaned.

Dr. Reynolds inspected the big man's hands and arms. Black matter was smeared on the back of one hand but there was no sign of tissue damage. "I'm not certain this is residue from a sting victim," she told the sheriff, "but if it is, it has lost its potency."

"Billy," the sheriff said, "are you sure you didn't hear or see anything else when you were in the tunnel?"

Wreckerman fast-forwarded the images in his mind,

the familiar night sounds when he had first regained consciousness after his fall, the unrelenting darkness and that foreboding clamor deep within the ground but now, free from the dank bowels of the earth, he wasn't certain anymore if those mysterious noises had been real or just the darkness playing wild tricks on his brain. "There was nothing else," Wreckerman answered.

CHAPTER 29

"BILLY NAGLE PROVED THE CREATURES are no longer under the factory or in the tunnels between here and the other side of The Swamp," the sheriff said to Drs. Reynolds and Potter. "So, where the hell are they?"

"Sheriff, we are dealing with an organism we know almost nothing about," Dr. Reynolds reminded the lawman. "It's possible the entire colony retreated to a central part of the nest for the night. It's equally possible heat within this building has driven them to another location. At this point, anyone's guess is as good as mine or Doctor Potter's."

"One thing is clear," Dr. Potter added. "This factory is not sitting on the main part of the nest."

"It might be best to turn off the heaters too," Dr. Reynolds suggested. "By reducing negative factors inside the building, there will be less chance for any further surprises should the bugs return."

Justin stepped forward, a clipboard and pen in hand. "There's something you need to see," he said to those gathered around the monitor. Adjusting angle to bring the clipped paper within the light, he displayed a roughed-out map of Union Town, the town no more than a crude circle with 'Dubois Farm' scribbled to the south and 'Industrial Park' to the north. A straight line connected Maurice's home to the factory area, passing directly through the town's center. A perpendicular line crossed this main segment to the general area of Red Dot Market, forming a partially finished, lower case 't'.

Silence reigned while the crew perused the penned-in map. The geometry was unnerving, too perfect to be coincidence.

"The tunnel we saw at the Dubois place," Dr. Reynolds said, "appeared to continue due south, away from town. What's out that way?"

"The landfill," Justin answered. He drew another circle where the landfill would be located and placed an 'X' over his rendition of the industrial park.

"And you said it is three and half miles from here to the landfill," Dr. Potter said.

"That's correct," the sheriff said, "and a half mile from Maurice's house."

"So," Dr. Reynolds said, "why would these creatures dig a tunnel between the industrial park and a landfill on the opposite side of town?"

"Maybe," Justin said, "they didn't dig a tunnel from an industrial park to a landfill. Maybe they dug a tunnel from one garbage dump to another."

"I don't follow you," Dr. Reynolds said.

"The fill-dirt on which this industrial park was built," Justin explained, "covers years of accumulated trash from during the time Union Sulfur was in business."

"So these creatures are attracted to garbage like normal bugs?" the sheriff asked, addressing both Drs. Reynolds and Potter.

"It's plausible," Dr. Potter replied. "These organisms have to eat something and that something may be associated with garbage, decaying organic matter no doubt; mold, fungi."

"Its teeth support that theory," Dr. Reynolds pointed out.

Dr. Potter said, "There's another part to this puzzle of which I'm not certain."

He paused.

"I have evidence this organism occurred in the jungles of Southern Venezuela where Doctor Jenkins and I were witness to a death similar to what you have seen here. Near that victim's remains I found a claw that matches those on these creatures. But that was over forty years ago."

"And the two are related?" the sheriff asked.

"The evidence shows they could be," Dr. Potter said.

"If that's the case," Justin asked, "why haven't they shown up at other sites? There are three landfills in Saint Landry Parish and probably thousands around the country, not to mention all of the other dumps around the world. Why are these things here, under a small town in South Central Louisiana and in Venezuela?"

No one answered.

Dr. Potter asked Jenkins, "What do you think, Mike? Is there a reason, geologically, why these creatures would be here and in Venezuela, exclusively?"

Dr. Jenkins shrugged. "There are not many geological similarities between Venezuela and Louisiana," he began. "Venezuela sits atop the Guiana Shield, mainly Precambrian crystalline rock covered with erosion sediments and alluvial deposits, river silt. Louisiana and the other gulf coast states sit on thick sedimentary deposits formed by a series of shallow seas that advanced and receded over the region for many millions of years."

"So there's no particular similarities between these two areas that would make them stand out from others?" Dr. Reynolds asked.

"Definitely not," Dr. Jenkins responded. "Most continents have examples of both of these types of strata."

"Then there has to be some other reason why these creatures are here," Sheriff Maxwell said. "Unless there are trash dumps in Venezuela's jungles."

"There are no trash dumps," Dr. Potter offered, "but there is a tremendous amount of decaying biomass."

"Which gets us where?" the sheriff asked.

"I wish I knew," Dr. Potter confessed. "This specimen may provide some answers." He holds up the trayed bug.

"I need to get back to the funeral home and begin my dissection."

The sheriff saw only one option. "Until we know more, I'm going to evacuate the town," he said. "If we ever had the advantage, we've lost it."

CHAPTER 30

SAM RAMEY, UNION TOWN'S RESIDENT beekeeper and part-time carpenter, sniffed the air in pre-dawn light. Frowning, he moved to his side yard, noting the stench was much more pungent outside his home than inside. He stepped through the gate of a Cyclone fence into his unlit back yard. The foul odor was even stronger here. Definitely not a skunk, or was it? Sam couldn't decide. The fumes reeked of musty mildew laced with sulfur and a dash of rotting vegetation.

Sam had long ago become used to the smell of sulfur. An outbuilding, known locally as The Shed, had been part of a sulfur extraction factory that occupied his property sixty years before. Though the lone surviving wooden structure still held the stench of brimstone, Sam found this present smell particularly strong, especially at five-thirty in the morning.

"Jet, here boy," Sam called to his black Labrador. The dog was at the rear of a half-acre enclosure, hackles raised, growling into the darkness. When his dog didn't respond, Sam called again, figuring another skunk had indeed come to rob his beehives.

The porch light above the kitchen door came on and Sheila Joules, Sam's fiancé, stepped outside onto a raised back porch, a kimono wrapped about her ample body.

"What's got Jet going?" Sheila yawned. A half-hour earlier Jet had set up such a ruckus, barking and howling, that Sam had climbed out of bed to see what was happening. A harsh word from a kitchen window had quieted the dog temporarily, but he was at it again.

"Skunk," Sam remarked tiredly. The lowlands were crawling with the animals and no amount of chicken wire or traps kept them out. Sam had tried everything, everything except poisons. This option killed too indiscriminately for Sam's liking. A twenty-gauge shotgun did just fine, thank you very much, and the skunks that escaped were tracked down by Jet. Jet hated skunks as much as his master and cut the varmints no slack. Still, Sam had to admit, he had never before seen his dog acting up like this.

"Jet, come," Sam called in his most stinging tone.

Jet began digging under the fence.

"Get him out of my flowers," Sheila wailed as dirt and marigolds flew. A leather strap Sam kept in the house had long ago taught Jet his limits but the dog was not heeding that lesson at this moment.

Sam hustled over to Jet and grabbed him by his collar, unceremoniously yanking him back. Jet fought against the restraint, barking wildly, struggling to return to his diggings. He wanted that skunk or whatever it was.

Sam bundled Jet into the house and slammed the back door closed. He stormed into a back room while Sheila knelt down and stroked Jet's head. "What is it, boy?" she comforted the big dog. The Lab whined, his eyes fixed on the door, anxious for a chance to get back outside.

Returning with his twenty-gauge, Sam broke the weapon and slid in a cartridge. "Keep Jet inside," he said, swinging the shotgun's barrel into place.

Sam pulled a flashlight from a kitchen drawer and donned his hat while Sheila stowed Jet in the back room. Jet would go even crazier if he knew his master was venturing out without him.

Sam hiked up a dirt track to the outbuilding, passing a one hundred fifty gallon kerosene storage tank and a stack of rusting, eight-inch diameter sulfur extraction pipes overgrown with honeysuckle. A similar pipe sprouted three feet above the ground in an adjacent clump of sage.

Sam slowed down his pace as he neared his hives, his eyes watering from the acrid miasma that seemed to seep from the ground under foot. He swung the flashlight's beam from one hive to the next, watchful for the slightest movement. No skunks.

Any relief Sam felt at not having to confront a family of polecats was swept away when he glanced over his shoulder at the soft, peach glow of dawn. Bees should have already been emerging from their hives for the day's foraging but he saw no sign of activity, none whatsoever.

Disregarding the chance of a sting, Sam opened the lid of the nearest hive, lifted out a frame, dropped it back into place and lifted out another. The combs were intact, full of honey, ready for harvesting but, except for the white larvae squirming in their cells, the hive was empty. Not a single adult bee remained, including the queen.

Sam moved to a second hive, then a third and still another. Slamming down the lid of the last box, he looked over the scene, dumbfounded. Every hive was abandoned, something he had never seen in his thirty years of bee keeping.

Dawn crawled skyward turning twilight into day as Sam stepped away from the beehives, certain the source of that god-awful smell was the reason for the mass exodus of his livelihood.

He followed his nose. Unlocking The Shed's slatted door, Sam swung it open, gasping at the stench that engulfed him. He reached an arm inside and flipped a switch. A flicker of fluorescent lighting caught the building's interior in a freeze frame, a picture which, at first, Sam thought could only have been an illusion; light and shadows dappled together upon the dirt floor in an irregular pattern of browns, blacks and brilliant yellow. But, when in another instant the light came on, Sam realized with astonishment his imagination had not played tricks on him.

Sam backed out of the doorway, aghast at what lay before him on The Shed's dirt floor.

Within the building, Sam's storage cabinet of empty honey jars and drawers of lids had toppled into a sinkhole. The sagging ground threatened to swallow the room's entire contents. From under a skid holding a centrifuge, a four-inch wide fissure cut a jagged line ten feet from the depression to a point just short of the rear wall. Rivulets of sulfur oozed from the rent, spreading out strangely colored tentacles and sending up noxious vapors that clung to the heavy air.

But there was more. Sam sensed it, rising from deep within the ground, the distinct sound of digging.

Sam rushed out of the structure and raced down the trail to his house. Throwing open the back gate, he bounded up the steps in two long strides. Sheila nearly jumped out of her skin when he barged through the kitchen door and pounced on the wall phone.

"What's wrong?" Sheila shrieked, alarmed.

"Someone's digging under The Shed."

"What?" Sheila had no idea what he was talking about. Sam held up a quieting hand. He dialed.

"Union Town Police Department," third shift dispatcher Carol René answered. Carol was Sam's cousin, on his father's side, and the woman who had replaced Doris

Greely at midnight.

"Carol, this is Sam. I need the law out here, now. Someone's digging around under The Shed. They've chased away all my bees."

"Who's doing what?"

"I don't know who it is but they're digging under The Shed," Sam repeated excitedly. "The whole damn building and everything inside are sinking into the ground."

"Sam, what on earth are you talking about?"

"Just send someone out here!" Sam slammed down the phone. Rushing into the bedroom, he grabbed a handful of extra shotgun cartridges from a nightstand.

"Sam! What the blue blazes is going on?" Sheila demanded. "What's going on in The Shed?"

"That's what I'm about to find out," Sam growled. He stomped out of the door and across the back yard, certain he knew why someone would burrow under his property. Sulfur.

For as long as Sam could remember, geologists and students of the science had been drawn to Union Town's unique geologic anomaly, as they called it. This site was supposedly the only place on earth where pure sulfur had been extracted at the turn of the century and the only location where, sixty years after exhausting the deposit, the spent sulfur had somehow been replenished. No one had yet come up with a viable explanation. Some believed underground pressure was forcing trapped sulfur from surrounding deposits. Others felt previous core sampling had been flawed and the deposits simply overlooked.

Whether geologic forces or human oversight, the fact remained the deposit was there, ripe for the picking and since Sam owned the mineral rights, he wasn't allowing anyone to tap into his mother lode without due payment. Sam's anger grew when he realized he had not only lost his bees but could be losing a fortune to sulfur thieves.

Sheila caught up with Sam at the back gate. She grabbed his arm. "You wait for the law," she ordered.

"I'm gonna kick their butts clear to New Orleans," Sam growled.

"You're gonna do no such thing," Sheila said. "You let the law take care of this."

"I have to stop them," Sam insisted. "The ground is caving in under The Shed. We could lose everything."

"You wait for the police." Sheila was not about to let Sam go any further with a gut-full of anger and a loaded shotgun in hand.

"Come and see for yourself," Sam said.

"Only if you leave that gun here," Sheila replied.

Sam reluctantly leaned the weapon against the fence and led the way up the hill.

Within Sam's house, Carol René's return telephone call set Jet to whining. Jet didn't like to be alone.

CHAPTER 31

DAWN EDGED A FAR HORIZON dimly illuminating the rotting trash of the landfill. A rancid smell of sulfur oozed from the pit, whispering death. Somewhere below Justin an excavated tunnel stretched from where he now stood to the industrial park on the opposite side of town. Wedged between these two landmarks were Coleman's Diner and Maurice Dubois' house, additional locations where the creatures had been discovered.

Justin pondered the barren dirt at his feet, wondering if the creatures underground knew he was there, could detect his shifting weight or hear the footsteps of Sheriff Maxwell and Sergeant Benoit as they returned from their surveillance trip of the pit's perimeter.

The remains of Spencer Neumann and Calvin Wissnant, along with a twenty-two-caliber rifle, had been located on the southern rim but recovery of the bodies had yet to be made. The two sanitation workers appeared to have been attempting to climb from the crater when they died too near a tunnel entrance for rescue personnel to venture close.

Dr. Jenkin's excited voice drew Justin's attention to

the landfill's utility shed. The geologist, Dr. Reynolds and Phil Linderson emerged from the outbuilding into the morning twilight. They hurried to the deputy, jabbering to each other, their flashlight beams skipping across the tread-marked earth.

Dr. Jenkins called to the sheriff. "Take a look. This is what Phil mentioned earlier," he said. They gathered together. Jenkin's hand trembled as he laid his find in the sheriff's palm.

The elongated object was mineral, rounded at both ends and river rock smooth. The potato-size stone was chipped at one end exposing three distinct inner laminates; a thin, outer cortex, a darker, grainy interior and a pearl-finished center.

Rolling the stone over in his hand, the sheriff shrugged. "Calvin must have thought it was worth something," he said. "He was a great collector of junk." The sheriff passed it on to Justin.

"That he was," Linderson said, "and it is good for us that he was."

"Sheriff," Dr. Jenkins said, "this is a very important piece of the puzzle concerning the creatures under the town."

"It's a rock," the sheriff stated, still seeing no significance in the discovery.

"Look at where it's chipped," Linderson cut in, pointing to the smooth core.

"Okay, I see it," Justin said. He passed the rock back to the sheriff. "It's that claw shaped thing you mentioned."

"That's right," Linderson said.

"It's a front claw from one of those creatures," Dr. Jenkins added.

"How did a claw get embedded in a rock?" the sheriff asked.

"It's not a rock," Dr. Jenkins said. "It's a petrified egg."

The sheriff's eyes widened. "You mean, petrified like a dinosaur bone?" he asked.

"Exactly," Dr. Jenkins replied. "One of my degrees is in paleontology, so I know a bit about fossils."

"You're telling me these bugs have been here since the dinosaurs?" the sheriff asked.

"Possibly not since the dinosaurs but certainly for a very long time, millions of years I'd say."

"So, where does that take us?" the sheriff asked.

"Since our discussion earlier this morning," Dr. Jenkins said, "I've been trying to understand why these creatures have been found at only two sites in the world and I believe I may finally have part of the answer." He regarded the surrounding scrub-land before continuing. "It has to do with the Union Town diapir."

"The Union Town what?" the sheriff asked.

"Diapir," Dr. Jenkins said. "A salt dome. It's the geologic formation that created the high ground on which Union Town and other regional towns are built."

The sheriff shook his head, not understanding the significance.

Dr. Jenkins explained. "Salt domes are enormous collections of salt within the earth's crust. They formed when salt deposited by ancient seas was compressed under tremendous pressures by thick cap rock. Shifts in the earth's crust can fracture this overlying cap rock allowing the salt to squeeze upward through the fault, like toothpaste from its tube. Because salt has a lower density than rock, the salt slowly migrates upward, like an air bubble in cold molasses. As it rises, it uplifts the ground above, as it did here at Union Town. Of course, this process takes millions of years."

"And there are salt domes in Venezuela?" Dr. Reynolds asked.

"No, there are not," Dr. Jenkins said. "As I mentioned earlier, the geology of both areas is quite different. But there is one similarity, sulfur. Salt domes are associated with petroleum and sulfur. Hence the sulfur mining in Union Town back in the twenties and thirties."

"What does that have to do with these bugs?" the sheriff asked.

"The gulf coast region of the United States has deposits of almost pure sulfur," Dr. Jenkins explained, "but the Union Town salt dome is unique. The sulfur extracted from this particular dome was not only one hundred percent pure, no dissolved impurities whatsoever, it reportedly also had an unusual greenish luminescence. For several hours after extraction it literally glowed in the dark."

"Bio-luminescence," Dr. Reynolds said, intrigued with this last bit of information.

"No doubt," Jenkins said. "But the cause of this phenomenon was never identified, though testing did prove it was neither bacterial nor fungal in nature."

Jenkins paused before adding, "Glowing sulfur has been found in only one other natural deposit."

"Southern Venezuela," the sheriff ventured, sure of the answer.

"That's correct," Jenkins said. "Doctor Potter and I were there with field teams forty years ago. My team was responsible for seismic mapping of petroleum deposits. We not only located petroleum but we also found pools of sulfur on the jungle floor."

"Is there not supposed to be sulfur in Venezuela?" Sheriff Maxwell said.

"In association with petroleum deposits and volcanic activity, yes," Dr. Jenkins said, "but not concentrated in rich deposits as we have here on the gulf coast. This Venezuelan deposit not only appeared to be an extremely large deposit, which is highly unusual for that region, but it was as pure as the sulfur extracted from under Union

Town and, it glowed."

"You say all that in the past tense," Dr. Reynolds stated.

"Yes I did," Jenkins said. "All subsequent research teams into the area failed to find any trace of the deposit. It simply vanished and has never been seen since."

"What does all that have to do with these bugs, or whatever they are?" Sheriff Maxwell asked.

"That I don't yet know," Dr. Jenkins confessed, "but there's one other interesting fact that links the two sites. Sometime during the 1930's, Union Sulfur sent to LSU's geology department samples of their 'glowing' sulfur as well as a half dozen chunks of what was thought to be basalt, dried lava. The rocks had jammed in the extraction equipment and the company wanted to know exactly what they were dealing with. There's never been volcanic activity in this region so the basalt should not have been here in the first place.

"Union Sulfur apparently found no further inclusions after this one incident because there was never any follow-up on their part and with time, the rock samples were shoved into a storage room and forgotten. Then a couple of years ago a grad student of mine resurrected the rocks for a closer look. What was thought to be terrestrially formed basalt turned out to be dunite Chassigny, a rare type of meteorite from Mars.

"What ties all this together," Dr. Jenkins continued,

"is that forty years ago, in South America, we found a dunite Chassigny meteorite in a creek bed a mile from the sulfur pools."

"And the meteorite from Union Town is similar to the fragment from Venezuela?" Dr. Reynolds asked.

"Not similar," Dr. Jenkins said, "Identical. They came from the same meteorite."

He paused again.

"Now, imagine if you will, millions of years ago, a meteorite from Mars breaking up as it enters the earth's atmosphere with fragments impacting the Earth at the point where we now stand and in Southern Venezuela."

"Wouldn't there be a crater?" Sheriff Maxwell asked. He found what Dr. Jenkins was saying more science fiction than plausible fact.

"With the advancing and receding seas in this region of America over the last few million years," Jenkins said, "the impact crater has been covered up and is no longer visible. And it's certainly feasible that the crater in Venezuela was covered by alluvium long before recorded history.

"It's also possible the meteorite's impact at this site is what fractured the underlying rock strata that led to the formation of this and other regional salt domes.

"I know all this sounds far-fetched," Dr. Jenkins admitted, "but those are the facts."

"So you're saying these creatures came to Earth in a

meteorite." the sheriff said. "From Mars. Millions of years ago."

"With the evidence at hand," Dr. Jenkins said, "yes, that is exactly what I am saying. If this object is indeed a petrified egg then these creatures have been here a very long time."

"That doesn't mean they came from some other planet," the sheriff said.

"No, it doesn't," Dr. Reynolds cut in, understanding her colleague had made some unusual but valid points. "But there is more than just this evidence. Since these organisms have exoskeletons, like arthropods, and show similar behavioral traits to social Hymenoptera, bees and wasps, my initial expectations were that they are cold-blooded. But, from what I've witnessed at the factory, in Justin's patrol car and at the funeral home, it appears I was wrong. These creatures are warm-blooded, at least what we would classify as warm-blooded, and that's a first. All previously known animals with exoskeletons, insects and the like, are cold-blooded and at colder temperatures show decreased metabolic rates while at higher temperatures they become more active. These creatures react in a totally opposite fashion. They become lethargic at higher temperatures before becoming completely dormant while displaying more rapid metabolic rates at colder temperatures, physical traits of warm-blooded animals.

"Then you throw in their bizarre morphology: an arachnid-like body with four legs instead of eight, insect-like stinger armed with a totally unknown venom and of course, binocular eyes. Simply put sheriff, either this organism is a never before discovered missing link to evolution here on Earth or it's completely alien to this planet."

A long silence followed bespeaking apprehension from all present of a situation far beyond their past experiences and current capabilities.

The sun's fireball broke free from the horizon, shimmering through morning mist spiraling upward over the sea of rubbish that formed a backdrop for the impromptu meeting. Somewhere in the distance a dog howled.

"Sheriff," Carol René's radio-transmission broke in. "Sam Ramey telephoned. He reported trespassers on his property."

The sheriff radioed back, "Carol, that's for Chief Gallo to deal with. I've got my hands full."

"I just thought, since you are in charge."

"Are the trespassers still there?"

"I don't know," Carol told him. "He seemed pretty upset. I called back but no one answered."

"All right," the sheriff grumbled, his mind on other types of trespassers than humans, "I'll get someone out there as soon as I can."

"Ten-four."

To Dr. Reynolds, Sheriff Maxwell said, "We can't halt our efforts to find out where those creatures have gone. Once we do, we cannot let them leave the nest."

"I'll get with Doctor Potter," Dr. Reynolds said, "and see what he's found out about the bug from the factory."

"Do what you have to do," the sheriff said, "but I want to be ready for any eventuality." He turned to Sergeant Benoit. "I need a couple of your men to monitor things here," he said.

"I'll take care of that," the sergeant replied.

"Doff, get back at the industrial park," the sheriff said, "and Justin, transport Doctor Reynolds to the funeral home. You might as well go by Sam's place on your way and see what his problem is. Don't mention the evacuation. No need to give Sheila reason for calling all over town before official word gets out."

"Where are you going to send everyone?" Justin asked.

"Folks here with no other place to go can stay at Opelousas High School's auditorium until all this is resolved," the sheriff said and to Benoit, "I'll have René track down Mayor Brandon and Chief Gallo. If we don't find them right away, I'll inform Union Town's support services of the evacuation. I'd appreciate it if you could contact your office and have your people coordinate the evacuation with Mayor Hernandez in Opelousas."

"Will do," the sergeant said.

The group broke up. The three-car convoy sped away toward town, Justin bringing up the rear. He reduced speed, allowing a freshening breeze to sweep away the billowing dust kicked up by the lead vehicles.

"There's something that has me worried," Dr. Reynolds said.

"What's that?"

"Last night," she said, "after we found that section of tunnel at the Dubois place, I mentioned it could possibly be a second nest, that these creatures might have reproduced and expanded their territory. It's clear now from what Billy Nagle said and what we've seen here, this is not a second nest but an extension linked to the one at the industrial park. Which leaves the question, why have these organisms suddenly become active? What is causing them to burrow to the surface?"

"Maybe they are going to swarm," Justin offered, recalling what the entomologist had mentioned the previous day concerning behavioral similarities between yellowjackets and this strange creature.

"You could be correct," Dr. Reynolds said, "but if this is part of their life cycle then why haven't they exhibited it before? Union Town has been here sixty years and there is no record of anything like this occurring before now. There's obviously some new factor that has sparked the colony's growth and expansion."

She wrinkled her brow in thought. "I wonder," she

continued, "if what we are witnessing is the result of evolution."

"So these things may not be from outer space after all?"

"We certainly don't know that, one way or the other," Dr. Reynolds said, "but assuming they did arrive on Earth in a meteorite, it's reasonable to expect certain genetic changes would be needed for them to survive and thrive on their new planet.

"The fact these creatures have never been found at any location in the world other than here in Union Town and possibly Venezuela indicates they have never established additional nests and this points to a previous low reproduction rate, at least for the last sixty years or so."

"So these things have been under Union Town all this time evolving?"

"In order for any animal species to adapt to natural changes in its environment, there must be beneficial mutations within its gene pool. That is, there has to be variations of genetic traits over successive generations that allow individuals in the species to change and adapt to new external conditions. During the last ice age many animal species went extinct due to their inability to adjust fast enough to environmental changes while others flourished due to sufficient beneficial genetic mutations.

"What we could be seeing here is an end result of

several million years of slow but steady evolution and a stable colony growth that did not require colony expansion. Then, with two new food sources here at the landfill and under the industrial park, the colony began to grow more rapidly and that has produced individuals suited to today's environment. This in turn has led to a need for colony expansion beyond this nest."

Justin reached blacktop and pulled out onto Colliers Road. "Would environmental changes up here on the surface have an impact underground?" he asked.

"Most definitely," Dr. Reynolds said. "Even if these creatures have remained underground since arriving, their subterranean environment would have been impacted by what occurred on the surface: water seepage, increased sedimentation from oceans, concentration of sulfur and increased salinity due to the rising salt dome. Depending on their particular reproductive dynamics, the essential traits for survival above ground might have taken a very long time to develop."

"So it's coincidence that this is all happening now."

"I believe it's more than just coincidence," Dr. Reynolds observed, "and probably has more than one cause. These creatures have shown no activity in recorded history and certainly not over the last sixty years, since Union Town was founded. Then a few years ago a new parish landfill was created here, increasing the creatures' likely food supply. That, I believe, coupled with sufficient evolutionary adaptations, is what triggered this whole incident."

"Would the same be true for the nest in Venezuela?" Justin asked.

"Yes, it would," Dr. Reynolds replied, "but the subterranean environment would be substantially different from this site in the absence of a significant quantity of sulfur and an associated salt dome. Exactly how that would affect the overall development of the colony is hard to say but I think it safe to say the evolution of the two colonies would be different."

"So we need to act fast or these things might spread," Justin said.

"As it stands now, yes."

CHAPTER 32

FARAWAY THUNDER ROLLED UP FROM Gulf Coast flatlands. Thunderheads built beneath dawn's pastel sky, stirring morning air and announcing a change in weather. Louisiana's late summer storms oft times spawn tornadoes that race across the countryside, ripping up everything in their paths but on this day Justin disregarded the distant warning. Other priorities beckoned.

Bouncing his cruiser through a dry rut on Bayou Lane, he turned into Sam Ramey's dirt driveway wondering why anyone would choose to live so close to the marshes of the Atchafalaya River. The only other house on this isolated road was Eloise Coleman's vacant brick split-level with its 'For Sale' sign sprouting from its front yard.

Justin halted his vehicle behind Sam's late model pick-up. The significance of the beekeeper's call became instantly apparent when the deputy and Dr. Reynolds stepped from the car. The air was rank with a smell of sulfur, much stronger than they had yet experienced.

Justin knocked on the front door. No one answered. He found the door unlocked and stepped inside.

The house was tomb silent.

He called out Sam's name, then Sheila's. Jet's muffled bark from a back room was the only response. When Justin opened the room's door, Jet bounded out and scampered into the kitchen. Barking wildly, the hound scratched furiously at the exterior door to get out.

Justin followed Jet, knowing the dog would lead him to its master. Through the kitchen window the deputy spied Sam and his fiancé. Sheila was staying well behind Sam, a hand pressed over her nose and mouth. Sam approached The Shed as if his worst fears might slither from its shadows.

Justin opened the kitchen door to warn Sam of possible danger. Jet plowed past the deputy, down the porch steps and raced across the yard. The big Labrador took the fence in one powerful leap and charged up the graded scape.

Sam looked toward his house, startled his dog had somehow broken loose. He spied a sheriff's deputy standing on the back porch waving his arms and signaling with urgency for him to return home. Sam waved back, beckoning the lawman to join him at The Shed and start making arrests.

Justin was well aware that if the creatures underground had opened a portal beneath The Shed, Sam and Sheila were in mortal danger. Drawing his pistol from its holster, the deputy discharged a shot into the air.

The results were immediate. Sam stopped dead in his tracks, uncertain what to do next. He wanted the law to catch whoever was stealing his sulfur but the deputy's intent was clear.

"This is enough," Sheila gasped from behind her hand. She grimaced when forced to take another breath. "The law's here. Let them handle it."

Sam cursed, reluctantly giving up his mission.

Sam and Sheila retraced their steps. Sam whistled for his dog to heel but the big Lab wasn't having any of it. He bounded past its owner and tore into the ground at the base of The Shed, throwing dirt in all directions and barking incessantly.

"It's about time you got here," Sam fretted to Justin as he entered the back yard. He picked up his shotgun and marched up the back porch steps.

Sheila caught up with Sam, out of breath, sweat pouring down her face. "Lordy, what on earth is going on?" she panted from exertion.

"Is that smell coming from The Shed?" Justin asked Sam.

"You're damn right it is," Sam growled. "I want you to find out who's down there and arrest them. I own the mineral rights to this property, ya know. And they're paying for every bee I lost."

"Did you see a hole in the ground?" Justin asked Sam. From the number of holes these creatures had already opened to the surface, something significant was happening.

"It's a sinkhole now," Sam said, "but if you don't stop them it's going to be a crater. I could lose all my hives."

"You and Sheila pack some clothes and get over to the courthouse," Justin said. "The state police have someone there to give you further instructions."

"I ain't going nowhere until you arrest whoever's digging up my property," Sam said defiantly.

"Sam, it's imperative you and Sheila get out of here, right now," Justin stressed. "There's a gas leak in the area and we are evacuating everyone." Justin figured a plausible lie would get faster results than the unbelievable truth.

"I've got your gas leak right here," Sam remarked, brandishing his shotgun.

"Get your things and get to the court house," Justin ordered. Indicating the shotgun, he said, "I'll take the gun." The single shot weapon would be of little use against attacking creatures and without his twenty-gauge Sam might not be so inclined to stick around and confront those he thought were depriving him of what was rightfully his.

"Sam," Sheila said, "we have to do what the deputy says."

"Then start packing," Sam said.

As Sheila hurried inside, Justin motioned Dr. Reynolds to join him and Sam outside.

Raising a questioning brow to what he realized was less than the truth, Sam said to Justin, “Exactly what's going on? The old Union Sulfur gas lines were disconnected years ago and there ain't no city lines anywhere near my property. And what about the digging?”

Sam Ramey was not budging until he had the truth, regardless how far-fetched that might be.

“Sam, listen to me,” Justin said, “there are giant bugs tunneling under the town. That's what's digging under The Shed, not someone after your sulfur.”

“Bugs? Yeah, right.”

“We don't have much time,” Justin explained quickly. “This is Dr. Reynolds, a bug expert from LSU. She is helping us find a way to kill these things.”

Sam looked puzzled. “You can't be serious.”

“I'm dead serious,” Justin said. He looked up the hill to where Jet was still raising a ruckus. The fact Sam and the dog were still alive indicated the creatures had not yet surfaced. That at least bought them precious time.

Dr. Reynolds was quick to realize this point also. “You heard digging underground, is that correct?” she asked Sam.

“Damn right I did. There must be a bunch of them down there.”

Dr. Reynolds nodded. “It's possible this is the main nest,” she said to Justin. “I need to have a look.”

Sam was not staying behind. Justin's bug story was poppycock to him and if the deputy didn't take action after witnessing the sinkhole and empty beehives, Sam would get on the phone to his brother, Darryl, in Shreveport. Darryl was a lawyer and a damn good one, far better, in Sam's opinion, than Tommy Crey, Union Town's own attorney.

The trio marched single file up the hard-packed trail, past the kerosene storage tank, Sam leading the way. A fresh breeze caressed late summer blooms of Queen Ann's Lace and pushed back the miasma that hung close to the rock-strewn ground. Distant thunder drew Justin's attention to the southern sky where the soft pastels of dawn played on the towering faces of flat-topped cumulus clouds. Rain before noon, he thought.

"It gets a bit snaky up here," Sam said for Dr. Reynolds's benefit.

"Good habitat," Dr. Reynolds commented, not the least bit intimidated by any unseen reptiles. "What's all this?" she asked, indicating the rusted piping. She had seen the same type of pipe on the corner of Front Street and Sunset Lane, the pipe on which a local church had posted their invitation sign.

"Extraction pipes from the old sulfur mill," Sam said. "Union Sulfur left the town looking like a giant pin cushion. Not much left now but piles of rust."

Dr. Reynolds regarded the weed-carpeted landscape

with entomological interest. She found it highly unusual that she detected no movement or tale-tell sounds of life in the underbrush; no chirping crickets and no vibration of a million insects moving about.

Sam and his entourage gathered around the beehives. Sam lifted the top from one hive and flung it aside. "Look at this," he said. "Empty, all of them." With determined strides, he marched to the building and flipped up the door's latch. A strong gust of wind rattled the structure's tin roof followed by the rumble of thunder.

Sam swung The Shed's door full open. Diffused morning light seeped into its interior, exposing a lone Mason jar teetering on the brink of a gaping hole. Sam gasped in further horror at the sight of the abyss into which his storage cabinet, apiary supplies and centrifuge had all tumbled.

"What the...!" Sam stammered when he beheld the sulfur-crusted chasm.

"They stopped digging," Dr. Reynolds said, straining to hear any sounds from below. "That's not a good sign. It could signal they are entering a reproductive phase. After that, they are likely to leave the nest."

Justin radioed the sheriff. "We found bugs."

"Where? At Sam's place?" came the immediate response.

"Affirmative. They opened a hole under The Shed."

"I'll have Derbigby and crew transport some gas

cylinders to your ten-twenty," the sheriff said. "You and Dr. Reynolds stay well away from the hole."

"Ten-four," Justin said. He scanned the darkening sky and added, "Sheriff, we're in for a pretty big storm."

"So I've seen," the sheriff replied. "It's certainly not going to help matters."

Sam asked, "Exactly what kind of bugs are down there?"

"All we know at this time," Dr. Reynolds said, "is that previously unknown organisms are tunneling under Union Town. Why they are here, we don't know. All we do know is that they are extremely protective of their nest and will kill anyone getting too close."

"Let's get back to the house," Justin said to Dr. Reynolds.

Sam hustled to the side of The Shed and grabbed Jet by his collar, dragging the barking dog back to the house.

Justin halted on the back porch. "You and Sheila get on over to the courthouse," he said to Sam. "State police are coordinating the evacuation."

"I ain't going nowhere," Sam stated bluntly. He shoved Jet into the kitchen and closed the door. "Those things chased away all my bees and are digging up my land. I ain't leaving until this thing is over."

"I've packed our bags," Sheila said to Sam as the group invaded the tiny kitchen. "You can get Jet's stuff."

"I'm staying here," Sam said and before Sheila could

respond he added. "Stay with your sister for a few days."

Sheila said, "What in God's name are you talking about? I'm not leaving you."

"The law needs me to show them where the steam generating plant was located," Sam lied. "Seems one of the old sulfur mill lines is still hooked up to the city line and its leaking. Once I'm not needed anymore here, I'll meet you at Sara's. Take Jet with you."

"What about the digging? Sheila asked.

"What we're hearing is the gas leaking," Sam stated with a straight face.

"Lordy, lordy," Sheila wailed. She rushed into the bedroom to get her packed bags.

"I ain't leaving," Sam repeated to Justin. The deputy nodded. Sam knew the surrounding terrain better than anyone and this knowledge could be of use.

Outside, the gusty wind rattled tall trees as an eerie early twilight descended over the town.

CHAPTER 33

A BROWN EXUDATE OOZED FROM the creature's mouth, pooling under its lifeless body.

"Do you smell that?" Olan asked. "Acetic acid.

"Yes, I do," Dr. Potter replied. He once again probed the animal with forceps, eliciting no more response than he had when he first noticed the purulent vomit.

Malcolm entered the embalming room. "How's your specimen?" he asked.

"I believe it just died," Dr. Potter said.

Five minutes earlier, when Malcolm had gone for coffee, the captive bug had obviously been in distress, its movements lethargic, its eyes no longer able to focus, but it appeared far from death.

"How important is having a live specimen?" Malcolm asked.

"Very important," the entomologist commented. "We'll have to capture another live one. As for this specimen, we'll dissect it and leave the decomposed specimen and the one I got from the factory for the CDC."

Dr. Potter turned the newly deceased specimen belly-up. While the entomologist taped down the creature's legs, Olan brought in his lab's 35 millimeter for stills and a video camera to capture the entire procedure. Snapping photos of the bug's underside from varying angles, he switched on the video and stepped aside to allow Potter room to work.

With pointed scissors, Dr. Potter snipped open the creature's soft underbelly just behind the midsection. He carefully extended the incision along the body's mid-line, over an underlying hard band forming the connection point for its rear legs and ended the surgical opening just forward of its distended stinger.

"Explain your work aloud," Olan said. He placed the mike close to Potter.

"Yes, of course," Dr. Potter said. He pinned back the belly's soft dermal tissue exposing brightly colored viscera; rich yellows, deep greens and brilliant blues.

"Is that blood?" Malcolm asked. White plasma dribbled out, emitting a sharp smell.

"If it is," Dr. Potter said, "this creature's blood has no hemoglobin." He nudged apart each organ with the probe, his hands trembling with excitement.

"Its anatomy looks almost human," Olan remarked. "That yellow tissue, lift it up."

Potter complied.

"That's gland," Olan exclaimed. "It could almost be spleen." Snapping another photo, he added, "The blue sac next to it could be its stomach and the tubular organ attached to that, the esophagus."

"This is way out of my league," Dr. Potter admitted. He exchanged the dissecting tools for Olan's camera.

Olan set to work, intrigued by the familiar anatomy. "I'm following a lumen from what appears to be the stomach," he explained for the benefit of the mike as he traced a tightly coiled tube to an anus at the stinger's base. The quarter inch diameter tube was netted in gray connective tissue and flanked by two green sacs attached to the stinger by narrow tubules. Olan touched the left sac with the probe. A clear venom oozed from the lance.

Olan cut open the cephalothorax to its mouth. Lateral incisions were required to fold back the hardened exoskeleton and expose twin hearts, gumdrop-size organs surrounded by rows of greenish tubules converging at the base of the head. Within this frothy mass, yellow tubes connected the nostrils to a rigid conduit fixed to the body's dorsal wall. A muscular gullet bisected the cephalothorax cavity, confirming the blue sac as the stomach.

Olan opened the stomach and extracted its black contents. He transferred the dark paste to a petri dish under the dissecting microscope and adjusted focus. Carefully, he teased the chime apart. "Fungus and black mold," he said. "It appears these creatures feed on decaying organic matter."

Olan laid down the dissecting tools. "I don't believe either one of us has the technical experience to properly evaluate what we are seeing here beyond what we have done so far," he said.

"Then let's give this one to the CDC also," Potter suggested.

The specimen and its stomach contents were covered with plastic wrap and placed in the refrigerator with its twin.

Olan checked the hour, 6:30 A.M. George Miles would be getting ready for work. "I'll call New Iberia and see if forensics has anything on that body we sent down yesterday," he said to Dr. Potter. He instructed Malcolm to take the entomologist to the foyer where accommodations were more comfortable.

"More coffee?" Malcolm asked Potter as he led the retired professor into the hall. The entomologist was no doubt as tired as he looked.

"I'm fine," Dr. Potter said. "I think I'll step outside for a bit of air."

Dawn's crimson tint highlighted the leading edge of anvil-shaped thunderheads in the southern sky. Dr. Potter took a seat on a nearby bench. His relief over the imminent arrival of federal authorities was tempered by concern that this unique scientific opportunity could become lost in bureaucratic protocol.

Thunder rolled in from the south, punctuated by an

emergency siren and a tinny voice broadcast over a loudspeaker. Dr. Potter wondered how well the evacuation was going.

✕

OLAN SAT AT HIS DESK, feeling the effects of no sleep in over twenty-four hours. He shook off his weariness and picked up the telephone's handset. He dialed Dr. George Miles' home phone number.

"Good morning, Kelly, sorry to call you so early. This is Olan Barnes. Is your father there?"

"Hi Mister Barnes, no, he's not," Dr. Miles' teenage daughter replied as she stifled a yawn. "Daddy left for the office about an hour ago. Do you want to speak with my mom?"

"That's not necessary," Olan said. It would have taken George only a half-hour to get to his office at that time of morning.

"Well, I gotta go. Bye." And Kelly hung up the phone.

Olan immediately called Dr. Miles' office. No answer. He dialed a second number printed on the forensic pathologist's business card, marked – LAB.

"Forensics. John Sweet speaking," said a voice on the other end of the line.

"Doctor Miles, please. This is Olan Barnes."

"Hold on," John replied before yelling, "Hey Doc, you

got a phone call."

An audible click from another extension indicated when Dr. Miles picked up his end, "George Miles," he said.

"George, this is Olan."

"Olan, you couldn't have called at a better time," Miles said. "I just finished going over some lab results from the liquefied body you sent us."

"I have a bit more information also," Olan offered, "but let's hear what you have."

"First thing," Miles said, "the skeletal remains you sent down arrived last night but with everything else, we haven't had time to look at them. As for the dissolved body, preliminary test results from yesterday kept my two best technicians working on additional samples and rechecks all night.

"It appears our initial conjecture was correct. There *is* an enzyme involved but it's not anything I can find in the literature. This thing has one hundred twenty sub-units."

"Is that big?" Olan asked, not being well-versed in the finer details of enzyme structure.

"Big?" Dr. Miles bleated. "It's huge! The most complex enzyme we know of is only sixty sub-units. This one's one twenty, twice the size. We're talking about a whole new class of enzyme, a whole new everything.

"And there's one more thing," Dr. Miles said. "This particular enzyme is non-specific, it breaks down all proteins and fats, indeed anything organic. One gram of this stuff could dissolve a horse. It's an amazing molecule."

"I have some other amazing information for you," Olan said, quickly going over the events of the previous night and the dead specimen's physiology.

"It looks like you have a real situation there," Dr. Miles said.

"Yes, we do," Olan remarked.

"I wish I had the time to come up." Dr. Miles said. "Keep me informed on any new developments. Meanwhile, we'll start examining the skeletal remains for any further information it can offer."

"Positively," Olan said. "Thanks for the help." He hung up his end and immediately his phone rang. He lifted the handset. Sheriff Maxwell was on the other end of the line.

"Olan, we've started evacuating the town," the sheriff said. "Justin located more bugs under Sam Ramey's property. It could be the main part of the nest. Derbigby is on his way over there with a load of gas and other cylinders are being staged at the landfill. I need you to take Dr. Potter over to Sam's place immediately. According to Dr. Reynolds, there's a good chance these things are preparing to leave the nest. I want confirmation of that."

"What about the Feds?" Olan asked.

"I just spoke with the governor," Sheriff Maxwell said. "Apparently there is still disagreement about jurisdiction between the CDC and the military. It's not clear exactly what to expect but from what I gather, someone from the Feds should be here in a few hours."

"Let's hope we can wait that long."

"That's why I need Potter over at Sam's place. We're still under orders to wait for the Feds but I can't let these things leave the nest."

Olan hung up the phone and found Dr. Potter seated outside. He explained to the retired entomologist Justin's discovery and the sheriff's orders for him to go to Sam Ramey's house.

A contrary breeze shook a nearby stand of tall pines, sending pine needles scurrying down Sunset Lane. A single bolt of lightning cut a jagged path across the face of black clouds. Twenty seconds later, thunder.

CHAPTER 34

"THAT'S THE PLACE." ANDRE LOUX pointed to Sam Ramey's house. Andre rode shotgun in Allen Derbigby's service van loaded with an impressive arsenal of gas cylinders, hoses and nozzles. Franklin Johnson had relocated to the landfill site with three reserve cylinders of fumigants and a support team of state police and emergency squad members. Reg Vaughn had a similar cache of fumigants and support personnel at the Dubois site. Tom Slyger provided support at the factory site.

Derbigby swung into Sam's driveway and pulled up sharply behind Justin's cruiser. The deputy and Sam Ramey emerged from the house. Lightning flashed.

"Where do you want this equipment?" Derbigby asked.

"Around back," Justin said. "Follow the dirt track to a wooden shed."

"And watch out for my bee hives," Sam said.

Sheriff Maxwell arrived with Dr. Jenkins. Olan and Dr. Potter followed close behind.

The new arrivals gathered at The Shed.

"Is this another entrance?" the sheriff asked the two

entomologists.

"This wasn't intentionally opened by these creatures," Dr. Reynolds commented. "They excavated a cavity under The Shed that caused the ground to collapse."

"But this is linked to the main part of the nest, correct?" the sheriff asked.

"I believe it is," Dr. Reynolds said, "but we haven't seen any bugs yet. This excavation could be an unused chamber."

"Mister Derbigby," the sheriff asked, "what is your plan?"

"We'll stage a couple of cylinders in The Shed with delivery hoses into the opening," Derbigby said. "If the main part of the nest is no deeper underground than this chamber, then injection will be possible. Exactly how we'll find the nest, I don't know."

Sheriff Maxwell regarded the threatening clouds. "Let's get things set up before this storm hits," he ordered. "Mister Derbigby, you handle this. Doctor Reynolds, you are to monitor things here and let me know if there are any changes. Doctor Potter, I'd like you and Doctor Jenkins to go with me to the landfill and Dubois sites to evaluate the situation there."

Doff's voice broke over the radioed. "Sheriff, we're behind Red Dot, where Billy was. The area is clear, just some rabbit bones and a three-foot patch of freshly exposed ground. If that is where Billy fell through, it's been resealed."

"Any sign of another entrance hole?"

"No sir," Doff responded. "What about Pete? I can probably get over there before this storm breaks."

"Ten-four. See what he or Clee knows and then get back to the factory."

"Ten-four."

"Are there any questions?" the sheriff asked his team.

Joel and Lonnie hiked up the hill to the gathering.

"Joel," Justin said, "you and Lonnie are supposed to be assisting at the landfill."

"Sheriff, there's another hole, in The Swamp," Lonnie said.

"We know about it," the sheriff said. "Behind Red Dot Market. It's no longer open."

"That may not be the hole Chief Gallo found," Lonnie replied.

"Gallo?" Sheriff Maxwell asked, shocked Gallo had finally surfaced after disappearing with Mayor Brandon. Not having either the mayor or his cohort around to aggravate the situation seemed the best policy to the sheriff but now he realized this had been a mistake. The mayor was not one to turn down an opportunity to strut his feathers at the expense of others, especially if that other person happened to be Sheriff Arthur Maxwell.

Lonnie knew he had messed up, big time. "Sheriff, I'm sorry. My uncle asked me to keep him informed about what's been happening."

"And?" the sheriff asked.

"I told him about Amory Planchard's boys finding something at Maurice Dubois' place and about Wreckerman," Lonnie confessed. "After that, he and Chief Gallo talked to Sammy and Seth."

"Why would your uncle set up his own investigation?" the sheriff asked pointlessly, knowing full well Mayor Brandon was up to no good.

"My uncle plans to catch one of those bugs alive," Lonnie confessed. He shrugged. "I have no idea why."

"Where is your uncle now?" the sheriff asked. "What about Gallo?"

"I don't know," Lonnie said, "but I do know Chief Gallo and the guys who were with him found a hole in The Swamp, over where those two bums live."

The sheriff couldn't believe what he was hearing. "Who was with Gallo?" he demanded, anxiety rising as quickly as his temper.

"Trey Frazier, Frank Dyer and... I'm not sure if Tommy Bendict was with them or not."

"When was the last time you spoke to your uncle?"

"A couple hours ago, I guess."

"Doff," the sheriff radioed, "Chief Gallo and at least two civilians could be in The Swamp. There could be another nest entrance there also. Confirm and report."

"Ten-four."

"Joel, you and Lonnie might as well stay here," the sheriff said, "and Lonnie, give your uncle a call. If he is home, I want to talk to him. If he's not, then call anyone who might know his whereabouts."

"Yes sir." Lonnie said.

The sheriff asked Dr. Reynolds, "How many other openings could we be dealing with?"

"Even as unusual as this organism is," Dr. Reynolds said, "I would not expect multiple access points. Every opening to the outside increases the colony's vulnerability. From what we have seen so far, there are only two confirmed entrances, the one in the factory and the other at the landfill. As for the other holes, Mister Dubois intentionally dug into the main tunnel and the opening here formed when the ground collapsed. We won't know about any other holes until Officer Green reports in."

"Mr. Derbigby, do we have enough gas if Doff finds another opening?"

"I believe so." Derbigby said.

Officer Green radioed again. "Sheriff, we're at the place where Pete and Clee live," he said. "It's deserted… hold on."

A long moment followed.

"Sheriff, there's some kind of dome. It's about nine feet in diameter and three feet high."

Dr. Reynolds asked the sheriff for his radio. "Officer Green," she transmitted, "can you tell what material the dome is made from?"

"It's yellow. Looks and smells like sulfur," Doff replied.

"Can you tell if it's sitting on top of a hole, a nest entrance?" Dr. Reynolds asked.

"I don't see any evidence of a hole. The dome is smooth as glass but too thick to see through. Did those creatures build it?"

Dr. Potter said to Dr. Reynolds, "They're capping the nest." And to the sheriff he said, "We need to find out what's happening at the other sites."

A radio call to the state troopers assigned to the landfill and Dubois farm and to Sergeant Benoit at the factory indicated there was no activity at any of these sites and the strong sulfurous stench at all three locations had abated.

"What does all this mean?" Sheriff Maxwell demanded of both entomologists.

"These creatures appear to be going through a transition," Dr. Reynolds said.

"Most likely, reproduction," Dr. Potter added. "That's why the nest is being sealed off."

"Do we need to rethink our strategy?" the sheriff asked.

"I don't believe we need a total rethink," Dr. Reynolds said, "just an adjustment, stage fumigants where Officer Green found the dome. That is likely the intended exit point."

"We can transfer a couple of cylinders from the factory," Derbigby said.

"That won't be possible," Justin spoke up. "Everything would have to be hauled in on foot and this storm will turn The Swamp into a quagmire."

"I need suggestions," the sheriff said to no one in particular.

"I believe we have time, sheriff," Dr. Potter said. "This is a fairly advanced organism which is likely to have an extended reproduction cycle. Our preparations at this point should be adequate. Once the Feds are on-site, we'll have additional support and a lot more resources. I suggest we maintain our current set-up, get cylinders to Officer Green's location as soon as possible and continue to monitor all of the sites."

"Then let's do it," the sheriff said, "but I want it clearly understood that if there is the slightest indication these bugs are going to leave the nest before the Feds arrive, we use every means possible to stop them."

Nods all around.

Sheriff Maxwell radioed Sergeant Benoit. "Blare, increase surveillance at the landfill, the Dubois site and all of the factories."

"Ten-four," the sergeant responded.

"Dispatch," the sheriff radioed.

"Yes sir, sheriff," Doris said. She had just replaced

René.

"Have you heard from Mayor Brandon or Police Chief Gallo?"

"I haven't," Doris said, "but hold on. René is still here."

René took the mike. "The chief came in just after midnight and collected some things from his desk. He said he was assisting you. I haven't heard from or seen him since."

"Doris, see if you can find either the mayor or Gallo. I also need you to track down Frank Dyer, Trey Frazier and Tommy Bendict."

"Will do," Doris answered.

Doff radioed again. "Sheriff, we have another human skeleton."

"Ten-four," the sheriff said. "I need you to stay there and monitor that dome. Do you have cover from the storm?"

"Not much but enough."

Coin-size raindrops pelted the dry ground. Pines swayed and oaks creaked.

"Doctor Potter, Doctor Jenkins" the sheriff said, "let's get over to the landfill and Dubois sites. I need confirmation they have indeed been sealed. Justin, keep me appraised of things here."

The sheriff and his entourage made a bee-line for his car.

Joel, Lonnie and Sam trotted to the house. Derbigby opened the van's rear door. Justin and Dr. Reynolds climbed inside. Derbigby slipped into the driver's seat and reversed the vehicle closer to the shed as a gray wall of rain swept across Old Simmesport Highway, obscuring all beyond it.

"That looks close enough," Justin said to Derbigby when the van rolled within six feet of the outbuilding. Derbigby switched off the vehicle's engine and hurried to the van's rear. He pulled a valve wrench from a tool box before unlatching the restraining strap for five cylinders of methyl bromide. He and Justin wrestled two of the cylinders from the van and hauled them and their hoses into The Shed.

Jagged lightning sliced through bruised clouds. The air was alive with Saint Elmo's fire. Sheets of rain from water pregnant clouds raced through Union Town.

"Get back in the van," Derbigby yelled to Justin over the din of the rain. "I can handle this. As soon as the rain slacks off, we'll stage the other three cylinders behind The Shed."

Justin hustled back to the van and jumped in. He swung its rear doors closed, The Shed visible through the van's rear window.

The torrent of rain settled into a steady downpour, puddling in low areas and running in brown rivulets to muddy pools in Sam's backyard. Constant lightning flashes and thunder kept nerves on edge.

“Justin, are things set up there?” Sheriff Maxwell’s voice broke through hissing static.

“Almost,” Justin responded.

“Ten-four,” the sheriff said. “We located the mayor.”

CHAPTER 35

MAYOR BRANDON'S POSSIBLE WHEREABOUTS HAD been offered to Sheriff Maxwell by Trey Frazier, a previous member of the mayor's clandestine team. With a family to worry about, Trey had more important things to deal with than participate in the mayor's personal vendetta.

Sheriff Maxwell had flagged down Trey as the self-employed auto-mechanic drove past the courthouse in his restored, early model pick-up with his wife, Jody, and their three children crammed into the cab.

"You looking for Mayor Brandon?" Trey asked the sheriff as the lawman pulled his cruiser alongside his vehicle.

"Have you seen him?" the sheriff yelled over rumbling thunder. He nodded greeting to Mrs. Frazier, a thin-faced haggard woman much older looking than her thirty-six years.

"Not since eleven last night," Trey told the lawman. "Have you tried Coleman's? Dick Driskoll showed up last night bitching about one of your deputies closing him down. Supposed to have found one of those bugs at his diner. The mayor was planning on catching a live one."

"So nobody went underground?" Sheriff Maxwell questioned.

"Frank, Tommy and I aren't fools," Trey snarled. "And Gallo ain't got the balls."

"Do you have somewhere to go until this is over?" the sheriff asked.

"I'm taking Jody and the kids to my brother's place in Krotz Springs," Trey said. "I'll be back to help out."

"You best stay in Krotz Springs with your family until all this is over," the sheriff said.

"I ain't letting no over-sized June-bug chase me out of my home," Trey stated. "I'm coming back. Some the other guys are already over at the industrial park to help out." He looked to the dark sky, adding, "We're in for a real gully-washer."

"Get on to Krotz Springs," the sheriff said, "and when you get back here, report to Officer Benoit, state police."

Trey put his truck into gear and sped away.

"Let's see what Mister Driskoll knows," the sheriff said to Drs. Potter and Jenkins.

Sheriff Maxwell made the four-block drive to Coleman's Diner. Mayor Brandon had made a poor attempt at concealing his car at the rear of the double-wide. The sheriff pulled up to the front door and the trio hurried inside just as the heavens opened up.

Lonnie's broadcast voice greeted the sheriff from a

walkie-talkie left atop the diner's service counter. No one was in attendance.

"Help," came Dick Driskoll's anxious voice. "Back here."

The sheriff moved quickly but carefully to the storage room's doorway.

Mayor Brandon and Dick Driskoll cowered behind a barrier of corrugated boxes wedged between cabinets and sidewall. Both men looked exhausted, the mayor subdued.

"Don't come in!" Dick cried. Two bugs perched on shelving along the opposing wall. The creatures' stubby antenna shifted with each new sound but there was something different about these bugs. Their exoskeletons had faded to a dull brown color and their cornea were milky-white. They still looked menacing enough but something was seriously different with them.

"Get us out of here," Mayor Brandon demanded of the sheriff.

"Where's Gallo?" the sheriff asked.

"How the hell should I know?" Mayor Brandon responded. "The son-of-a-bitch was right behind us. Dammit, hurry up and get us out of here!"

The sheriff drew his pistol.

"Don't shoot," Dr. Potter said. "This may be our last chance to catch live specimens."

"Shoot the damn things," Brandon ordered, feeling

more himself with the sheriff's gun in attendance.

Dr. Potter ignored the mayor. "Do you have any way of heating this back room?" he asked Driskoll.

"What the hell do you want to do that for?" Dick asked.

"Just answer the man," Mayor Brandon barked, having already heard how the bugs had been dealt with in the factory. "Can you heat this place or not?"

Dick was taken aback at the mayor's rebuff. "Yeah, there's a portable heater under the sink," he said.

Dr. Potter spoke in a slow but urgent voice, loud enough to be heard over thunder and rain. "Without making any sudden moves, I want you to open the cabinet and take out the heater."

"The bugs," Dick said with a look of alarm. "I know what happens if I get stung."

"Just get the heater, dammit!" Mayor Brandon spat.

Dick blew out his disdain for being handed this dangerous job. Keeping a cautious eye on the two creatures, he slipped out from behind the barricade just far enough to hook a finger around a cabinet door handle. He swung it open. Inside, greasy rags shrouded half-filled bottles of cleaning compounds stacked around the electric heater.

Dick carefully set the rags and bottles aside and pulled out the heater, never taking his eyes off the twin bugs. Setting the heater on the floor, he returned to whatever protection the corrugated boxes offered.

"An outlet," Dr. Potter said.

"Behind the freezer," Dick answered, "and I ain't moving no damn freezer."

"Do you have an extension cord?" Sheriff Maxwell asked.

Dick said, "Under the front counter, somewhere."

Dr. Potter quickly found the thirty foot electrical cord. He straightened its prongs and inserted it into a wall socket above the grill. He played out the cord to the storage room. With sufficient slack in hand, he tossed Dick the cable's free end. The sudden activity caused one bug to flare its wings, threatening flight.

"You're going to get us killed," exclaimed Mayor Brandon.

Dr. Potter realized the mayor was right. "Plug in the heater," the entomologist said. "Then turn it on high."

Nervous sweat beaded Dick Driskoll's brow as he reached out beyond the makeshift shelter again and picked up the heater's cord. He connected the unit to the extension cord and twisted the thermostat's knob, bringing the unit to life.

"I'm going to leave this door cracked open," Dr. Potter said to the two prisoners. "As soon as you see the creatures' eyes constrict get out of the room as fast as you can."

Potter smiled, anticipating he would soon have two more specimens in questionable health but at least alive.

CHAPTER 36

DERBIGBY APPEARED AT THE SHED'S open doorway. As Justin swung open the van's rear door in preparation for the pest controller's return, the gray twilight burst apart with a brilliant flash and an instant thunderclap. A high-topped pine towering above The Shed exploded as lightning coursed down its trunk, sending wooden splinters showering over the outbuilding and trembling the ground as if the earth shivered in fright. Derbigby leaped back inside.

Within the van, a manual pressure sprayer toppled over and the tool box slid forward. The view of Sam Ramey's house through the windshield was replaced with that of the rain-soaked ground.

"We're sinking," Dr. Reynolds screamed. A ghostly yellow vapor rose around the vehicle as its front end disappeared under ground. The vehicle's steep angle tossed its two occupants forward and the three cylinders of methyl bromide broke from their mooring, plowing through scattered gear and pinning Dr. Reynolds to a front seat. The creaking van bucked and disappeared underground.

⨯

ALLEN DERBIGBY CRINGED AT THE thunderclap so near the hairs on his arms stood up. The heart of the storm was now directly overhead, the wind, rain and lightning unrelenting. Derbigby moved to the gaping hole, his fear of the bugs rising like the deluge outside. Erratic lightning illuminated the interior of the wide cavity encased in sulfur. To his relief, he observed no movement, no bugs.

Derbigby laid a gas cylinder on its side and attached a hose to its valve. He tossed the hose's bitter end into the cavern, a feeble attempt at controlling this situation and one he hoped it would not be needed.

When Dr. Reynolds scream, Derbigby ran outside into the downpour in time to see the van sucked underground.

CHAPTER 37

THE SERVICE VAN STRUCK BOTTOM with a tremendous crash, tossing Justin and Dr. Reynolds about like loose cannon. A cylinder of methyl bromide was catapulted forward, barely missing Dr. Reynolds head, and toppled onto the passenger side floorboard. Through the gaping hole above rain and mud battered the vehicle.

Justin and Dr. Reynolds extracted themselves from jumbled equipment, their hearts pounding from their predicament. The van's rear door was awry, having been ripped from its bottom hinge and leaving them exposed to bug attack.

Justin moved to the open doorway. Light seeping through the aperture above revealed muddy rainwater racing along the cavern floor in an increasing grade.

Derbigby appeared at the hole. "Are you all right?" he shouted down. "I'll get rope."

Justin signaled their condition. He ducked back inside the van.

"We have to get on the roof," he said to Dr. Reynolds.

"Wait," Dr. Reynolds said. She pointed beyond the van to two, pale-brown bugs clinging to the sulfur-crusted ceiling twenty feet away. The sentries' antennae flicked as they advanced but their movements were awkward and unexpectedly cautious. Entrance into the nest should have marked her and Justin for immediate destruction.

Justin drew his pistol. "Look at their eyes," he commented when the bugs moved into more revealing light. Each bugs' eyes were cloudy-white.

"They can't see us," Dr. Reynolds said, unsure if these creatures were suffering from disease or some normal physical change.

Justin holstered his pistol and turned his attention to their immediate task while keeping a wary eye on the two bugs.

The mangled door offered a foothold for Justin to boost himself waist level to the vehicle's roof. Rain and debris from above splattered over him. He hoisted his six-foot frame up searching for a handhold. The ruined door shook in protest to this further abuse. With a sharp creaking sound, its top hinge snapped from its mounting and the door crashed to the floor, skidding away like a runaway sled on wet ice.

Dr. Reynolds grabbed Justin's arm, trying to save the lawman from the murky depths.

"I can't hold you," Dr. Reynolds yelled, struggling with Justin's weight and her own precarious balance.

Justin had no footing on the slick floor. He fell

against the van's rear bumper causing the vehicle's wheels to break from their anchorage on a backward slide. Clinging to Dr. Reynolds' arm and the van's bumper, Justin caught a glimpse of Allen Derbigby's terrified face staring down at him as they slipped into darkness.

With Dr. Reynolds help, Justin hurled himself inside the van as the vehicle skated five hundred feet through the corridor and broke out into an impressive cavern filled with an eerie, greenish phosphorescence. The van shifted direction ninety degrees on an increasingly steep grade, bounced over an edge and carved ruts in the sulfur-crusted flooring as it descended into a lower, stadium-size grotto where it halted on a more even keel.

Dr. Reynolds coughed. The noxious smell of sulfur and stench of rotting vegetation was nearly overpowering. Above ground lightning strikes rumbled through the earth like aftershocks of an earthquake.

"Where are we?" Justin questioned in astonishment. All around them lifeless bodies of decomposing creatures littered the floor. High overhead, thick-shafted stalactites of phosphorescent brimstone swept from a honeycombed ceiling and fused along the back wall into an elongated sphere towering one hundred feet above the cluttered flooring. A sulfur extraction pipe pierced the ceiling between van and giant casing like a prison bar, ending a foot above the floor.

"We're in the heart of the nest," Dr. Reynolds said

with more awe than fear. She leaned out of the van's open door for a better look. Within the huge sphere, hundreds of pale white creatures clustered around a central core, waving their antennae in rhythmic palpitations. Unlike the bugs seen before, these individuals had smaller eyes and no wings. They worked continuously, collecting ivory-colored capsules from one end of an undulating sac and ferrying the fist-size nodes through a rear portal and darkness beyond. Above this activity a webbed sling hung from the orb's apex cradled a brown globe, ten times larger than those being carried away.

"That's the queen!" Dr. Reynolds said of the membranous sac. "She's laying eggs."

The queen was an oddly-shaped version of her attending offspring but a hundred times larger. Her short stubby legs hung limply at her side, mouth agape as she accepted dark globules of nourishment from her cortege. Prompted by strokes to her forty-foot long body, her eyes transfixed on some distant point as peristaltic contractions within her membranous abdomen conveyed ripened ova to her waiting attendants.

"That larger egg hanging from the top must be the future queen," Dr. Reynolds said of the dangling orb. "All the others will likely hatch into ordinary workers."

"So the colony *is* growing," Justin said.

"Growing and dying," Dr. Reynolds remarked. "These dead workers are the soldiers, being replaced with a new generation. That's why they sealed the other openings and why those bugs where the van fell through didn't look well. They are dying too."

"So most of the bugs guarding the nest are dead?" Justin asked.

"I don't think so," Dr. Reynolds said. "That would leave the nest totally unprotected. There are likely soldiers guarding the main tunnels."

"Why haven't they detected us?" Justin asked.

"The rumbling from the lightning strikes must have covered-up our entrance," Dr. Reynolds replied. "It is also likely those white workers don't have well-developed eyesight or sensitive antenna."

"Then let's get out while we can," Justin said. "The sheriff has to know what we found. This may be our best chance for wiping out these things once and for all."

"I have to get photos," Dr. Reynolds said. She rummaged through the scattered gear. "I saw a camera in here somewhere."

"There's no time," Justin said, amazed at Dr. Reynolds total lack of urgency.

Dr. Reynolds wasn't listening. "There should be enough phosphorescent light to photograph without a flash."

Justin grabbed the entomologist's arm. "Forget the pictures," he ordered. He slipped out of the van onto the polished floor. "We're getting out of here."

"But this may be the only chance to get photos of this phase of the colony's cycle," Dr. Reynolds insisted.

Joel Dubbonet's voice crackled over Justin's radio. "... you read me?"

"Where are you, Joel?" Justin responded in a whisper. He turned down his radio's volume.

"We're in the tunnel, where the van fell through," Joel replied. "Are you two all right?"

"Affirmative."

"Are there bugs?"

"Affirmative," Justin radioed, leaving out the details. "Be careful, there are two up where you are."

"We don't see any," Joel responded. "Do you need assistance?"

"Stay where you are," Justin said. "Let the sheriff know there's a queen and she's laying eggs. Maybe Derbigby can bring the fumigant down here."

"You have to get out first," Joel said.

"We're coming out now," Justin said. "Are you sure there are no bugs up there? We saw two near the hole."

Allen Derbigby's voice came over the air. "Justin," he said, "when the van started to slide I saw..."

A creature leaped at Justin from the vehicle's roof. Too weak to fly, it swerved mid-air and crash-landed inside the van. Dr. Reynolds smashed the giant bug with a hammer from the tool box.

Jumping from the van armed with the hammer, she

batted the second creature from the van's roof and Justin stomped on its head.

"Let's go," Justin urged.

CHAPTER 38

THE DAMP CLAY-PAN OFFERED UNCERTAIN footing up the furrow carved out by the van and slippery scabs of sulfur flooring made the only avenue of escape even more precarious. One false step would send the unfortunate trespasser slip-sliding downward back into the nest.

Justin and Dr. Reynolds picked their way up the skewed path, testing each step, ever vigilant to detection from within the orb. Rumbling from lightning strikes had faded with the storm's passing, no longer covering up any sounds from the intruders and putting their nerves further on edge.

"I have you spotted," Joel radioed Justin. A flashlight's bright beam revealed the emergency squad member's position above. "Do you need any…? Christ have mercy!" he exclaimed upon beholding the frightening sight below. He fixed his light's beam on activity within the sulfur bubble.

"Turn off that light," Justin radioed anxiously. He glanced over his shoulder, instantly welded in his tracks. Alerted by the probing light, the queen shifted her massive head to focus on the movement below. Her lucent eyes dilated like an alert feline and raising her head, jaws agape, she emitted a low resonating sound that turned Justin's blood to ice.

A loud clamor rose from behind the great sulfur ball. The darkness beyond heaved as if a living entity. Hordes of hissing bugs swarmed forth into the main chamber, their brown bodies carpeting their dead nest-mates, eyes latched onto the intruders. Unable to fly, these obvious fledglings ascended the walls in a swift flanking maneuver.

"The van," Justin yelled to Dr. Reynolds.

Justin and Dr. Reynolds scampered back to the van. With its rear door stripped away the vehicle offered little protection but it was their only refuge, the only point where the attack could be fought on only one front.

The first wave of bugs hit the van with wings flared and claws ripping at tires and frame. They swarmed around the vehicle like locust, piling atop each other and threatening to breach the top of the van's bumper.

Justin fired his pistol into the attackers, doing little to slow their progress. In desperation he rolled a cylinder of methyl bromide out of the doorway. The heavy container crushed the carpet of bugs piling up behind the van and bowled over scores more but another wave quickly replaced their fallen comrades. Justin followed this with the second cylinder and then the third.

Dr. Reynolds whacked a stray bug with the hammer,

keeping others at bay with well-aimed swings. For all her and Justin's efforts though, it was clear their position would be overrun.

A wild, whooping yell burst forth from the cavern's upper level accompanied with the boom of heavy weapons. Joel and Sam Ramey charged down the carved out channel firing twelve-gauge shotguns into the attacking swarm. Buckshot rained down, ripping holes in ranks that were rapidly filled.

"Come and get us!" Joel shouted.

With amazing swiftness the bugs hurled themselves in-mass up the grade at Joel and Sam, too many to be halted by the two men's gallant endeavor. But the bugs had been lured from the van buying Justin and Dr. Reynolds precious time.

Sam and Joel fell back, guns blazing, bug parts and white goo splattering walls and flooring.

"Hold them," Joel yelled to his partner. He fumbled cartridges from his pocket. Shoving fresh rounds into his gun's magazine, he fired another volley. An uprooted sulfur slab shifted unexpectedly underfoot and Joel went down, an easy target.

Sam charged the bugs' advancing line, firing his weapon as fast as he could pump it.

A bug leaped onto Joel's right foot. Its claws pierced his boots and dug deep into flesh. As the bug's stinger distended, dripping with poison, Joel turned his weapon on himself and pulled its trigger. The bug disintegrated along with half of Joel's foot.

With Sam supporting Joel, the two men retreated into the upper chamber and headed for the exit hole. There was nothing more they could do.

CHAPTER 39

THE BUGS RENEWED THEIR ASSAULT on the van. No avenue of escape remained for Dr. Reynolds and Justin. Since the attack began, the creatures had darkened in color, nearer to the individuals at the factory site, indicating their exoskeletons were hardening. Their ability to take flight was imminent.

Dr. Reynolds tossed her insignificant weapon aside. It would take more than a miracle to save them now and a miracle was not to be found in that hammer.

Turning her attention to the sulfur encasement, Dr. Reynolds realized the ability of this queen to direct her subjects verified something more than just instinctive behavior. These creatures were controlled by a lone sovereign, proving that at least the queen had some degree of cognitive thought.

An idea sprang into Dr. Reynolds' mind, an inspiration born from her knowledge of animal behavior and one that just might alter the inevitable. "Shoot the sphere," she told Justin. "Shoot the top, near the large egg but don't hit it."

"I only have three shots left," Justin warned.

"Shoot!"

Justin squeezed off a shot. The bullet shattered a pan-size hole in the orb, blowing apart smaller eggs being carried to safety. Greenish liquid dribbled from the broken ovum, stirring the attendants into a fury. The queen let out a horrible hiss. Her troops hesitated, uncertain of her intentions.

"You don't like that, do you?" Dr. Reynolds shouted as the queen's eyes met hers. "Shoot again," she said to Justin, "but let her get a good look at your gun. Aim closer to the large egg."

Justin fired again. The bullet's force rattled the cradled egg.

The queen tossed her head in anger. She focused on the figures within the vehicle and their peculiar weapon pointed directly at her unborn heiresses. Emitting a series of low-pitched wails, her troops hissed displeasure at not being able to finish the attack. The throng fell back, ready for the signal to renew their offensive.

"What's happening?" Justin asked.

"Species preservation," Dr. Reynolds breathed with heartfelt relief. "I was right, that largest egg is a new queen, no doubt vital to colony survival. Since this queen launched the attack, I figured she could do the same for a retreat."

The wings of the stifled fledglings had acquired a glossy sheen indicating they had sufficiently dried to enable flight and though their aerial skills were still underdeveloped, the bugs appeared to be quick learners as they took to the air.

"We've got to make a run for it," Justin said. Within the great sphere royal attendants gnawed at the webbed cradle in order to free the egg and move it to safety.

A bright flash of orange-red luminescence flicked across the upper chamber. There were gunshots. Reinforcements were advancing through the tunnel.

"Justin, can you make it out?" Sheriff Maxwell's voice came over his walkie-talkie.

"We're going to try," Justin responded.

"We're burning the bugs in the tunnel with kerosene and shooting others," the sheriff radioed over frantic voices. "Derbigby says there is an oxygen mask in the van. In a wooden chest. Do you see it?"

The wooden cabinet Sheriff Maxwell spoke of was bolted to the van's side frame, its door padlocked. Justin smashed in the cabinet's door with a powerful kick. Inside he found a box of latex gloves, bottles of Phostoxin tablets, assorted tools and a self-contained breathing apparatus. He pulled out the yellow air cylinder with its attached pressure hose, regulator and mask.

"We can toss down another SCBA," the sheriff said. "After that you can discharge methyl bromide."

"Negative" Justin radioed. "We have no cylinders."

"Hold on," the sheriff transmitted.

"Justin," Derbigby radioed, "you have three cylinders."

"Not anymore," Justin responded.

"Justin," the sheriff asked, "what do you suggest?"

"How much kerosene do you have?"

"About one hundred fifty gallons but you need another SCBA."

Without commenting on the obvious, Justin said, "Between the bugs and us there's an extraction pipe protruding down through the ceiling. Sam should know where it is up top."

"Go on."

"The pipe ends just above the floor. Toss me down a loaded shotgun and another SCBA. Pour as much kerosene as you can down the pipe. When I tell you, drop in a flare."

A pause.

"We're doing it now," the sheriff radioed.

"You need to get topside," Justin said to Dr. Reynolds.

"I'm staying," the entomologist told Justin. "That queen is up to something."

CHAPTER 40

LONNIE NETHERO LIFTED HIS OXYGEN mask and wiped his brow. "Tell the sheriff the upper level is clear," he called up to Dr. Potter.

Potter hurried off.

Lonnie and Reggie Vaughn had completed a final sweep through the upper chamber, incinerating bugs with kerosene loaded into pressurized sprayers. A handheld flare set the flammable liquid alight and a fire extinguisher snuffed out the flames before the sulfur lining ignited. The small amount of sulfur that had caught fire created an atmosphere laced with acrid, foul smelling sulfur dioxide.

"KEEP IT COMING," THE SHERIFF shouted. Arriving volunteers joined the human supply line of state police and emergency-squad personnel conveying buckets and jerry cans of kerosene from Sam's storage tank to the rusty extraction pipe atop the hill.

Sam hacked the last of the undergrowth from around

the casing and tossed aside his machete. He took the first bucket of kerosene and tipped it in. "How much?" he asked Sheriff Maxwell. He handed off the empty bucket and accepted a second.

"Just keep pouring," the sheriff answered.

Sheriff Maxwell returned to The Shed where Stan Wilton and his firemen had assembled a Scott-breathing unit and flares. The sheriff loaded a shotgun before mounting the ladder. He called down to Reginald, "I'm passing you down some gear."

"Sheriff," State Policeman Benoit said, hurrying up from Sam's house. "I just spoke with a Doctor Kell, with NASA. The nest is not to be disturbed. He said they'll be arriving in about an hour."

"I'll try to remember his request," the sheriff said as he handed Reginald the SCBA and flares. Lonnie accepted the shotgun.

Officer Benoit nodded understanding. "What can I do?"

"Check how Sam is doing with the kerosene."

Benoit hustled off.

"Stan, I need you to prepare your men to go underground," the sheriff said to the fire chief. The sheriff climbed down the ladder. The air within the excavation was laden with the rank odor of rotten eggs and kerosene.

"The kerosene's going in," the sheriff radioed his chief deputy. "Do you have a visual?"

"Negative," Justin replied.

"I have your gear," the sheriff said.

"Toss it down from the upper chamber. Be careful, these bugs are really agitated."

"Sheriff!" Benoit called down. "The pipe is full. It's not draining."

"How many buckets went in?"

"Twenty-one."

CHAPTER 41

ACTIVITY WITHIN THE GIANT ORB had not ceased and though the task of moving the royal spawn to safety was unfamiliar, therefore slow for the creatures, each passing minute brought Justin and Dr. Reynolds closer to an inevitable fate when the bugs would turn their attention back to them.

Justin's plan was proving a blind alley. No kerosene had yet appeared from the extraction pipe, indicating blockage between ground level and its lower end.

Justin's radio crackled to life again. "I'm in the main chamber," Sheriff Maxwell radioed. "I can see the van. Do you still want to try this?"

"Affirmative," Justin replied. He was painfully aware the added disturbance of tossing the gear down could bring an abrupt end to the standoff but he saw no other option.

A cloth-covered bundle arced through the air from the shadows above and landed with a thud amid bug carcasses.

"Can you reach it?" the sheriff radioed.

"Affirmative," Justin responded.

Justin handed Dr. Reynolds his pistol. “Keep this aimed at that egg. You have one shot left so whatever you do, make it count.”

“You need to hurry,” Dr. Reynolds urged.

Justin exited the van through the driver’s door. With a wary eye on the uneasy army, he slipped free of the vehicle and made his way toward the lifesaving gear fifteen feet away.

The giant matriarch was not missing a thing. With her royal eggs almost to safety, she was unwilling to give further ground. She raised her massive body and emitted another yowl. Her minions rushed forward.

Justin gave up his attempt and scrambling back to the van, jumped in the driver’s seat. He slammed the door closed.

The earth vibrated under the bug army’s unchecked advance. Holding her aim on the royal egg, Dr. Reynolds snatched up the hammer, unwilling to die without a struggle.

Justin cranked the van’s engine. “Hold on!” he yelled. He jammed the vehicle’s transmission into first gear and stomped on the accelerator. Wheels spun as Justin cut doughnuts into the sulfur flooring, slinging chunks of brimstone and earth and knocking back the advancing bugs.

Dr. Reynolds laid down the pistol and wedged herself in the van’s rear, the hammer at the ready. Justin’s spinning, erratic driving was keeping the bugs from gaining entry but for how long?

Hundreds of bugs were crushed under the vehicle's tires. Those nimble of enough to fly hurled themselves into the van's windows and paneled sides. Dr. Reynolds slashed at the ones attempting to gain entry from the rear.

Upon witnessing the possible escape of the invaders, the queen produced another shrill yowl that brought thousands of immature reinforcements from the inner darkness.

"I can't hold them back any longer," Dr. Reynolds screamed. More bugs had achieved flight.

The van bounced through a deep rut and spun wildly, careening off the great sphere. Dr. Reynolds was thrown against the van's side and Justin's pistol spilled out through the rear doorway.

Justin's cut and swerve driving in the great grotto had successfully prevented the bugs from gaining entrance into the van but with the flood of reinforcements, their time had all but run out.

Through the mud-splattered windshield and eerie green haze, a beckoning target materialized. "Drop a flare down the pipe," Justin radioed the sheriff. "Drop a flare." He floored the van's accelerator, careening off mounded dirt and sulfur. Gaining what control he could, he straightened his course.

"Your mask," Justin yelled to Dr. Reynolds.

The entomologist secured her oxygen mask.

The van slammed full speed into the extraction pipe. The impact buckled the vehicle's hood, rupturing its radiator and shattering its windshield into a web of interconnected shards. The heavy-duty pipe was catapulted into the air and snapped off at its junction with the cavern roof, crashing to the floor. Instantly, a hundred gallons of kerosene rained down filling the underground air with its pungent mist.

Justin reverted to his cut and thrust driving tactics but the vehicle's tires had lost traction on the kerosene-soaked floor and he no longer had steering control.

The van slid sideways through a deep, rutted channel, splashing the petroleum distillate over a wider area. The vehicle spun wildly, swerving through another rut and coming to an abrupt halt against the base of the incline.

The bugs rushed the stranded van.

A point of brilliant light emerged from the severed pipe. The super-heated flare tumbled downward from the ceiling, filling the cavern with its red iridescence and igniting vaporized kerosene into a fiery ball that leaped to the saturated floor. Flames raced along trails of the flammable liquid turning the cavern into an inferno and incinerating all in its path.

A singed bug darted through the van's open rear and ricocheted off the ceiling light, crash-landing onto the floor. The beast launched itself at Dr. Reynolds, its front claw grazing her cheek before it fell dead.

The van's kerosene-soaked tires ignited. Black smoke and the sharp bite of burning rubber and sulfur dioxide filled the cavern. Justin coughed and gasped for air. Dr. Reynolds shoved her oxygen mask over the lawman's face. He took a deep breath, his eyes teary, his chest tight.

Outside the blackened van, the fires withered as precious air was used up, turning the underground into another type of death trap. All movement within the cavern had ceased. Those bugs not incinerated had succumbed to the deadly vapors.

Sharing the breathing gear, Justin and Dr. Reynolds retrieved the lifesaving air-pack and shotgun.

Dense smoke from smoldering sulfur rose to the cavern's upper chamber, improving visibility below.

"Justin, do you read me?" Sheriff Maxwell radioed. "The smoke in the upper chamber is too thick for us to make entry. Are you two all right?"

JUSTIN LIFTED HIS FACE-MASK. "AFFIRMATIVE," he transmitted. He chambered a round in the shotgun. Unlike Dr. Reynolds' scientific curiosity, he had a personal score to settle.

CHAPTER 42

PLUMES OF YELLOW VAPOR ROSE from reddish-brown pools of melted sulfur. The chamber's own faint luminescence back-lit a wispy smog emanating from the scorched army half-buried under ripped up flooring and scored out earth. Destruction within the nest was complete.

Justin made his way through the miasma, his senses tuned to the slightest movement from every quarter, a finger on the shotgun's trigger. Dr. Reynolds followed. They passed the three cylinders of methyl bromide rolled from the van. Added insurance if any of these creatures were still alive.

The orb's familiar outline emerged from the ghostly haze. Justin inspected the imposing structure. The strange cocoon had been untouched by the flames but the van's impact had opened a gaping hole causing its internal framework to collapse. Amid the rubble lay bodies of dead attendants and their monstrous queen in her final death-throe, her mouth agape, eyes dilated to black disks.

Still filled with spawn, the monarch's translucent

epithelium revealed twin hearts pumping white plasma through a network of arteries and veins. With each beat, the cardiac contractions became slower, more feeble, as life ebbed from the giant beast.

Justin stepped into the great sphere, cautious of compromised framework above. He pressed the end of his gun's barrel against the queen's head.

"Don't damage her," Dr. Reynolds pleaded. "She's invaluable for research."

Justin would just as soon finish the job here and now but the massive creature was near death and if her corpse could reveal important information about these bugs, so much the better. Dr. Reynolds could have her trophy in one piece.

Justin waded through the rubble to the orb's rear portal where the royal egg lay. The ovum's shell was cracked and drooled a thick, green liquid.

Stooping down, Justin trained his flashlight's beam through the passage in the orb's back wall and into the dark chasm beyond.

"That's the nursery," Dr. Reynolds said, looking over his shoulder.

Air within this acre-size chamber held only a hint of smoke and through the wispy haze could be seen rows of neatly stacked eggs. Wingless hatchlings crawled aimlessly among the ovum, searching for those who would feed them. In the queen's desperation to save her nest, she had sacrificed all of her able-bodied minions and in doing so, left her new brood to perish by some other fate.

Dr. Reynolds lifted up one of the dark, fibrous globules offered to the queen by her attendants. "Our assumption was correct," she said. "This is fungus." She plucked a sliver of brimstone from the glob. "Interesting. Sulfur makes up a portion of their diet."

"We need to get topside." Justin said. Dr. Reynolds insights were indeed interesting but they had been underground long enough.

"Justin, what's your situation?" Sheriff Maxwell's voice broke over the radio. "The smoke up here is beginning to thin out."

"The kerosene worked," Justin replied. "Just about everything down here is dead or dying. Someone needs to check the tunnels."

A pallid point of light appeared in the upper chamber.

"Can you see my light?" the sheriff radioed.

"Affirmative," Justin replied.

"Use my light as a bearing. Be aware the respirator from Derbigby's van only has a thirty-minute air supply. The Scott I threw down is good for an hour."

"Ten-four," Justin radioed.

"Look," Dr. Reynolds exclaimed. "It's hatching."

A dollop of green fluid spilled forth from the cracked

royal ovum. The slimy albumin sloughed away revealing a wrinkled, three-foot miniature version of the queen but with a brilliant-blue head. It freed itself from bondage and snorting open its plugged nostrils, let out a loud chirping squeal.

"We have to get it topside into fresh air," Dr. Reynolds urged.

"You need to get out now," Justin said. "We'll handle this."

"I can't leave her," Dr. Reynolds said, referring to the hatchling.

"You don't have enough oxygen to wait any longer," Justin said.

Dr. Reynolds grudgingly abandoned her position, her attention now on locating an undamaged bug specimen from the main hall on her way to the top. She picked up Justin's pistol as she searched.

The hatchling's chirps echoed through the vast hall, a forlorn sound of a newborn calling for its mother. Drawn by the sound, Dr. Reynolds halted and looked back. Her breath caught in her throat. "Justin!" she screamed.

The queen's massive head struck Justin full-body, knocking him from the orb, his mask askew. He struggled to his feet, his blood chilled. Revived from near death by her offspring's calls, the huge matriarch towered over the lawman, her eyes clear and her jaws snapping. She snaked from her odd palace with cold intent.

Justin chambered a round in the shotgun. The queen struck like a viper. Her razor-sharp pincers sliced deep into Justin's left shoulder, wrenching the shotgun from his grip and severing his radio's mike cable. She lunged at him again. He side-stepped, tripped on the uneven flooring and went down.

"Hey, you ugly bitch!" Dr. Reynolds shouted. The entomologist had slipped behind the queen to her shattered orb and now stood over the royal hatchling, Justin's pistol pointed at the newborn's bobbing blue head. As if aware of its plight, the young heiress squealed louder.

The mighty queen swung around to face this new threat.

"Come and save her," Dr. Reynolds yelled.

The monstrous bug lowered her head like a bull ready to charge. She hissed furiously. She understood the power of that odd weapon and her own precarious position but this was not a fight she could afford to lose. She shifted her trunk and pinned down Justin's legs. Drawing closer to the deputy, she opened her sickle-size pincers, making clear her intentions.

On his back, his lifeblood flowing from his lacerated shoulder, Justin stared into the monster bug's mile-deep eyes. He saw no mercy. No escape, only death as wrought by her once great colony. And Justin saw more, the deaths of ten people, the injury to his partner and...

Justin pushed aside the pain in his shoulder and raised up his torso with his good arm. He was not getting out of this alive but there was something that might end this queen's reign. He took a deep breath and with all the focus he could muster, he let go a wad of spittle with deadly accuracy, striking the big bug's right eye.

The monarch recoiled at this unexpected defense but quickly recovered.

"Your move," Dr. Reynolds called out to the beast. She stepped back from the royal heiress, offering false hope to the monarch her offspring was hers. The queen shifted her weight from Justin and turned toward the orb, remaining within striking distance of the deputy.

The queen's movements were slower now, labored. A white foam dribbled from her mouth. A cloudy patch had appeared around Justin's spittle and was quickly spreading across the big bug's right eye. The advantage of this deadly game had shifted.

"Justin," Dr. Reynolds called, "the shotgun. Can you make it to the van?" The shotgun lay ten feet from him on a sulfur slab. It was his only weapon and the vehicle, his only refuge.

Justin signaled he would try.

"Over here, you ugly beast," Dr. Reynolds yelled.

The drool from the queen's mouth dripped from her pincers in frothy rafts. Her right eye had turned completely opaque and her huge body quivered but even with her affliction, it was clear she was still lethal.

With flagging strength, Justin dragged himself over the shattered floor, his blood-streaked left arm of no use. He reached the shotgun, his strength draining fast. Aware he could go no further, he painfully turned onto his back and gained a sitting position. Somehow he found the strength to heft the firearm onto his bent knee. The scatter-gun felt as heavy as lead.

"Come on, you can have your baby," Dr. Reynolds yelled, trying to keep the great queen's attention on her but whatever the poison was doing to the big bug's brain, it's maternal instinct had switched from species preservation to complete destruction of the cause of this disaster. She swung around, slinging foam from her mouth and in total rage, charged Justin like a run-away freight train.

Clinging to his quickly fraying thread of consciousness, Justin knew to get lucky was to live. He steadied the firearm on his knee, aiming as best he could at his target and forcing himself to fight the darkness closing in on his brain. Time for him stood still. His hands trembled and as his cognizance faded into blackness, he squeezed off a shot.

A thunderous gray ball erupted beneath the huge bug, the explosion from the bursting methyl bromide cylinder disintegrating the monster's lower body into a spray of white fluid and shattered ova. Like a felled tree, her head and torso crashed down at Justin's feet, its eyes still locked onto the lawman. Unrelenting, the mighty sovereign hauled her wasted trunk ever closer to Justin, jaws snapping, hell-bent on this man's destruction.

Sheriff Maxwell, garbed in a breathing apparatus, pressed a twelve gauge shotgun between the great creature's eyes and splattered her spongy brain over the broken floor. Stan Wilton was quick to throw a spare Scott Air-pack over Justin's battered face before starting medical procedures to stabilize him for the trip topside. Dr. Reynolds was given a fresh breathing unit and she remained at Justin's side to the outer world.

CHAPTER 43

Within a wedge of sunlight on Sam Ramey's kitchen windowsill a ceramic honeybee held a hopeful smile that drew wide the flowerpot's toothy mouth. Leafy bougainvillea spilled from the bee's back, hanging over its outstretched wings and partially obscuring words written on its flank – "What you bee is honey to me."

Dr. Potter's troubled features stared out of the window at a contingent of military personnel draped in containment suits and staging equipment in front of The Shed. Four equally suited figures, one of them Walter Kell, had entered the nest a half-hour before and had yet to reappear. Isolation from the goings-on outside was not something Dr. Potter had expected and every minute Kell and his team remained underground increased the retired professor's ire. Sighing frustration, Potter rejoined Drs. Reynolds and Jenkins at Sam Ramey's kitchen table.

"What's happening?" Dr. Reynolds asked, as frustrated as her ex-professor.

"More people and more equipment," Potter replied. "What the hell are they doing?"

"I wouldn't worry about that," Special Agent Thom Dempsey said as he entered the kitchen. A representative from NASA, Thom was thirty-five years old, of medium build with a stern face and military crew-cut. Having shown up with a small military contingent only minutes before Dr. Walter Kell's arrival, the government agent had immediately taken control of Sam Ramey's property and all points in and around Union Town. Additional government and military personnel in attendance had been deployed on all roads leading in and out of the town. Union Town was under siege of a different kind.

"What do you people intend to do?" Dr. Potter asked angrily. Potter and Company had been detained in Sam's house for well over an hour with no explanation or indication of when they would be permitted to join the activities outside.

"That's no concern of yours," Dempsey stated.

"It most certainly is," Potter bleated. "Do you people know anything about these organisms? Do you understand the threat they pose?"

Disregarding the entomologist's questions, Dempsey continued, "You will each be debriefed and once you leave here you are to speak to no one about this incident without prior clearance from NASA, is that understood?"

"Mister Dempsey," Dr. Jenkins spoke up, "I'm not in the legal profession but I do know the government has no right to silence us about what occurred here."

Dempsey maintained his strict demeanor. "I suggest each of you cooperate," he said. "Any breach of these orders will lead to your arrest and imprisonment."

"On what charge?" Dr. Reynolds piped up, piqued she and her colleagues were being treated in such a cavalier manner.

"Federal Regulation, Title 14, Section 1211, Extra-terrestrial Exposure Law," the federal agent replied matter-of-factly. "Possession of or coming in close proximity to any extra-terrestrial entity requires you to be quarantined and in this case, disclosure in any way of this incident will land you in prison for a year and a five thousand dollar fine." Thom Dempsey was not one to joke, a fact that was very clear to his audience.

"Surely you can't expect us to have gone through what we did and just forget about this 'incident', as you call it," Dr. Potter said. "This is too important for science and for us."

"What you care to forget or remember after being debriefed is up to you," Dempsey said. "What you tell unauthorized personnel after you leave quarantine is not."

"And the townspeople who were around these creatures?" Jenkins asked. "What about them?

"We're handling that," Dempsey said.

A heavyset air force colonel with a shock of silver hair and a black brief case entered the kitchen. Upon seeing the military officer, Dempsey pursed his lips and exited the house.

"I'm Colonel Jack Canter," the new arrival said. "I apologize for not getting here faster."

Potter leaped to his feet. "What's going on here?" he demanded. His dander up, he was going to get answers, and fast. "The treatment we have received has been totally inappropriate. We're being treated like criminals."

"I apologize for any misunderstandings," Col. Canter said. "If Dempsey has been less than tactful it's because he excels in that area." Col. Canter set his briefcase on the floor, by the table. "There's been a bit of confusion as to why orders had not been followed and the nest was destroyed."

"There were lives at stake, for Christ sake," Potter cut in.

"I understand that now," Col. Canter replied. "I spoke with state police and Sheriff Maxwell. It's regretful, the turn of events, but apparently it was necessary." Canter took a seat, as did Potter, somewhat reluctantly.

"There's a newly hatched queen still in the nest," Dr. Reynolds said. "Do you know if she's still alive?"

"From the last report, everything in the nest is dead," Canter replied. "Our team is inspecting the remainder of the tunnel system for any signs of life."

Potter frowned. "Meanwhile, we're stuck in here," he said. "We have valuable information about this organism."

"Which gets to why I'm here," Canter said.

"Are you arresting us too, under this Extra-Terrestrial Exposure Law?" Potter asked, still upset the US government would stifle civilian work on this strange creature.

Canter raised a questioning brow. "Did Dempsey threaten you with that law?" he asked.

"Yes he did," Jenkins replied.

"That's Dempsey," Canter commented with a shake of his head. "He's good at intimidation. Congress enacted the Extra-Terrestrial Exposure Law in 1969, just prior to the Apollo moon landing. At the time, there were fears lunar material brought back to earth might contain latent viruses or bacteria that could create health risks here on Earth. The law was enacted to control those materials. Don't worry about Dempsey's threat. The law was revoked by Congress ten years ago, in 1977."

"Then why are you here?" Dr. Reynolds asked.

"And why are we not allowed outside?" Potter said.

"Corporal," he ordered a guard at the kitchen door, "no one is to enter this room without my authorization. Please close the door and wait outside."

"Yes sir," the young soldier replied and swung the door closed.

Canter laid his briefcase on the table and pulled out a gray folder. "What I'm going to show you is classified information," the air force colonel said, "and I apologize but I have to be Mister Dempsey on this point. You have to agree that anything you are about to see or hear will not leave this room." He waited until he had an affirming nod from each participant.

Canter laid the open file on the table for all to see. Affixed to the top page was a black and white photo marked with a date of August, 1957. The photographed object was remarkably similar in appearance to a front leg and shred of torso from one of their creatures. Canter handed the snapshot to Dr. Reynolds.

A second, more recent color photo showed a badly decomposed creature on a cutting board covered with fish scales. A fillet-knife laid purposely alongside indicated the bug's size.

"Where was this found?" Dr. Reynolds queried, passing the first photo to Potter and taking the second.

"Texas, twenty miles west of Brownsville."

"And this one?" Dr. Reynolds said, holding up the color photo.

"Corpus Christi," Canter replied. "Three years ago."

"No live specimens?" Potter asked.

"No," Canter said. "The only physical evidence previously on file is the leg in the first picture."

"And this decomposed specimen?" Dr. Reynolds asked.

"Unfortunately," Canter said, "the evidence was discarded by the fisherman who found it and never recovered. The photo came to us from Harvard Museum of Comparative Anatomy where it was sent for identification."

"Are you aware of the possible origin of these creatures?" Jenkins asked.

"We know it is highly likely they are extra-terrestrial biological entities," Canter said.

"From what limited evidence you previously had," Potter said with raised brow, "what led you to believe an extra-terrestrial origin? The specimen in the first photo could be an appendage of a previously unidentified crustacean and as for this second photo, it would be impossible to tell what it was unless you had seen one of these creatures before."

Canter slipped a printed document from the file and handed it to Potter. "This is analytical data of the exoskeleton in the first photo," Canter stated.

Office of Scientific Intelligence

DEFENSE DEPARTMENT – UNITED STATES OF AMERICA

Sample: GP.002Y3

ANALYTICAL METHODOLOGY: NMR AND ENZYMATIC DEGRADATION TEST

RESULTS: Linear polymer of glucose, 12,000 residues,

Beta-(1-4) linkages

Amino acids: cysteine, methionine, cysteine, lysine, histidine

Trace elements: S, N, P, Na, Fe

Potter studied the data. “Remarkable,” he said with amazement. Trading with Dr. Reynolds for her color photo, Potter waited for her response.

“Linear polymers of glucose with beta linkages,” Dr. Reynolds read aloud. She looked around the table. “What are we dealing with, an animal or a plant?”

“It seems,” Dr. Potter said to Col. Canter, “these creatures’ exoskeletons are made of cellulose.”

“So I’ve been told,” Canter replied, “the same thing plants are made from.”

“That’s correct,” Potter said. “Cellulose is nothing more than long chains of glucose folded back on themselves. The chains are so complex only a few organisms can digest them.

“As for insects, spiders, crabs and the like, their exoskeletons are composed of chitin, similar in structure to cellulose but with a bit of nitrogen thrown in. Even though there is some similarity in structure, cellulose is found exclusively in the plant kingdom and chitin only in the animal kingdom, at least until now.”

“This explains why the dead specimen Deputy Hebert found was full of fruit fly maggots,” Dr. Reynolds commented, nodding her continued amazement. “A very interesting organism indeed and the fact human saliva is lethal to these creatures indicates an equally unique metabolic system.”

“I didn’t know human saliva was poisonous to them,”

Canter said.

"Justin Hebert, the deputy taken to the hospital," Dr. Reynolds said, "noticed this phenomenon while trapped inside a factory building by these creatures and I witnessed the effect of saliva on the queen. It literally sent her into convulsions."

"How could saliva kill an animal like this?" Col. Canter asked.

"The fact these creatures have an exoskeleton composed of cellulose indicates a biological system that is likely highly reactive with Alpha-amylase or one or more of the other enzymes in saliva," Dr. Reynolds said.

"Interesting hypothesis," Dr. Potter said and for Canter's benefit added, "Alpha-amylase is the key enzyme in saliva that breaks down starches which are similar to cellulose but not as complex."

A long silence followed.

"Will it be possible for us to get involved in more detail?" Potter asked, hopeful the colonel had some clout within the government. Possibly Walter Kell could be of help.

"I believe we can accommodate your wish," Colonel Canter replied. He pulled yet another photo from the folder and laid it in front of the retired professor. This recent picture showed low-lying terrain littered with rusted drilling equipment and surrounded by dense jungle. A dilapidated bus laden with passengers and topped with sundry goods ascended a low hill, stirring up a cloud of dust. In the foreground a brown-skinned man with shiny teeth and a baseball cap held a jar half-filled with what appeared to be chunks of sulfur.

"This picture was taken a month ago outside a small town on the Isthmus of Tehuantepec, Mexico," Canter said.

He paused.

"I believe you're already familiar with phosphorescent sulfur."

AFTERMATH

JUSTIN STEPPED ONTO THE BACK porch of his home, a steaming cup of coffee in hand. Taking a seat on a patio chair, he breathed the cool morning air, his thoughts on the New Year begun and the one just past.

As he sipped his coffee, he glanced through the sliding glass doors to packing boxes cluttering his living room. Moving day had arrived and the only task remaining was for the packing crew to load his belongings into a transport van. So would end his residence in Opelousas.

Justin knew he would miss small-town America and quiet mornings like this but for him the sacrifice was well worth it. Baton Rouge was not his idea of a comfort-zone but Dr. Jennifer Reynolds was there and she could not abdicate her professorship as easily as he could turn in his badge.

He set his coffee cup atop a shipping box next to his chair and raised his left arm, flexing his fingers and stretching sore muscles. His shoulder was healing well, if slowly, and according to his doctors, continued physical therapy and exercise would allow him full use of his limb.

Justin had not returned to Union Town since that fateful August day when he had somehow escaped death's clutches. No more than a hazy memory now, his only recollection of those final moments was the trembling ground beneath him and Dr. Reynolds' terrified scream. The very next image was from a hospital bed, his torso wrapped like a mummy and arms sprouting clear tubes. Sheriff Maxwell had been there, as had Olan Barnes and Bill Moley, all seated on chairs along a wall. Dr. Reynolds had come later in the afternoon, a daily ritual she kept until Justin's discharge two weeks later.

Justin smiled his good fortune of meeting Jennifer Reynolds. Those hospital visits, though hardly romantic, had led to weekends at his home in Opelousas and one month ago to the day, at Jenny's New Year's Eve party, to their engagement. The events in Union Town six months before had worked out well for Justin but how so for the others who had shared in that traumatic drama?

Gerald Wilson, now a married man living in Lafayette, had not yet fully recovered from his wounds. The venom-affected areas on his arm and face still oozed clear plasma but he hoped the next round of skin grafts would make him fit for duty as a Louisiana State Policeman. Gerald and Cindy were expecting their first child sometime in July.

Sheriff Arthur Maxwell chose not run for re-election due to a promise to his wife, Gail, to find a safer job and after a lifetime in law enforcement, he and Gail moved to Slater, Colorado to manage a dude ranch, something they had talked about for years. Gail's interest was in making Native American pottery and she had opened a gift shop in the ranch's lobby while her husband managed the guests' outdoor activities with time off in the fall for elk hunting.

Mayor Bill Brandon had not been as fortunate in making career decisions. With Dick Gallo still missing, talk was Union Town's chief of police had followed the mayor's orders and gone into the nest and to his death. The police chief's remains had yet to be located but that didn't keep state police from investigating the allegations. In the process, authorities uncovered pedophile material with evidence directly linked to the "honorable" mayor. Two days before Thanksgiving, Mayor Bill Brandon was arrested for possessing and distributing child pornography.

During the weeks following the incident, Union Town Funeral Home saw a string of unusual funeral services in which the deceased were represented by photos propped up on closed coffins. Even Pete Baxter and Clee Roden were in attendance, their grave plots donated by Saint Matthew's Catholic Church. These two vagabonds finally had a permanent address.

Tom Slyger changed his company's name to "Bug Beaters" and featured as his mascot a toothy insect very similar in appearance to those that had infested Union Town. Tom's six pest control operators now serviced four parishes in the State of Louisiana.

Within days after the events that August day, Union Town gained nationwide notoriety within UFOlogy cults as a site where extra-terrestrials had actually touched down. This fact was supposedly substantiated when the Army Corps of Engineers razed the factory buildings in the industrial park and filled in ground subsidence and holes in and around the town. They even replaced the industrial park's old enclosure with a razor wire-topped security fence decorated with 'US Government – Posted' signs.

Cultists and the just-plain-curious streamed into Union Town for months afterwards hopeful of seeing little green men strolling along the town's sidewalks or levitating saltshakers at Coleman's Diner. Some even spoke of the Second Coming of Christ.

Dick Driskoll's eatery, Union Town Motel and most other businesses around town boomed with the waves of sightseers. Campsites sprang up in the pine thickets west of town keeping Police Chief Doff Green busy with trespassing complaints and littering. One amorous couple had been arrested for making love in broad daylight along the old industrial park's fence line, a point where cosmic rays supposedly focused on the child they were procreating.

As for the remainder of those who participated in the 'incident' that fateful day, they returned to their lives and jobs. Phil Linderson started an advanced invertebrate zoology class at Union Town High School and Bill Moley won first prize at the State Fair in Baton Rouge for his monster tomatoes. Bill's part-time partner, Malcolm Friar, moved to New Orleans to attend Delgado Community College's Department of Funeral Services while Gene Lancer chose Donna Forrest, over her sister Shirley, to be his wife. Gene and Donna relocated to Westwego where he opened a photo shop. Buck Greely entered a career in professional wrestling as 'The Zydeco Kid' while Billy (Wreckerman) Nagle kept the UFO'ers glued to their seats with his story about surviving a stroll through the heart of the nest, and Dick Gallo…

Trey Frazier had said it best – "Gallo ain't got the balls." The then Union Town chief of police had had no intention of following the illustrious Mayor Brandon to Coleman's Diner or anywhere else. No sooner had Brandon started for the eatery than Chief Gallo offered up a verbal resignation from his job, picked up personal items from his desk and steered his personal car out of town. With one stop to refuel in Baton Rouge, he took Interstate 210 and headed west. No one in Union Town ever heard from Gallo again.

Justin's telephone rang, pulling him from his reflections. Returning into the house, he located the phone behind a stack of boxes.

"What are you doing?" Jenny asked from the other end.

"Finishing my first cup of coffee and wishing I were in Baton Rouge with you," Justin replied.

"Do you feel up to a bit longer trip?" Jenny queried.

"Where to?"

"Mexico."

THE END

www.ingramcontent.com/pod-product-compliance
Lightning Source LLC
LaVergne TN
LVHW010558100826
845148LV00014B/2759

* 9 7 9 8 2 1 8 1 4 1 8 6 8 *